Ela Area Public Library District
275 Mohawk Trail, Lake Zurich, IL 60047
(847) 438-3433
www.eapl.org

ROBERT B. PARKER'S LULLABY

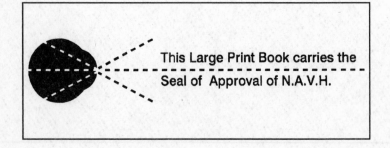

This Large Print Book carries the
Seal of Approval of N.A.V.H.

A SPENSER NOVEL

ROBERT B. PARKER'S LULLABY

ACE ATKINS

THORNDIKE PRESS
A part of Gale, Cengage Learning

Detroit • New York • San Francisco • New Haven, Conn • Waterville, Maine • London

GALE
CENGAGE Learning·

Thorndike Press® Large Print Core.
The text of this Large Print edition is unabridged.
Other aspects of the book may vary from the original edition.
Set in 16 pt. Plantin.

LIBRARY OF CONGRESS CATALOGING-IN-PUBLICATION DATA

Atkins, Ace.
  Robert B. Parker's lullaby / by Ace Atkins.
    pages ; cm. — (Thorndike Press large print core) (A Spenser
  novel)
  ISBN-13: 978-1-4104-4814-9 (hardcover)
  ISBN-10: 1-4104-4814-2 (hardcover)
  1. Spenser (Fictitious character)—Fiction. 2. Mothers—Crimes
against—Fiction. 3. Private
investigators—Massachusetts—Boston—Fiction. 4. Boston
(Mass.)—Fiction. 5. Domestic fiction. 6. Large type books. I. Title.
PS3601.T487R63 2012b
813'.6—dc23   2012010210

Published in 2012 by arrangement with G. P. Putnam's Sons, a member
of Penguin Group (USA) Inc.

Printed in the United States of America
1 2 3 4 5 6 7 15 14 13 12 11

To Joan.
Always the inspiration.

1

I spotted the girl even before she knocked on my door. I was gazing out my second-floor office window down at Berkeley Street, eating a cinnamon donut and drinking coffee with a little milk and sugar. The girl looked lost among the businesspeople and tourists hustling along the icy sidewalks. She wore a pink Boston Red Sox cap and an oversized down parka with a fur collar, and stared up at the numbers on the office buildings where Berkeley intersects Boylston.

When she stopped at my building, she folded up a piece of paper and crossed the street with a lot of purpose. I had an open box of donuts and an uncashed check on my desk from Cone, Oakes. I'd done a little work for Rita Fiore and had been paid handsomely.

The winter had been dark, bleak, and endless, but sometime in the last hour I had actually seen the sun. My computer was playing Helen Forrest singing with the Harry James Orchestra. Life was full of promise.

I had a bite of donut just as I heard the knock on the door.

I opened it.

"You Spenser?" asked the girl in the pink Red Sox cap.

"The one and only."

"People say you're tough," she said.

"Did they mention handsome and witty?"

"That you aren't afraid to use a gun."

"Only when my feelings get hurt."

Her accent was South Boston, maybe Dorchester. Henry Higgins could have told me her exact address. I figured her for fifteen or sixteen. She stood about five-foot-five with straight reddish brown hair spilling from the Sox cap. Her eyes were green and very large, made slightly ridiculous with heavy eyeliner.

"You really a private investigator?" she asked.

"Says so on the door."

"And you didn't get your license from the Internet or anything?"

"No."

"Were you a cop or something?"

"Or something."

"Thrown off the force for drinking?"

"No."

"Police brutality?"

"No."

"Then why aren't you a cop now?"

"I don't play well with others," I said. "Would you like to come in?"

She peered around me into my office, checking out my desk, two file cabinets, and the couch where Pearl slept when it was take-your-dog-to-work day. I extended my hand toward my guest chair and sat behind my desk. She joined me.

The girl had a full face with ruddy cheeks, a couple of moles on the right side. A cute kid if she'd sit up straight. But she slouched into her chair and nervously toyed with a Saint Christopher medal. "Who busted your nose?" she asked.

"Jersey Joe Walcott," I said.

"Who's he?"

"Former heavyweight champ," I said. "Before your time."

I pushed the box of donuts toward her. She looked down at my carefully chosen assortment. Then she looked back at me, still playing with the medal, and shook her head. I let the silence hang there for a moment. I figured if I waited long enough, she might tell me why she was in need of my services.

9

After a long pause, she did.

"Somebody killed my mom."

I took a deep breath and leaned forward. "When?"

"Four years ago," she said.

"I'm sorry."

"I want to find the bastards."

"Okay." I nodded. "Why now?"

"Nobody listens to kids," she said. "I'm older now. You do this kind of stuff, right?"

"I'm good at making people listen," I said.

"How much do you charge?"

I told her the usual rate. She began to dig through her pockets, pulling out five crumpled twenties and a ten, flattening the cash on my desktop. "Will this get you started?"

I glanced down at the money and again nudged the box of donuts her way. This time she accepted, choosing a chocolate-frosted. I complimented her choice. Giving away a whole donut was a major philanthropic gesture. I hoped she appreciated it.

"What's your name?"

"Mattie Sullivan."

"You take the Red Line into the city, Miss Sullivan?"

"How'd you know that?"

"I am a trained investigator."

I drank some coffee. I pulled a yellow legal

pad and a pen from my left desk drawer. Ever the professional. "Why don't you tell me what happened."

"They left her up on The Point," she said. "By U Mass, where they tore down all those old buildings. You know?"

I nodded.

"She was stabbed to death."

I nodded some more. I took some notes.

"She'd been raped," she said. "They think."

Her face showed little emotion, telling the story as if she'd read it in the newspaper.

"I'm very sorry," I said.

"That was a long time ago."

"How old are you now?"

"Fourteen."

I turned my chair as I listened and could see the morning traffic on Berkeley. People continued to make their way down the sidewalk as an MBTA bus passed, churning dirty slush in its wake.

"What did the police say?"

"They arrested this guy the next day," she said. "Mickey Green. He's doing life at Cedar Junction."

"And you don't think he did it?"

"I *know* he didn't."

"Why?"

"Mickey is a screwup, but he's a good guy,

11

you know?"

"Not much to go on," I said.

"I saw her with a couple men that night," she said. "I saw them snatch her up and push her into the back of a car. She wasn't with Mickey. Mickey wasn't with her that whole night."

"Who were they?"

"You gonna do this?" she asked.

"Maybe."

"These are real mean guys."

"Okay."

"And young, too."

" '*O Youth! For years so many and sweet.*' "

"You're an older guy. I'm just sayin'."

I tried not to take offense. I was fourteen once.

"I don't know their full names," she said. "They just go by Pepper and Moon. Coupla shitbag drug dealers in the neighborhood."

"What neighborhood?"

"I've lived in the Mary Ellen McCormack my whole freakin' life."

The McCormack was down at the bottom of South Boston, close to Dorchester, a tough old brick housing project that headlined a lot of shooting stories in the *Globe*.

"The last time I saw Pepper was six months ago. I don't know about Moon."

"Why not go back to the cops?"

"I did. A bunch of times."

"What'd they say?"

"That Mickey Green is a true douchebag and got what he deserved. One time they gave me a pat on the head and a card about some shrink so I could 'talk about my trauma.' After a couple of years, they just stopped calling me back."

"You can vouch for Mickey's character?"

"He was friends with my mother," she said. "They used to drink together at Four Green Fields. He helped her when our pipes would bust or if she needed groceries."

"Tell me what you saw that night."

"I saw her come into my room," she said. "I'd put my baby sisters down to sleep after dinner, and my mom came in and went through my drawers for money. She didn't know I saw her, but I was pissed. I followed her outside and was gonna yell at her, but before I could, I seen Pepper and Moon grab her and drag her to their car. They threw her in the backseat. They were yelling back and forth, but I couldn't hear what they were sayin'. Or what she was sayin'. One of the guys hit her. It was a real mess."

"I'm sorry." There wasn't much else to say.

Mattie dropped her head and nodded. She

13

rubbed her hands together. Her nails, which were painted with black polish, had been bitten to stubs. She didn't look like she'd smiled since elementary school. Her parka had seen a lot of winters; her wrists peeked out from the blackened sleeves, buttons barely hanging on. The knees of her jeans had been patched.

"Where are your sisters now?"

"We all live with my grandmother."

"Your mother's mom?"

She nodded.

"Dad?"

Mattie rolled her eyes.

"So four years later, you just decide to set this straight?"

"Me and Mickey been talking about it."

"You visit him in jail?" I asked. I leaned forward and made some notes.

"He started writing me letters and sending me birthday cards and crap," she said. Mattie ran her finger under her reddened nose. "He kept on saying how sorry he was and all, and that he would've never hurt my ma. And so I wrote him back and said, I know. I told him about Pepper and Moon. I said I tried to tell but no one was listening. Jesus, I was only ten."

She studied my face as I thought about what she'd said. I figured she was seeing the

14

chiseled features of a man she could respect. She finally rolled her eyes and went for the money. "You're not the only tough guy in Boston," she said.

"There's another," I said. "But we work as a team."

She left the money and looked at me with those sad, tough eyes. Her shoulders slouched some more, and she dug her hands deeper into the pockets of her old parka. The pink hat looked shabby. She reminded me a lot of Paul Giacomin when I'd first met him. Nobody in his corner.

"Anyone else see your mom taken by these guys?"

"I don't know," Mattie said. "Nobody wants to talk about it. And nobody wants to help."

She blinked hard, and rubbed her eyes with her tiny, balled-up fists. She sighed. "This was a stupid idea."

"Wait a second."

She stood up, eyes lingering on me. I pushed the money back across my desk.

"You're in luck, Mattie Sullivan," I said. "I'm running a special this week."

"What's the special?"

"Investigative services in exchange for more of these," I said, holding up a donut.

"Are you shitting me?" she asked.
"I shit you not."

2

"I sure am lucky to know you, Spenser," Quirk said. "Otherwise, I wouldn't know what to do with myself."

"I like to make people feel useful," I said. "Commander of the homicide squad can be such a lonely job."

"I got the file set up for you in a conference room down the hall," he said. "I hope that's to your liking."

I lifted my eyebrows and tilted my head. "Service with a smile."

"Had to have the thing printed out, too," Quirk said. "You know cops these days use these devices called computers. You heard of them?"

"Sure," I said. "I've seen pictures."

Quirk was a big guy with bricklayer's hands who always looked buttoned-up and spit-shined. In the decades we'd known each other, I had never seen him with so much as a wrinkle. He was dressed in a navy suit with a white dress shirt and red-and-blue rep tie.

"Do you mind me asking why you're looking into this?" Quirk asked.

"I have a client who thinks you got the wrong man."

"I've heard that song before."

"You read the report?"

"I was the one who printed the son of a bitch out."

"What'd you think?"

"I think you're wasting a perfectly good afternoon."

"Solid?"

"The vic was stabbed, raped, and run down with a car," he said. "We got her blood all over the suspect's vehicle."

"Blood match the deceased?"

Quirk looked at me like I should be wearing a cone-shaped hat. "*Hmm.* Gee, maybe we should've thought about that."

"You mind if I grab some coffee?"

"Help yourself."

"Bad as always?"

"Worse."

The homicide unit kept their offices in a big open space on the third floor of the new police headquarters building off Tremont Street in Roxbury. The old headquarters had been within walking distance of my office and was now a boutique hotel called the Back Bay. The old headquarters was all gray stone with a lot of rugged charm. The new headquarters had all the aesthetics of an insurance company.

I spent the next two hours reading through the incident report, the coroner's notes, and the detectives' file. The file contained a copy of Julie Sullivan's arrest record. She'd been arrested four times for possession of crack cocaine. And five times for prostitution and once for public intoxication.

Two weeks before she'd been killed, Julie Sullivan had entered into a plea deal on drug charges. She was set to enter a drug treatment facility in Dorchester a week later. I noted the name of the facility and date on the yellow legal pad I'd brought.

I also noted the dates and places of her drug arrests. The reports told me little else.

I wrote down Julie's date of birth. She'd been twenty-six when she died. Her body had been found at a construction site off University Drive on Columbia Point. Not only did her blood match the blood on Mickey Green's car, but tracks found at the scene matched his tires.

Mickey Green's file was pretty thick. He'd been convicted of breaking and entering at eighteen, aggravated assault at nineteen.

And twenty. And at twenty-one — twice. He stole some cars. He robbed a convenience store. He spent time in the pokey.

Green had been spotted at a drive-through car wash at Neponset Circle an hour before his arrest. But some of Julie's blood and matted hair remained on the car, despite his efforts.

Outside the window, flags popped tight on their poles. Cold wind tossed trash and dead leaves down cleared sidewalks past banks of dirty snow. A sheet of newspaper lifted in the wind and disappeared under a Buick.

I'd been doing what I do for a long while now. In that time, I'd grown pretty good at knowing when I could poke holes in investigations and admitting when poking would do little good. This one had been fashioned of steel and concrete. I tapped my pen against my legal pad and let out a long breath. The case I'd just worked made me feel dirty and shabby but had also left me with a full bank account and a little time. The girl just wanted someone to listen and check things out. Despite everything I'd just read, she believed her mom's killers were still out there and a family friend had been left holding the bag. Pretty weighty stuff on a fourteen-year-old. Sometimes a few hours of honest work was better than a bar of soap.

I leaned back into the seat. I was making a few more notes when Quirk strolled into the conference room and handed me a business card. On the back he'd written a cell phone number.

"Bobby Barrett," Quirk said. "Works out of District Eleven. He can tell you about this Mickey Green guy."

I took the card and thanked him.

"How far you get with the file?"

"Far enough," I said.

"Like I said, the case is solid."

"My client says she saw the victim with thugs a few hours before her death."

"Then who the hell is Mickey Green?" Quirk asked. "The ice-cream man? Did you read his sheet?"

"I didn't see any other suspects."

"I don't think there was a reason," Quirk said. "He was driving the car used to kill her."

I nodded.

"Girl like that gets around at night," Quirk said. "You saw her priors. She could have had a lot of company before she ran into Green at that bar."

"I don't see a motive."

Quirk smiled. "How many killings ever have a good motive? People get pissed off. Shit happens."

21

"I'll inform my client."

"I'm not trying to bust your balls," Quirk said. "I know you want to do right by the kid. I just don't want you wasting your time."

"I'll talk to Barrett," I said. "I'd also like to talk to someone in the drug unit."

"What about the case detective?"

"Didn't see much detecting done in the file," I said. "I want to know some of the players in Southie. Drug unit would help."

"Yes, sir," Quirk said. "Your wish is my command."

"Quirk, you really make me feel special."

Quirk told me to go screw myself.

3

Locke-Ober was classic Boston, like the Old North Church or Carl Yastrzemski. There was a time when they didn't allow women, but fortunately those days were over. The décor still had that men's-club feel, with wood-paneled walls and brass trim. The waiters wore white.

I had gone home and exchanged my Boston Braves cap, leather jacket, and jeans for gray wool pants, a light blue button-down with a red tie, and a navy blazer sporting brass buttons. I had showered, shaved, and polished the .38 Chief's Special I wore on my belt, behind my hip bone. The drape of my blazer hid it nicely in the hollow of my back.

I looked as if I deserved a solid drink. I ordered a dry Grey Goose martini and sat at the old bar, staring at an oil painting of a nude woman. The woman looked strong and curvy, with ample breasts and only a thin silk sash around her waist.

I heard Monk being played somewhere as my martini arrived. Very cold and slushy with ice, extra olives. I looked into the bar mirror and lifted the glass to myself.

"What should I make of that?"

I turned and smiled. Susan took the barstool next to me.

"Why would any club exclude women?" I asked, signaling the waiter for a glass of chardonnay.

"Repressed homosexuality," she said.

"Mother issues?" I asked.

"Could be both," Susan said. "A martini?"

"Cheers."

"What's the occasion?"

"Tonight we dine courtesy of Cone, Oakes."

She smiled as a glass of Chalk Hill was placed in front of her. The tune switched from Monk to Coltrane. The room was warm and pleasant. Our voices seemed to be absorbed into the old walls as we talked, waiting on our table. I had envisioned a filet, medium rare, with creamed spinach and mashed potatoes. Another martini. Maybe two.

"Wow," I said, taking all of her in.

Susan wore a black sheath dress with sheer black stockings and high-heeled suede pumps. A chunky necklace of black onyx and small diamonds rested on her collarbone. I leaned in and kissed her on the cheek. She smelled of lavender and the promise of a long evening in good company.

"Aren't you going to buy me dinner first?"

"For this kind of dinner," I said, "I'll expect something spectacular."

"Have you ever been disappointed?"

"Of course not."

"Or exhausted?"

"Nope."

"Then yes, cheers," she said, toasting me.

I raised my glass in reply.

"Since when do you like olives?"

"You know me," I said, taking a big sip. "I like to switch it up."

"And drinking a bit faster than usual."

"I made a promise to a kid that I cannot fulfill."

"What was the promise?"

"I told her I would look into her mother's murder."

"What's the problem?"

"There's a man already serving life for the crime," I said. "She believes him to be innocent."

"Oh."

"Quirk showed me the case file," I said. "I'd have had a better chance of freeing

Bruno Hauptmann."

"But you only told her that you would look into it."

"Semantics."

"Ah." She nodded. "You want to help her."

Susan sipped her wine and studied me. Her black eyes were very large and luminous, framed by dark lashes and elegantly arched eyebrows. She gave me a crooked smile before taking another small sip.

"So tell me, how old is this girl?"

"Fourteen."

"Quite young to be hiring her own detective. She come alone?"

I nodded. "Straight off the Red Line from Southie."

"And can she pay you?"

"Sort of."

"You didn't ask."

"We settled on a fair price."

"How'd she find you?"

"Apparently I'm known in the best Southie circles as a toughie."

"What happened to her mother?"

I told her.

"Jesus Christ."

"Spoken like a true Jewish American Princess."

"A parent's death is always tough, but a violent death as seen by a ten-year-old

26

would be seismic," Susan said. "Is there a father?"

"Nope," I said. "Dead mother was a single parent."

"Who's looking out for her now?"

"She's pretty independent," I said. "Lives with her grandmother, who's largely absent. She takes care of her younger sisters and stays in school. It's not *Ozzie and Harriet,* but what is?"

"She must be pretty strong-willed," she said. "She wants to right things herself."

"Even if they're wrong."

"You don't believe that she really saw her mother forced into a car by those other men?"

"Yep," I said. "I believe she saw it, but I'm not sure it proves anything. A woman with Julie Sullivan's rap sheet doesn't exactly run with the Brahmins."

"Then you must see something in her story, or you wouldn't have taken the case."

"Not in the case," I said. "In her. She needs someone to listen."

"And you like her."

"We bonded over donuts and the Sox." I nodded. "So, yeah. She's tough and smart. You meet a kid like that and think about all that's in her way to succeed. You take the same kid and put her in another home. . . ."

"Loving parents and a nice colonial in Smithfield?"

"Something like that."

Susan took another micro-sip. "Has she had contact with the convicted man?"

"I understand she visits him in prison," I said.

"Stoking the fantasy."

"What fantasy?"

"To become her mother's savior."

"Hold on, let me take some notes," I said. "You shrinks and your fancy talk."

Susan shrugged. I ordered another martini. Susan caught me studying the oil painting of the curvy nude woman. She smiled at me and nodded at the painting.

"Now, that's a real woman," Susan said. "Naked as a jaybird and fighting for liberty."

Susan turned to me. She could tell I was barely listening.

"I just don't want to get this girl's hopes up."

"Be honest with her," Susan said. "If she's clear about your intentions and what you can do, then you can't hurt her."

I put my glass down on the bar and leaned in to her ear. "You know," I said, "you're pretty smart for a Harvard Ph.D."

4

I met Officer Bobby Barrett the next morning at Mul's Diner on West Broadway in
South Boston. Mul's was a hash-and-eggs
joint with a neon sign on the roof and walls
made out of stainless steel. I ordered black
coffee and took it outside to talk to Barrett,
who was leaning into his prowl car to moni-
tor the radio. The morning was crisp, hover-
ing around thirty degrees. Our breath
fogged as we talked.

"Mickey Green," Barrett said. "What a
piece of work."

"You ever arrest him?"

"A few times," Barrett said. "Chickenshit
stuff, mostly. Lots of warnings. But you can
bet when some shit was going down, Green
was there. A neighborhood fuckup. The kind
of guy who'd try and sell a Christmas tree
in July."

"A killer?"

"What do you think?" Barrett said. He

looked about forty-five, with a shaved head and a significant belly.

"Seemed more like a thief."

"Every man in jail says he's innocent."

"Quirk said you helped out in the investigation."

"Someone dropped a dime on him." Barrett shrugged. "We got a call from a pay phone; somebody said that Mickey Green killed that woman. Whatshername?"

"Julie Sullivan."

"Sullivan, right," he said. "I went out looking for Green, checked in at a few bars, and damn if I didn't catch him at a car wash over by the circle. I mean, Christ. The guy was right there washing the blood off his Pontiac."

"Uh-oh."

"Big-time," he said. "Makes you wish this state would reinstate the death penalty."

"Motive?"

Barrett grinned a little and shook his head. "The vic was what is commonly known as a crack whore. The perp was a user, too. Mix those two together and you get a Southie dance party."

"So it was all about drugs?"

"When your mind is fried, could be anything," he said. "I once saw a guy kill another guy over a jar of fucking peanut butter."

The inside of Mul's Diner looked warm and peaceful, something out of a Hopper painting. People ate breakfast and drank coffee in vinyl booths. On the other side of the fogged windows, they read the paper or chatted on a slow Saturday morning. I turned and faced the empty brick storefronts that lined the street, marching in a steady, slow decay.

I lifted the collar on my leather jacket and took a sip of coffee from a paper cup.

"You ever hear of a couple guys named Moon and Pepper?"

"What is that, a rap group?"

"Drug dealers."

"I could ask around."

I handed him my card.

"I don't think Julie Sullivan was top priority for the boys in homicide."

"A Southie girl living the life never is," he said. "I don't even think it made it into the *Globe*."

"It got a brief."

"So why do you give a shit?"

"I'm handsomely paid by the deceased's family."

Barrett nodded. "Must be nice."

"Not to mention, I'm bold and stout-

31

hearted."

"Quirk said you were a smart-ass but a real straight shooter."

"That's true."

"He said you used to work for the Middlesex DA's office but didn't like to follow orders."

"Also true," I said.

"Maybe the reason I'm still on patrol at forty-five."

I shook Barrett's hand and thanked him before driving south on Dorchester Avenue, passing a big sign welcoming me to South Boston in English and Gaelic.

5

The Mary Ellen McCormack had been built back during the Depression, endless rows of squat brick buildings surrounded by black iron fencing. Old snow had been scraped and banked along the sidewalks and around an open basketball court, where a little boy rode a tricycle. A woman in a tattered ski hat stood nearby, smoking a cigarette and keeping watch. A patch of brown grass poked out of a bare spot beyond the court. Old twisted trees in the courtyards loomed barren and skeletal.

I parked off Kemp Street, in front of an official-looking building with an open wrought-iron gate and quickly found her second-floor unit. A television played inside as I knocked.

Mattie opened the door, a bit surprised to see me. She was wearing a black sweatshirt, faded jeans, and a silver tiara. She swiped the tiara from her head and nodded me in, through the kitchen. I spotted in front of the television an assembled pink play castle, where twin girls crawled out from a door flap, waiting for Mattie to return. Mattie tossed the tiara onto the kitchen counter by some dirty cereal bowls and an open carton of milk. Her face was flushed.

"I can come back," I said. "You look busy."

"Just babysitting and crap until Grandma gets up."

A gaunt woman lay asleep on a flowered sofa, one bony arm across her eyes, mouth open, a knitted blue blanket over her feet. She had a tattoo on her forearm of praying hands holding a rosary with the word JULIE beneath it. Grandma looked to be in her late forties.

"What'd you find out?" Mattie asked. She placed her hands on her narrow hips.

"May we sit?" I said, looking to the small kitchen table.

"I'd rather stand."

"Grandma have a rough night?"

"Are you kidding?" she asked. "She just got in."

"Night shift?"

"Yeah. The night shift at the pub."

"We all must serve God's purpose."

"Listen, let's get to it," Mattie said. "I got to get the girls cleaned up and ready for a birthday party over in the next building. It's *Dora the Explorer*. They love freakin' Dora."

The twins rattled around in the pink castle. Occasionally one would emerge and then crawl back inside. They both had short reddish brown hair but wore different pajamas. One kid was Dora and the other was a Disney princess. I didn't know which one. I used to really be up on the latest Disney princesses.

"I read your mom's file," I said. "I talked to some cops."

"They're idiots."

"Maybe. But they had a pretty solid case on Mickey Green."

"If I just wanted the cops' side of things I wouldn't have dragged my ass up to the Back Bay to hire you," she said. "I already know what they think, and that's not worth shit to me."

The furniture in the room that wasn't slip-covered looked to be from the late 1960s and well worn. A stack of folded kids' clothes sat in a laundry basket next to a pile of towels. There was a bicycle chained to a radiator and three plastic milk crates filled with dolls and toys. On one wall hung a framed picture of the Pope, a charcoal etching of Fenway, and a framed picture of an attractive young woman with bright red hair wearing a bright red sweater. It was the kind of studio portrait they take at shopping malls or discount stores. On closer inspection, I noted it was a senior portrait taken for South Boston High School.

"She was pretty before she fucked herself all up," Mattie said, coming up beside me. I could tell she was biting the inside of her cheek. She blinked hard three times. "That crap ages you. Makes you nuts. After a while, even your friends quit on you."

She was breathing like someone trying to steady herself.

"I can't promise anything," I said.

Mattie Sullivan studied my face before nodding. I was glad to see she'd cleaned the dime-store makeup off her eyes.

"I know she looked cheap, and I know the cops thought she was a whore. But that was bullshit. She loved us. She was trying to get clean. She was going to rehab when they came for her. They never even gave her a chance to make things right."

"What things?"

"Everything."

"Money?"

"I don't know," Mattie said. "Probably."

I nodded.

"She was a mess. She knew she had to do better. She was trying."

Mattie didn't look at me. She looked at her mom's picture, at the pink castle teetering with play, then down to her grandmother on the couch. "I didn't ask you for a miracle. Okay?"

"Amen," I said.

"The cops didn't do a thing but point to Mickey Green because he was easy," she said. "Meanwhile, the two animals who did this to my mother are still out there."

"How long have you been friends with Mickey?"

"Did I say he was my friend?"

"You said you visit him in prison."

"I've been a few times," she said and shrugged. "He was a screwup. But he wouldn't kill anyone. Especially my mom. He had feelings for her. That's why he hung around and tried to help."

"Does he write?"

"Yes."

"May I see the letters?"

"You mind me askin' if that's okay with Mickey?"

"Not at all."

"I know what you're thinking," Mattie said. "But I'm not a retard. Okay? You find Pepper and Moon, and you'll find the men who did this. What the cops did to Mickey wasn't right by him or my mom."

37

"How can you be sure?"

"Like I said a hundred times, I seen these two guys push my mother into their car. She was fighting them and yelling. Next thing I know the papers are saying Mickey Green did it. I'm thinking, Mickey Green? All he did was help my mom out with groceries and work on her car."

"Were they together?"

"You mean was she boinking him?" she asked.

"Yes."

"I don't know," she said. "Maybe. He was kinda sweet and goofy."

"You remember the car they were driving that night?"

Mattie shook her head.

"Grandma see anything?"

"We weren't living with her then. Okay?"

"Okay."

"Okay like you're done with me? Or okay like you're going to start doing some real detective work and quit just listening to the cops?"

"You're a tough boss."

Mattie looked me over. She almost smiled. "I got to be tough," she said. "If I wasn't, the twins would run wild and this place would turn to shit."

I nodded. Besides the toys and pile of

towels, the apartment was very clean. The twins looked to be socialized and up on their shots.

"You have some more pictures?" I asked. "Anything from the last year of her life?"

"Sure," Mattie said. "But she looked like shit."

"Where'd she hang out?"

"Four Green Fields. She went to happy hour like it was Mass."

Mattie turned to the dinette table and reached for her parka and pink Sox cap. The twins had again pushed aside the flap of the play castle and watched their big sister with hands under their chins.

"Going somewhere?" I asked.

"With you."

"That's not how I work."

"Too bad."

"What about the birthday party?" I said. "Who gets the twins ready?"

"I can help," she said. "You need me. Hey, Grandma?"

Mattie walked over and pushed at the gaunt woman's shoulder as she brushed past me to the door. Grandma stirred. I thought of a hundred ways to lose her or to explain just how I did my job. I could force the issue.

Mattie stood outside the door and pointed

to the center of my chest. "Whatta you want? Me to hold your hand? C'mon."

"Yes, Your Highness."

6

Four Green Fields looked like a hundred bars in Southie. There were neon and mirror bar signs, Sox and Celtics posters, two electronic dart boards, a video boxing game, and two ragged pool tables back by the toilets. I was pretty sure Philippe Starck had not designed the space. A well-worn barfly sat at a long row of empty stools, while a pale skinny guy with tattoos curling from shoulder to wrist beneath his sleeveless black T-shirt tended bar. He had a narrow patch of hair on his chin and a gold ring in one eyebrow. He looked up from a cutting board where he was slicing lemons. "No kids," he said.

Mattie acted like she didn't hear him and saddled up to the bar. "I'll have a Coke, please," she said with a big fake smile.

"Didn't I say no kids?" the bartender said.

"Just give me a soda and shut up," Mattie said.

41

He looked at me. I shrugged and offered my palms. "I'd do what she says. She just beat me twice in arm wrestling."

Tattoo Boy looked me over and shook his head. His T-shirt read DROPKICK MURPHYS. "Whatta you want?"

"I'd like a gimlet that's half gin and half Rose's lime juice," I said. "It beats martinis hollow."

"I got whiskies and Popov vodka, I got Guinness, and I got Sam Adams, I got —"

I held up my hand and stopped him there and asked for a beer and a shot, a soda for Mattie. He poured Mattie a Coke over ice, making a big deal about adding two straws and wrapping the glass with a napkin. Mattie rolled her eyes when he walked away. "What a dick," she said.

"It's just an act," I said. "Deep down, he's insecure."

Mattie shrugged.

"So this was your mom's place?" I asked.

"Yep."

"You know Tattoo Boy?"

"Nope."

I called for the bartender. Tattoo Boy looked up from the cutting, letting us know we were a real distraction. I wondered if he could chew gum and walk at the same time. I decided not to inquire.

42

"When you get a second, sir."

He sliced up one more lemon and walked slowly from the end of the bar. The drunk never looked up from his coffee mug. He was old, weathered and whiskered, and wore a filthy brown coat that may have been blue once upon a time. Or perhaps red.

"You want something?" he asked.

"Besides world peace and greater harmony with my fellow man?"

He sucked on a tooth and crossed his arms over his chest.

I slid a four-by-six photo of Julie Sullivan across the bar. She had her arm around a pudgy guy in a slick black shirt. He had a fat neck and a doughy, smooth face. The man's hair looked as if it had been shellacked. Julie Sullivan's eyes were glassy, the guy's meaty paw resting on her breast. Good times.

"You know her?"

He leaned in a little, stared for a second, and shook his head.

"What about the guy?"

He shook his head again. "Looks like a real douche."

"You've got a keen eye," I said.

"How long you been working here?" Mattie asked.

"What's this about?" Tattoo Boy asked.

"I'm looking to add captions to my photo album," I said. "This is my partner, Annie Leibovitz."

"What the hell are you talking about?"

"He's a detective, numb nuts," Mattie said. "And that's a picture of my ma. She used to make happy hour at this shithole, every day from the time she was out of high school. You know her or not?"

"I'll be the good cop," I said.

Tattoo Boy reached for the photo and held it against the green-and-white neon of the Guinness sign. He shook his head and gave it back to Mattie. He was very good at shaking his head.

"She leave you?" he asked.

"You could say that," Mattie said.

"My mom, too," the bartender said. "She left us a box of Frosted Flakes and a bottle of sour milk and said she'd be home by supper. She moved to fucking Florida."

"Thank God you turned out all right," I said.

He nodded at me with great understanding.

"Who's worked here the longest?" I asked.

"Shirley," he said. "She's been here for like thirty years."

"When does Shirley get in?" I asked.

"She's on Monday nights," the bartender

44

said. "But don't piss her off. She keeps a Louisville Slugger under the cash register for smart-mouth types."

"What does that have to do with me?"

He frowned at me.

"You know a couple locals named Pepper and Moon?" I asked.

He shook his head, but his gaze wandered. His lips pursed in thought.

"You sure?"

"Lots of folks come in here," he said. "I don't know all of them. I mean, Jesus."

"Seems like you'd recall those names."

"Everyone has fucked-up names in Southie."

"What's your name?"

"Ted."

"Well, there you go."

Ted returned to his lemons, slowly slicing away. The old bum at the bar lifted his mug. I was glad to see the movement, since I was beginning to think he might be a figment of my imagination.

"Where to, Princess?" I asked.

"Don't get cute with that," she said. "I was babysitting."

"I can't help but be cute," I said. "It's part of my genetic code."

"How about being a detective?"

"Okay. Your mom got any friends who still

live around here?"

"Sure."

"Aha." I reached for a cocktail napkin and a pen. "In my business, we call those leads. You want another Coke?"

"Nope." She leaned in to her straw and then turned to me. She narrowed her eyes. "How old are you anyway?"

"Methuselah was my kid brother."

"Who's that?"

"Methuselah played ball with Branch Rickey."

When I was a teenager, anyone who'd graduated high school seemed ancient. I tapped the pen to the napkin. "Tell me about your mom's friends."

She did.

The bar was very long and very quiet as I wrote. The sounds of the freight trucks barreling down the road shook the bar. Tattoo Boy occasionally looked up and gave me the stink eye.

I winked back.

7

The fourth person on Mattie's list was Theresa Donovan. We chose to meet with her first through a highly selective process: The first person on the list wasn't home, and Mattie didn't know where the next two lived. Theresa worked at a corner convenience store on Old Colony not far from Joe Moakley Park. The store was a small brick building with a glass front that offered great deals on both cigarettes and lottery tickets. Beer was on sale, too. Yippee.

We had to talk to Theresa from behind bulletproof glass while she rang up customers. After a few minutes things slowed, and she unlocked her cage and came out and gave Mattie a hug, being careful not to burn her with her newly lit cigarette.

"This is Spenser," Mattie said. "He's helping me find out who killed my ma."

"Whatta you mean?" she asked. "Mickey Green killed her."

"That's bullshit, and you know it."

Theresa looked at a wall clock and then back to Mattie and then back to me. She blew out some smoke from the side of her mouth. "Don't be a smart-ass, kid. Your ma wouldn't've liked that. Why are you digging that up now?"

"If you were such great friends, why don't you try and help?" Mattie asked. "You know Mickey Green wouldn't hurt anyone. Tell the truth instead of spewing bullshit on him."

I shrugged. "She has a true gift," I said.

Theresa took the cigarette out of her mouth and pointed the red end at me. "You payin' this guy?"

"Yeah," Mattie said.

"You a lawyer?"

"Do I look like a lawyer?"

"You look like a pro wrestler."

I nodded. She had me there.

"I'm a private detective," I said. "Not that it's any of your business."

Theresa eyed me and shook her head with disgust. She wore a pair of gold hoops that went nicely with her threadbare blue sweatshirt, well-worn knockoff designer jeans, and dirty Nikes. She was a good-looking girl who'd probably been much better-looking before all the junk food and beer.

48

Her hips had grown wide and her skin was uneven and blemished. She'd quit bleaching her hair some time back, and a good inch of her roots had started to show. But her face remained sharp, set off with a nice pair of sleepy blue eyes. Her eyes had a smart sexiness to them, studying me as I studied her.

"You were a friend of Julie's?" I asked.

"I was Jules's best friend."

"School?"

"All the way through Southie High," she said. "Our families went to Gate of Heaven."

"You know Mickey Green, too?"

"Everybody knew Mickey."

"And you obviously think he's guilty?"

"You're goddamn right." Her mouth twitched just a bit, her eyes not meeting mine. "Of course."

"You don't know what you're talking about," Mattie said. "You tossed her in the fucking garbage and wouldn't help her. Mickey was her friend."

"Mattie, you were ten years old," Theresa said. "You don't know how I tried. It didn't amount to shit. She was sick in the head, kid. She didn't want help from nobody."

"That's crap," Mattie said. "She was headed for that rehab place."

" 'Cause the judge made her."

49

Theresa squashed a cigarette under her heel. She lit another. The convenience store was brightly lit with hard, artificial light over rows and rows of cheap food and soda. The stuff probably had a shelf life into the next millennium. The air smelled of overcooked hot dogs, stale smoke, and old grease.

"You know anyone who was still friendly with her when she died?"

Smoke escaped out of the corner of a smile on Theresa's face. "Sure."

"Who?" I asked.

"Mickey Green and about a hundred other guys."

"Bitch," Mattie said. Her face flushed, and her eyes grew bright. She was biting the inside of her cheek again. "You're a liar."

"Your mom liked men," Theresa said. "Sue me."

"Not that I don't appreciate your help," I said to Mattie. "But would you mind waiting for me outside?"

"Hell I will," Mattie said. "I got the right to hear her lies."

An old woman walked into the store, and Theresa found her way back to the register and locked the door behind her. The old woman wore a spiffy rabbit-fur coat over a flowered housedress. She bought twenty dollars' worth of lottery tickets, a carton of

50

Newports, and an *Us Weekly* magazine. Brad and Angelina were having relationship issues. Charlie Sheen was headed back to rehab.

Mattie dropped her head and lowered her shoulders and barreled out the front door. I walked in front of the Plexiglas and gave Theresa the million-dollar smile. The full wattage of my charisma was needed to repair the damage.

"You should be ashamed of yourself," she said.

"I heard if I don't stop, I'll go blind."

"You shouldn't take that little girl's money."

"What kind of best friend were you to Julie Sullivan?" I asked.

The question hung there for a moment in the smoke. She glared at me.

"Surely you've heard of two local baddies named Pepper and Moon?" I asked. "Or don't you allow riffraff in here?"

She smoked the cigarette down to a nub as she studied me. Smoke fogged the inside of the bulletproof cubicle. She shook her head. The glass had yellowed with age and smoke. "You don't get it, do you?"

"The million-dollar smile usually works."

"You know what kind of shit you're kicking up? That little girl walks around Southie and starts asking questions about those two and pretty soon you'll see her picture on the back of a milk carton."

"So you know them?"

"Sure."

"And they're bad guys."

"Hannibal Lecter was a bad guy," Theresa said. "These guys are evil."

"But you don't believe they had anything to do with Mattie's mom?"

"What's the difference?" she asked. "They were friends with Mickey Green. They all lived together in a three-decker over on G Street. They sold crack and heroin. That was Julie's candy store, where she'd do about anything to get a hot shot. You see what I'm sayin'?"

I nodded. "Where can I find them now?"

"I haven't seen them in years," she said. "I don't care what Mattie thinks, I don't want to be dragged into this. I got bill collectors on my ass and a dad who's got the dementia."

"Mattie says Mickey wasn't with her mom that night."

"How would she know?"

"Who were her regular friends before she was killed?'

"You check Four Green Fields?"

"Yep."

"You keep asking there and you'll find people who knew Jules. Good-time Jules. Lots of folks knew her."

"What about away from the pub?"

"You check with Gate of Heaven?"

I shook my head.

"Priest there did some kind of outreach thing," Theresa said. "I heard she was getting better before she got worse. Mattie wasn't wrong about that."

"When did she make the turn?"

"She'd always been wild," she said, finding a seat on a wooden stool by the register. Her voice sounded distant behind the glass. "But she stopped having any pride in herself after this car accident. I mean, she would've never given a guy like Mickey Green the time of day. He followed her around like a kid, walking her home from the store, fixing shit in their apartment."

"What car accident?"

"I don't know everything," she said. "It was like ten years ago. I just know it messed her up. Got her more into drugs and shit. Then she got straightened out again after the twins. A real roller-coaster thing."

"You know Mattie's father?"

"No," Theresa said. "And neither did Jules."

I nodded.

Theresa turned her head to the parking lot where Mattie sat on the hood of my car. It was getting late, and the streetlamps on Old Colony started to flicker to life. Mattie was smoking a cigarette and staring at nothing. She looked very small and awkward fiddling with the lighter. Her coat seemed ill fitting and shapeless and brought to mind Paul once again.

"Don't get her hopes up, okay?" Theresa said. "I heard she was spreading rumors about those guys, and that doesn't do nobody any good."

"You know their real names?"

"Moon is just Moon," she said. "Big fat guy. Looks like a whale. He used to be a bouncer at Triple O's before it closed."

Three teenage boys strolled and smirked inside and tried to buy a six-pack and some condoms. Theresa sold the boys the condoms and they shirked away. I walked over to the bubble gum aisle and looked for some Bazooka. They didn't carry it. Bazooka Joe would have offered guidance.

I walked back to the register.

Theresa turned off the intercom and leaned to the cutout in the Plexi. "Red Cahill. They call him Pepper."

I nodded. She studied my face and let out a long breath.

"These are some seriously connected people who don't like old shit being kicked up."

"Connected to whom?"

" 'Whom'?" Theresa asked. "You gonna buy anything? 'Cause if not, you can't just loiter around. My heart feels like it's gonna jump out of my throat talkin' about this shit."

I smiled at her. "It's been a pleasure."

"Are we finished?" she asked.

8

"In the future, how about I handle the questioning," I said.

"If I hadn't come with you," Mattie said, "Theresa wouldn'a said shit."

"Do you have any idea what happens when I smile at women?"

Mattie didn't answer.

"It comes with a permit," I said. "I use it sparingly."

"She needed a little kick in the ass," Mattie said, reaching to turn up the heat as we drove. She sank down into the passenger seat, pink Sox cap low over her eyes. She tapped her black-nailed fingers against the window glass as she stared out at the road. The night had grown dark outside the car as we headed south back to the Mary Ellen McCormack.

"How about you just point me in the right direction," I said. "And I do the legwork."

"Nope."

"Thanks for the help," I said. "But I'm going to have to talk to some rough characters. People of low reputation."

"Wow," Mattie said. "I'm scared."

"You hired me to do a job," I said. "You need to respect the way I work."

"You need me," she said. "I know people."

"I would have to play shamus and bodyguard," I said. "I prefer one job at a time. And don't fool yourself. I know a lot of crummy people, too."

She didn't say anything.

"You hungry?" I asked.

"Nope."

"I'm hungry," I said. "It's late. I'll start again Monday."

"I got school Monday."

"I don't," I said. "Being an adult has its privileges."

We followed Old Colony, passing check-cashing businesses and liquor stores and secondhand car dealers. I turned onto Monsignor O'Callaghan Way and slowed by the front gate of the housing projects. The old brick buildings looked to be built from the same design as Depression-era hospitals and mental asylums. In the last decade or so, someone had added a few murals and a modern-looking sculpture. Neither did much to dress up the place.

I stopped the car and offered her my hand.

Mattie removed her ball cap and shook my hand. She tucked her reddish hair behind her ears and slipped the cap back on.

"I wasn't tryin' to screw with you," she said.

"Never dream of it."

"Theresa was just trying to give you the same bullshit she gave my ma."

"Maybe she told me some things."

"What things?"

"I got stuff to check out," I said. "Leads to follow. Hoodlums to rough up."

Mattie rubbed her cold nose and nodded. She reached for the door handle. "You call me tomorrow?"

I smiled. "You bet, kid."

"Spenser?"

"Yep?"

"Please don't call me 'kid.'"

She pushed the door open and stepped onto the curb. I turned up the collar on my leather jacket and put my hands in front of the heating vent. I watched Mattie Sullivan open a spiked gate with a key and walk down a path lined with skinny leafless trees. A group of teenagers were lounging on a playground in their parkas and puffy coats. Five or six of them blocked Mattie's path.

She busted through them like Gale Sayers, splitting the group in half, and kept walking with her head down and her hands in her pockets.

I smiled.

I cranked the engine and drove north on the expressway to the Back Bay, where the boutiques on Newbury Street were still full of shoppers and the dinner crowd was heading out for cocktails in their cashmere coats and hats. The trees of the Public Garden were still strung with white Christmas lights. Tonight was Susan's night to volunteer at a women's shelter in Charlestown, and she'd left me a message to expect a very important houseguest at my apartment.

I parked on Marlborough Street and headed up the steps to find Pearl the Wonder Dog waiting for me with a squeaky rubber chicken in her mouth.

I scratched behind her ears and gave her a cookie. Peanut butter and bacon sounded like a terrific combo to me.

"What's for dinner?" I asked.

Pearl didn't answer. She panted.

Seeing I was on my own, I opened the refrigerator. I pulled out a sweet potato, a yellow onion, and some andouille sausage we'd bought at Savenor's in Beacon Hill. Since Susan wouldn't be dining with me, I reached for a bottle of Tabasco.

"First things first," I said to Pearl. She looked at me earnestly and tilted her head.

I went to the bar and poured myself a measure of scotch and then added a lot of ice and a lot of soda. I flicked on the stereo and sipped the drink while listening to a Tony Bennett LP, "I'm Always Chasing Rainbows."

I placed the sweet potato in the oven and tried Vinnie Morris. He didn't pick up.

I asked his voice mail about Red Cahill and a heavy named Moon. His voice mail did not respond.

I listened to Tony for a while, then put on a pot of stone-ground grits. I sliced the andouille and chopped the onion and cooked them both in some olive oil. I added a splash of Tabasco and some salt and a lot of black pepper. When the sweet potato was done, I peeled and chopped it and added it into the mix. I found some maple syrup from Vermont and drizzled some into the pan, along with a dash of brown sugar.

I lowered the heat and checked on the grits.

I set a single place at the table with good china and gave Pearl another cookie as I dolloped the andouille-and-sweet-potato mixture on top of the steaming grits.

Tony sang a sad song. But he sang it with hope.

I was halfway finished when the phone rang.

"Excuse me," I said to Pearl. Pearl eyed the grits.

I picked up the phone.

"Do you go out looking for flaming piles of shit, or do people leave them at your door?"

"Hello, Vinnie."

"Jesus."

I reached over the table and finished the scotch.

"What you got?" I asked.

"Red Cahill and some guy named Moon. Right?"

"Red likes to be called Pepper," I said. "Like red pepper. It's cute, right?"

"There isn't shit cute about Red Cahill," Vinnie said. "Whatta you want with these animals?"

"Coming from you, that is high praise."

"I ain't the man I used to be."

"Me and you both," I said.

"Since Joe got old, the city is a little screwy," Vinnie said.

"It was screwier with Joe Broz."

"Maybe, but he consolidated."

"Big word," I said.

"I try," Vinnie said.

"And now?"

"You read about that shooting in Dorchester last month?"

"Five men," I said.

"Yep."

"Town is changing again," I said.

"Yep."

"And hot Pepper has something to do with this?" I asked.

"Bingo."

"He a shooter?"

"Maybe better than me," Vinnie said.

"Nobody is better than you."

"I'm just saying."

"So who's in charge?" I asked.

"You're not gonna believe this."

"I hate stories that start out that way," I said. "Will this give me indigestion? Because I've got a top-notch meal waiting for me."

"Gerry Broz is reclaiming his old man's territory."

"Red Cahill works for Gerry Broz?"

"And Gerry Broz is no friend to you," Vinnie said.

"He may hold a grudge," I said.

"He's been wanting you dead for a couple decades."

"I *may* have shot him."

"There is that," Vinnie said.

"Indeed," I said.

9

Monday morning, I dressed in a pair of gray sweats and laced up my New Balance running shoes, taking along some street clothes in a gym bag. At eight a.m., I met Hawk at Henry Cimoli's place on the waterfront. We waited until the yoga class had finished their meditation and deep breathing and then took over the back room. Hawk hung the speed bag, and I lifted the heavy bag, Hawk hooking the chains onto the swivel.

We turned on the lights.

"You ever think about takin' up yoga?" Hawk asked. "Deep breathing, meditation. All that shit."

"No," I said. "You?"

"I am the model of inner peace."

"Even when kicking the crap out of someone?"

Hawk grinned. "Especially then."

The yoga teacher was young and slim, with long red hair wrapped into a bun. She shut off the meditation music and carried the CD player out with her. On her way out the door, she and Hawk exchanged smiles.

"Why didn't she smile at me?" I asked.

"You an acquired taste," Hawk said. "My sexual energy is recognizable and immediate."

"Of course."

"How many rounds?"

"Let's hit six," I said. "We take turns on the speed and heavy. Maybe some shadow work."

"You still talkin'?" he asked.

I nodded, and we slid into the rhythm we'd developed over the years. I found the punching, footwork, and breathing to be a kind of music. Hawk's hands worked on a speed bag like Gene Krupa on drums. My hands weren't quite as fast, but my punches were solid. By the third round, I was sweating. Hawk glistened.

His bald black head shone. His biceps and forearms swelled from his T-shirt. But I did not hear a grunt. Hawk was effortless in both speed and violence.

We finished the workout with some bench presses and arm work. Hawk and I tossed around the medicine ball, quick passes back and forth. Some of the young ladies watched as we worked.

"Poetry in motion," Hawk said.

"No," I said. "I don't think they've ever seen a medicine ball before."

"Good thing Henry keeps one for us."

"Nostalgia," I said.

After a fat guy in swim trunks left us in the steam room, I told Hawk about Mattie Sullivan and Moon and Red "Pepper" Cahill. Gerry Broz, too.

"Just where'd you shoot him?" he asked.

"Right in the Public Garden."

Hawk grinned and shook his head.

"Leg," I said.

"You saved the motherfucker's life," Hawk said. "Joe Broz knew that."

"Joe thought I'd have to kill him," I said. "But he wanted Gerry to try for me anyway. Thought it would make him a man."

"That's love," Hawk said.

I nodded and wiped my face with a towel, leaving it over my eyes and settling back into the cedarwood bench.

"Feds been lookin' for Joe Broz's ass for ten years," Hawk said. "I see him on *America's Most Wanted*."

"I think he's dead."

"Men like Joe Broz don't die, man," Hawk said. "He down in Florida givin' it to some old widow."

"You know Gerry was back into the rackets?"

"Figure he be back," Hawk said. "He don't possess many skills."

"He ain't Joe Broz."

"No," Hawk said. "He ain't."

"Vinnie says Gerry was behind that shooting in Dorchester."

"You goin' straight ahead at this?" Hawk said. "If so, a brother might need to consult his schedule."

I took the towel from my face and wiped my eyes. "Not yet," I said. "I want to poke around it. See what jumps out."

"You gonna use your red-skinned protégé?"

"Z's in Montana," I said. "Business with his family."

"So you gonna screw around and then call me when your ass in a sling?"

"Exactly."

"Be good to talk to this guy, Mickey Green," Hawk said. "See what he know."

"Thought had crossed my mind."

"Maybe he was neck-deep in this shit, too."

"Probably."

"Where she live in Southie?"

I told him.

"Never been real fond of black folk there."

67

"You know it's not the same," I said. "It's black and white and Asian. Gay and straight. Yuppies moving into condos on the harbor."

"Still a tough place to grow up."

"You think Mickey Green will agree to see me?"

"What else he got to do at Cedar Junction," Hawk said, "besides play with himself?"

"I still want to call it Walpole."

"Don't have the same ring," Hawk said. "Walpole sounds tough. Cedar Junction sound like a peckerwood jamboree."

After the workout, I showered and shaved and dressed in jeans and a sweatshirt. I slipped my running shoes back on and clipped my .38 Chief's Special onto the rear of my belt. I slid into my leather jacket with the zip-in liner and reached for my Boston Braves cap.

I felt calm. My breathing had slowed. My heart beat at an easy rhythm, and my head was clear. I now needed only coffee and some corn muffins to fuel my day.

When I returned to my car, I found the little red light blinking on my cell phone, so I called my voice mail. Spenser, master of technology.

"I need to see you," Mattie Sullivan said. "Don't freak out or nothin', but they won't let me leave the counselor's office. I told them I'm fine, but a couple douchebags tried to run me over this morning. I ripped my pants. No big deal, but thought you should know."

I circled back to Southie.

10

Mattie told the school counselor I was her uncle, and the counselor bought it. I'd like to think it was the wisdom in my eyes or the deep calm resonance of my voice. Or maybe the counselor just thought Mattie could use a day off. She'd shown up for science class in torn khakis, her knees and elbows skinned and bloody.

We found a Dunkin' Donuts on Perkins Square where Broadway and Dorchester Street converge. We sat at a stand-up bar overlooking Broadway, watching people line up at the check-cashing business. Next door was a hardware store, and across the street was a pizzeria called McGoo's in the bottom of a three-decker. There was also a bank, a barbershop, and a Goodwill in the little shopping district. The skies hinted at a cold rain.

I chose two corn muffins and a black coffee. Mattie chose a grape-jelly-filled. The folly of youth.

"Did you see these guys?" I asked.

"Sort of."

"Was it Pepper and Moon?"

"Nope," she said.

"How do you know?"

"Do I look stupid?"

"What'd they look like?"

"The guy driving was older," she said. "Gray hair and kinda scruffy. Other guy I couldn't see so well. He mighta been black. Or maybe Mexican or somethin'."

"How do you know they were trying to hurt you?"

"I figured that out about the time the car's grille nipped at my ass."

"Excellent point," I said. "Then what?"

"What do you think?" Mattie asked. "I jumped into a fucking ditch."

"What kind of car was it?"

"I don't know. Car was blue or silver."

"You see the license plate?"

"As I was jumping into the ditch?"

"Wouldn't matter," I said. "Probably stolen. What did they do after they passed?"

"They braked real hard and doubled back," she said. "Ditch was outside a construction site on Dorchester, and I ran like hell through it. I cut over to G Street through some people's backyards, and that's

71

how come I tore my pants."

"And still made school on time."

"Yep."

"That's dedication," I said.

We sat quietly for a while. A homeless man in an Army jacket wandered in and shelled out dimes and pennies for an old-fashioned and two donut holes. Several city buses passed the big plate-glass window, spewing black smoke and churning slush. The teenage girl at the counter looked bored until a couple teen boys walked up to the counter.

"How's Grandma?"

"She didn't come home last night."

"That okay with you?" I asked.

"Sometimes it's better when she's gone."

"You got other family?"

"Sure."

"Anyone who can help?"

"Help with what?"

"You and your sisters."

"I don't need any help."

"You raising them?"

"I don't raise them," Mattie said. "I look out for them."

"What's the difference?"

"I'm their big sister," she said. "It's what you do. I don't really have a lot of time to think about it. You just do it."

I watched her finish the donut. I sipped

some more coffee. One of the boys at the counter was trying to make time with the girl selling donuts. He said he'd love to have her number in his cell. She turned him down flat.

Mattie was listening and grinned a bit. She was a very good listener, aware of everything around her.

"How do you guys make do?" I asked.

"We get a government check," Mattie said. "Grandma cleans houses and offices some."

"Has she always been a drunk?"

"Not like now," Mattie said. "She didn't drink so much after my mom died. We had social workers dropping in and stuff. People from church bringing food and whatever. She can dry out if she wants."

"What happened to them?"

Mattie shrugged. We watched more cars pass by the window and the homeless guy artfully begging for more change. The kid at the counter would not give the donut girl a rest. She finally gave up her number. Persistence.

"What do you do for fun?" I asked.

"What do you mean?"

"You like sports or going to Mass? You belong to any clubs? Do you have a boy-friend?"

She made a snort that could almost have

been a laugh. I smiled at her.

"No boyfriend?"

Her pudgy face colored a bit as she re-adjusted her elbows on the counter. She reached up to chew a black nail.

"But you do like the Sox?"

"Sure."

"What do you think about Adrian Gonzalez?"

"For a hundred and fifty mil, he better pull his weight."

"You ever been to Fenway?"

"Oh, yeah," she said. "With all my extra money. I got season tickets."

"You know you've got to quit asking around about these guys without me," I said. "That's not a good idea right now. Not very safe."

She shrugged.

"I'll drive you to and from school," I said. "Something happens at home, you call me and then you call nine-one-one. I'm going to try and work out something with a patrol officer I know."

She nodded. "Okay."

"How are you feeling right now?"

"Fine."

"You think we could stop by the local station house and look at some photos?" I asked. "Have you file a report?"

She nodded.

"After that, let's do something about those clothes. I can run you back to your apartment to change."

"Where we headed?"

"Field trip," I said.

11

I had made many visits to Walpole and its lovely state prison. It had opened sometime back in the fifties and had that classic prison feel. Big concrete walls, concertina wire, heavy iron doors with brass handles. The entire place stank of funk and sweat. The Boston Strangler had once called it home. They still made license plates.

Mattie had been there, too. She knew the drill.

I'd arranged for us to meet with Mickey Green during visiting hours. I'd called while waiting outside Mattie's apartment for her to change. We walked through metal detectors and a hand search. I checked my .38 at the door.

Mattie was impressed. The guard was not, and he asked for my permit.

"You carry that gun all the time?" she asked.

"I have a slight inferiority complex."

A guard motioned for us to enter through another door into a long room lined with Plexiglas windows and telephone handsets. A thick-barred window had been opened a crack on the visitors' side to let in fresh cold air.

I let Mattie take the seat. I stood behind her.

Mickey Green wasn't much to look at. Average height and skinny, he wore some sparse blond hair on his face that some might describe as a beard. He eyed me with hooded, hawkish eyes and then sat in front of Mattie. He picked up the phone gingerly, as if it could be bugged.

He figured me for the fuzz.

I thought that word had gone out of fashion a long time ago. Mattie told him that I wasn't. She explained the situation. Green began to relax, eyes flicking up to my face and nodding. Mattie asked him if he needed anything and if he was taking care of himself. Green smiled at Mattie. She smiled back. He looked up again at me and nodded his approval.

I switched places with her, and she moved to stand behind my right shoulder.

"Mattie says you got a raw deal," I said.

"She knows I got fucked," Green said, scratching his neck. "You gonna get me out of this shithole or what?"

"But Walpole is so beautiful this time of year."

"Change seats with me."

I shrugged. His eyes met mine, and he nodded back. "Okay," he said. "What do you want from me?"

"If you lie to me or lead me in the wrong direction, you're only screwing yourself."

Mickey Green nodded again. He looked earnest in his bright orange jumpsuit. It was tough to look earnest in orange.

"Were you with Julie Sullivan the night she died?"

"I've been through this."

"Not with me. Were you with her?"

"Nope," Mickey said. He leaned toward the glass as if it would amplify his voice. "I did not kill her. I loved Jules."

"That's why you helped out the family sometimes?"

"I did what I could, you know," he said. "I'm good with my hands."

There was a solid offering of a joke, especially sitting in prison, but I refrained. I only nodded and asked, "You sell her drugs?"

"No."

"But you lived with two known drug dealers?"

78

He nodded.

"And you've told Mattie that those two men killed Julie?"

"Yes."

"Moon and Red Cahill."

He nodded again. "It's complicated, man."

"My mind is nimble," I said. "Try me."

"Huh?"

"How am I to believe you were not connected in their business endeavors?"

"I'm a fucking mechanic," he said. "Red is my cousin. We split the rent."

"But that's where Julie got her drugs."

"Well, sure."

"And you didn't stop that?"

"How was I gonna stop her when I couldn't stop myself? I ain't her fucking priest."

"Fair enough," I said. "The Suffolk County DA had a tight case on you."

"Bullshit."

"You were washing blood and hair off the car used to run her down."

I felt a hand on my shoulder and turned back to Mattie. I wish she'd stayed in the car. But Mickey obviously trusted her, and I didn't know if he'd see me without her. She nodded to him. He stared at her, smirked, and shook his head.

"They listen on these things," he said.

"And I don't like talking with my pants down."

"Can you at least explain the car?"

"Red borrowed it that night."

"And the next day, you just decided to give it a wash?"

"Red asked me to check the belts and get it cleaned," he said. "I was sleeping one off, and he comes in and pitches me the keys and tells me to take care of the car."

"Nice."

"And he paid me fifty bucks."

"You tell the cops this?"

Mickey Green rubbed his insignificant beard and blew out his breath. "No."

"Because he's your cousin?"

"Because he would've killed me."

"That would be a deterrent," I said. "And now?"

"Now I don't give a shit," he said. "I can't do life in here."

"I need names," I said. "I need to know people who would've seen Julie that night."

He nodded, meeting my eyes.

"If you want to protect Red," I said, "that's fine. But do you think he'd do the same for you? Has he ever come to visit?"

Mickey shook his head. "Only people come to visit are my sister and Mattie."

"I think you need to start looking out for

yourself," I said.

Mickey looked as if he'd just tasted something sour, but the sourness passed, and something brightened his face that seemed like a decision. "You got a pen?" Mickey asked.

"Always prepared, that's my motto." I reached into my jacket.

"You better watch your fucking back," Mickey said.

"Hold on, let me write that down."

Mickey smirked. He leaned forward and lifted his eyes up to the glass.

"You ever hear Red mention the name Gerry Broz?" I asked.

"Broz, as in Joe Broz?" Mickey said.

"Yep."

"Is he Broz's son or somethin'?"

"Or somethin'."

"Never mentioned him."

"So Red and Moon worked alone back then?"

"Yep."

"What's Moon's real name?" I asked.

"Leslie Murphy."

"Not a very tough name."

"You seen him?"

"Haven't had the pleasure."

"Looks like a rhinoceros on steroids," Mickey said. "He once sexually assaulted a guy who played for the Pats with a pool cue."

"Ouch."

"Fuckin' A," Mickey said. "I heard that guy didn't shit straight for a month."

"Names?" I asked. "People who knew Julie then, and people who saw you that night."

"Like an alibi?"

"Yeah, Mickey," I said. "Just like that."

12

Tiffany Royce worked in a nail salon near Andrew Station in a long row of storefronts populated by a couple of pubs, a corner convenience store called the Cor-nah Store, and an auto-glass shop. If you looked north along Dorchester Avenue, you got a pretty good idea how far we were from downtown. Across the turnpike and channel, the late-afternoon sun warmed silver- and gold-mirrored windows. The cluster of office buildings looked like the Emerald City.

"So Mickey Green was your boyfriend?"

"Sort of," Tiffany said.

" 'Sort of' for how long?"

"I don't know," she said. "A long time. Maybe six months."

"Were you together when he was arrested?"

"He came over a few times," she said. "Him going away saved my life."

"How's that?"

"We had a lot of good times," she said. "We liked to party. I mean, I was twenty. Isn't that what you do?"

"I don't know," I said. "I haven't been twenty for a while."

Tiffany had brown hair with highlights and was short and small-boned, with angular features and a sharp nose. She had green eyes and very long, ornate nails, as you would expect. She wore stylish dark blue jeans with red stitching and very tall pink heels. Her very tight pink V-neck sweater showed off a good bit of lace bra, also pink. Her breasts were high and very large for such a delicate girl.

I tried not to leer. But the devil lived in details.

Mattie sat in a waiting area of two faux-leather chairs patched in several places with duct tape. She read a celebrity gossip magazine as she eavesdropped, Sox cap down over her eyes like an infielder. Her legs were crossed, the right foot kicking up and down with nervous teen energy. I didn't like her tagging along, but she'd insisted, arguing that she knew the neighborhood better than I did.

In the back of the salon, two Vietnamese women worked on the feet of a couple of hefty ladies in glittery sweatshirts. The ladies jabbered on their cell phones and flipped through more celebrity rags. One lady peered over the top, perhaps confusing me for Brad Pitt.

"He ever get rough with you?" I asked.

"Mickey?" Tiffany asked. She laughed.

"Never?"

"Never," she said. "Are you kidding? I would have kicked his ass. He's not that guy. You know? He's kind of like Charlie Brown, bad things just seem to happen to him. He never looked for trouble."

"You ever know him to beat up another girlfriend? Get in a bar fight?"

She shook her head. "You want a manicure?" she asked. "You have some rough cuticles."

"Might harm my reputation as a tough guy."

"Lots of men get manicures," she said. "There's no shame in it."

"Might lead to a Brazilian wax."

Tiffany opened up a cardboard box with the sharp end of a nail file and started to arrange colorful little bottles of nail polish on a wall display. I wondered if Susan had ever thought about painting her nails dark purple. Probably didn't call it purple. Maybe eggplant. Better yet, *aubergine*.

"That your daughter?" she asked.

"Julie Sullivan's kid."

Tiffany's small white face flushed. "Jesus. I hadn't seen her in years. She know who I am? Me and Mickey?"

"Don't worry. She thinks Mickey Green is an innocent man."

"Jules Sullivan's kid thinks Mickey is innocent?"

"Yep," I said. "Makes you wonder."

"Never made sense to me," she said. She folded her arms across her chest as if she'd grown cold. "Lots of shit in Southie happens that don't make sense. Mickey was pretty far gone. Figured it was the drugs that changed him. You know anything about heroin?"

"Know enough not to try it."

"You ever do any drugs?"

"Took Benzedrine in the Army," I said. "I prefer a good whiskey. Beer, too. I'm not picky."

"Better than sex."

"Excuse me?" I asked.

"The rush," she said. "It's ten times more powerful than sex."

"Maybe you're not doing it right," I said.

"Took me most of a year to get clean."

Tiffany unlocked her arms and continued to arrange the little bottles of nail polish. She had to lift up on her toes to reach a top

86

shelf, showing off a wide butterfly tattoo on her lower back. I searched for more clues.

"Mickey said you were with him the night Julie was killed."

She stopped arranging and turned, staring at me.

"Is that true?"

She nodded.

"He slept on my couch."

"What time?"

"I don't remember."

"Was it past midnight?"

"I think," she said. "He sometimes came over like that. You know? Knocking on the door, saying he loved me. Wanting some booty."

"And you were intimate?"

"You mean did we fuck?"

"Or maybe a cordial game of naked Twister."

"Not that night."

"Did he act strange?"

"Mickey's a strange guy," she said. "He always acted strange, especially when he was drunk. He was pretty messed up. Said he needed me. Blah, blah, blah."

I nodded. "You see any blood on him? Did he seem nervous or agitated?"

She shook her head. "He came over for one thing. Telling me he loved me. Wanted to marry me and a bunch of shit."

I nodded. "Was he serious?"

She laughed again. "He was serious about getting into my pants. I knew he was doing the same thing with Julie. It was no biggie."

"What time did he leave?"

"Early," she said. "I know it was light out. Said he was gonna buy some eggs, make breakfast, and never came back."

"You tell this to the police?"

She shook her head.

"Why not?"

"No one asked," she said. "I don't think even his lawyer cared. Same shit I'm telling you. Charlie Brown."

"You know Red Cahill?" I asked.

"Sure, Mickey's cousin."

"I hear he's a top-shelf individual."

"He's an evil piece of shit."

"How bad can a guy named Red be?"

"He was a fighter," Tiffany said. She took a seat in the receptionist's chair and spun to the right and then to the left. She lifted her eyes, waiting for me to digest that fact. "Hung out at the old McDonough's Gym when we were kids. Won all kind of trophies. That Golden thing. You know."

"Golden Gloves," I said.

"Yeah," she said. "Heard he went pro but didn't go that far."

"What's he do now?"

"Sells drugs," she said. "What else?"

"And Moon Murphy?"

"He and Red work together," she said. "I don't think I've ever seen them apart. They're a team, you know. That guy freaks me out, looks at me like I'm a slice of hot pie. He's not right in the head. You better watch it. He knows you're looking for him, he might get rough."

"I'm sure I can reason with him."

"Red's the brains," she said. "Whatever he has left. Moon just does what he says."

I asked her about more people from the Four Green Fields drinking crew. She gave me some names. I handed her my card. The one with just my name and phone number. I had decided against the magnifying-glass or skull-and-crossbones logos.

"Private eye," she said. "For real?"

"Yep."

"You really think Mickey is innocent?"

I looked over to Mattie. She caught my eye, listening to every syllable, and then looked back at a magazine advertising *Hawaiian Dream Deals. Golden Shores. Memories to Last a Lifetime.*

"To be honest, I really don't know," I said. "I'm pretty sure he didn't get a fair shake in court."

"I would like to think that wasn't him," she said. "I mean, we were together for a while. What would that make me? If you're with someone who does something like that, the way he killed her, that shit infects you. Men take off once they hear I used to be with Mickey. No one in Southie has forgotten."

I nodded.

"You think Julie's kid would want a manicure? I'll do it free."

"You sell black nail polish?" I asked.

"Nope."

"Then probably not."

I walked outside into the cold, ankle-deep in slush. Mattie followed, and we stood on the street for a moment, our breath fogging in the cold as we looked north to south. Light sliced across the far-off Boston buildings and then faded across the tripledeckers and old brick buildings of Southie. Mattie jammed her hands into her coat pockets.

Three teen girls toting backpacks crossed our path. Each girl took special care not to glance at Mattie. But Mattie eyed them until they crossed Dorchester Avenue. As they walked, one girl turned to the others and whispered. The girls all looked back and laughed, barely covering their mouths.

"You know those girls?"

"Bitches."

"How about I walk you home?" I asked.

"What about the pub?"

"What about it?"

"You said we'd go back and talk to the bartender at Four Green Fields," she said. "Shirley? It's Monday like that douchebag with the tattoos said."

"Oh, yeah."

"I saw you looking at that woman's ass in there."

"I am a keen observer."

"What did you learn?"

"She has a thing for butterflies."

"Come on," Mattie said. "It's happy hour. Do I have to do all the thinking here? Jesus."

13

The Celtics were playing Miami, and the pregame show blared from a flat-screen television that seemed out of place with the faded beer posters and dusty neon signs of Four Green Fields. Behind the old bar, Shirley held court, peering up at the television while drinking a cup of coffee from a mug that read GRANDMA KNOWS.

"Good evening," I said. "Lovely night."

She cut her eyes at me, nodded, and went back to watching the game. Shirley was a big white-haired woman with thick arms and skin as fine as parchment paper. She wore a boxy flower-print top and a massive gold cross around her neck. A well-worn Louisville Slugger took the place of honor next to her ashtray, the grip wrapped in silver duct tape.

"Use that much?" I asked, nodding in the bat's direction.

"When I need to."

"I bet it might upset you if I asked for a Grey Goose martini. Up with a lemon twist."

"We got what's on the shelf, beer, and soda."

I did not see Grey Goose on the shelf. I ordered a Sam Adams with a shot of Bushmills, and a soda for Mattie.

Shirley nodded, making a great show of getting off the barstool behind the counter and reaching into the cooler for the beer. She poured the shot and then sprayed some Coke into a tall glass of ice for Mattie. Mattie leaned onto the bar with her elbows. We exchanged glances. She bit her lip and nodded for me to get on with it.

I laid down a ten and the picture of Julie Sullivan with the slick-haired man.

"You know these people?"

Shirley shook her head. She went back to her barstool. With great effort, she sat back down with her coffee and listened to Mike Gorman and Tom Heinsohn discuss the Celtics' rebounding troubles.

"That's your technique?" Mattie said, whispering.

"Terrific, isn't it?"

"It sucks."

"What do you expect for a bag full of donuts?"

"You haven't even earned the holes."

I shrugged. I drank half of the shot and chased it with the beer. I had always liked Bushmills. I kept a bottle in my office for cold, rainy days. Medicinal purposes.

"Shirley?"

She cut her eyes back at me.

"How about another beer?"

"You aren't finished with the first one."

"I like to plan ahead." I winked at her.

She groaned, got off the barstool, and reached into the cooler for another beer. She managed to do all this while keeping her eyes on the pregame.

"Julie Sullivan was a regular," I said. "Four years ago, she was killed."

Shirley's eyes turned back to me. She studied Mattie. She turned back to me.

"So?"

"I'd like to find some of her friends," I said. "This is her daughter. I work for her."

"You a lawyer or somethin'?" Shirley asked. " 'Cause I fucking hate lawyers."

"It's your lucky day," I said. "I couldn't pass the bar. I'm just a detective."

Shirley nodded. "I don't know what to tell you. I remember that name, that girl that was run down. But lots of people drink here. How am I gonna know what was going on four years ago? I've been tending bar here for thirty years."

"You must love your work," I said.

"Yeah, it's a pleasure to meet so many smart-asses."

I smiled and shrugged.

"You want more soda, sweetie?" Shirley asked.

Mattie nodded. Shirley added ice to the glass and sprayed in more Coke. The bar seemed like a cave, light and sound flashing in spurts whenever the battered front door opened, the cold, bright wind cutting through the stale heat, body odor, and cigarette smoke.

"How about Red Cahill?" I asked.

She looked at me. She didn't answer.

"Moon Murphy?"

"I just serve drinks, doll."

She wandered back down the bar. But she did not take a seat on her throne again. She hovered there for a few minutes, watching the television and burning down a long, thin cigarette. She served two beers to a bald-headed man who retreated to a back corner. She looked over to me and then at the television set. After a few more minutes, she picked up the phone.

The phone call was short. She returned to her throne.

A sign above her read NO DOPE SMOK-

ING, NO BAGGY PANTS, AND NO FUCKING CUSSING. MISS MANNERS.

"Do you mind waiting outside for me?" I asked.

"Why?" Mattie asked.

"I believe things are heating up."

"I don't need a babysitter."

"Wait in the car," I said.

"I'll wait right here."

I finished the Bushmills, not wanting her to see what came next but figuring she'd be safer right here anyway. Tom Heinsohn was on to why the Celtics need to play more cohesive ball in the face of LeBron James. Injuries had thinned the ranks. Ray Allen was questionable with a bruised knee.

"Maybe Heinsohn should suit up," I said. "Come out of retirement."

Shirley didn't respond. She kept her eyes on the flat screen with a dull stare. Mattie drank her Coke and watched the game. I watched the game, too, keeping an eye on the old metal door.

Fifteen minutes later, the door opened. A very large man walked inside Four Green Fields. He had on a black leather jacket that could serve as a circus tent. He had a thick, doughy face with black stubble and small, dumb eyes. He didn't close the door behind him, and a lot of cold air rushed into the place. Another man followed, skinnier and smaller, who pulled the door shut. He had thinning hair shaved tight to his head and a pockmarked face.

They approached the bar.

"Now," I said to Mattie.

I must've said it with a little force behind it. Mattie's face burned with color.

"That's him," she said. "Fucking fat ass is Moon."

"I'd arrived at the same conclusion using deductive reasoning," I said. "Now go."

Mattie got up and backed away. I took a sip of the beer. Moon Murphy took one side, and the skinny guy took the other. The bar had one other patron. The drunk in the shadows.

The men crowded me.

I began to whistle "Moonlight in Vermont."

Moon Murphy jabbed his elbow into my side as if he were stretching. He turned and studied my profile, unblinking, watching me. I could hear the creaking of his leather jacket. His breath was something to behold.

"Do you find me that attractive?" I asked.

"Why don't you go back to Beacon Hill, shithead."

"Don't let my good looks fool you," I said. "I only seem rich."

"That little girl gets hurt, and it's your own fault."

I shook my head. "That little girl gets one scratch on her, and you'll be wearing your ass for a hat."

He grabbed my biceps. I shook his hand loose and stepped back. Moon gave me a very mean look in return.

I shot him a left jab in the temple. His buddy lunged at me, and I hammered a hard right cross to his eye. The skinny guy staggered back. Moon came for me, so I found some open space on the concrete floor. Moon was one of those guys who tried to pass off fat for muscle. Most of the time they didn't have to fight, only look mean. He probably practiced a menacing look in the shower. I bobbed to the right and nailed him with a solid left hook in the gut. He lunged for me and punched me in the eye. It was sloppy and wild but hurt just the same. I sidestepped another punch and peppered him with a couple left jabs and a solid right cross. And another solid right. And another solid right. And a nice uppercut to his fat throat. Moon's feet left him. He made a noise that sounded like "Eck."

Skinny jumped on my back, screaming.

I bent at the waist and tossed him over my shoulders. He skidded a few feet on the concrete floor and fumbled for a gun. My .38 was already out and aimed dead center at his forehead.

I held out my hand. He gave me the gun, a Glock. Very unoriginal.

"You tell Red Cahill I want to meet."

I tossed a business card down at Moon. He was thumbing at his bleeding mouth and still trying to look tough. It was hard to look tough lying flat on your ass.

"You son of a bitch piece of shit," Mattie said. Her cheeks were flushed bright red. She rushed forward like she wanted to get a few kicks in.

I grabbed her elbow. "Easy."

"You son of a bitch," she said. "You killed her. I saw you."

I pulled her toward the door. She was stronger than she looked.

I kept a hand on her upper arm, my .38 still loose in my other hand, as we walked to the car and crawled inside. She played with the ends of her hair under her pink cap. Her hands shook.

I cranked up the heat. A line of cars parked along Dorchester were still covered in snow. I pulled out and drove back toward the McCormack Housing Projects. Mattie sat quietly beside me for a moment before she asked, "Why didn't you ask him anything? Isn't that what you do?"

"Believe it or not, this is my own special strategy," I said. "He wouldn't have answered anyway. This was about making my presence known in Southie."

"I guess you did that."

"Yep."

"They'll come for me, won't they?"

"Nope," I said. "They'll come for me. I'll find someone to watch your family. Just in case."

"And how does that help us nail those bastards?" she said.

"It's easier when you can get the bad guys to come to you," I said. "And I'm ready for them."

My right hand was swelling as it gripped the steering wheel. I felt a mouse forming under my eye. "I just keep circling, waiting for an opening."

"Jesus, I don't want 'em to kill you, too."

"Yeah," I said. "That would be nice."

14

I stopped off at Broadway Market on Harvard Square, stocked up on some booze, and let myself into Susan's Victorian on Linnaean Street. She still had a half hour of shrinking left, and I passed the time in Pearl's company. I drank. Pearl the Wonder Dog worked on the head of a rubber chicken. It squeaked, which made Pearl very happy.

I dropped some ice cubes into a glass, added some bitters, and then added a good measure of Wild Turkey. I hadn't had much bourbon in a while, sticking with scotch. But somehow I thought the return appropriate.

I dropped several more handfuls of ice in a champagne bucket and covered it in water. I took my bourbon and the ice bucket to the kitchen table, where I soaked my knuckles and drank. Pearl tilted her head, studying my bruised face. I thought I spotted concern in her amber eyes. We sat together for a long while, listening to the silence of the house, punctuated by the occasional creaks that would come through the old wood in the wind, and the brittle sound of sleet against the glass.

And then footsteps.

"You want a steak for that eye?" Susan asked. She removed her diamond earrings and placed them on the kitchen counter.

"That seems like a terrible waste of a steak."

"How about an ice pack?"

"Aren't you going to say, 'Tough day at the office?' " I said.

"You want to talk about it?"

"Don't you get tired of listening to problems?"

"I am handsomely paid for my professional services."

"I'm a nonpaying client."

"There may be ways to bring your account into good standing."

"Hot damn."

She was still dressed in her professional duds, a black wool crepe wrap dress, tied at the waist, and black tights. She wore a strand of small pearls and a thin gold chain. She kicked off her black leather pumps, knocking her down a few inches.

She patted Pearl's head. And then she patted mine.

"You might say, 'That must have hurt,' and then I'd say, 'You should see the other fella.' "

"How's the other fella?" Susan asked.

"Pissed off."

"And that's bad?"

"That's bad."

"You want to order a pizza?"

"Read my mind."

"You don't look to be in a cooking mood."

"I'm in a drinking mood."

Susan freshened my drink, then let her black hair down from the chignon at her neck. I loved to watch her hair spill over her shoulders. I studied the construction of the wrap dress.

"So one tug on that little sash?" I asked.

"And the dress comes off, palooka."

"Yippee."

She found an open bottle of white in the fridge and joined me at the kitchen table. Pearl rested her head in Susan's lap.

"How's the kid?" she asked.

"Tough but scared," I said. "Someone ran her off the road this morning. I tried to stick around. But she wanted to be back with her sisters and didn't care for me to be a houseguest."

"Can you call someone?"

"I know a patrolman in Southie who's going to check up on the family," I said. "It's not much. But it's something."

"What about Hawk?"

"Hawk in Southie?"

"He may stand out."

"Hawk stands out everywhere," I said. "Besides, I may need him."

"What happened?" she asked.

I told her.

"Your charm failed with Shirley."

"And with Moon."

"So now they know you're onto them."

"They knew anyway," I said. "The kid had been asking around. She's got a hard head."

"Which you respect."

"Nice trait to have," I said. "But I wish she'd tone it down a bit. She could get hurt."

"I don't think Mattie has a choice," Susan said. "Didn't you say her mother was largely absent before her death?"

"Depends on what period of her life," I said. "She would go through periods of sobriety and then hit rock bottom."

"And Mattie has two sisters and a grandmother?"

I nodded again. "The grandmother is there because she's the only family available but not exactly a role model. She's a lush. When I tried to talk to her, she was passed out."

"Father?"

"When I asked, Mattie laughed like it was a stupid question."

"And it's ridiculous to ask why the system has failed her?"

"If the system worked, I'd be out of a job."

"You're working for the classic parental child," Susan said. "Probably thought she could assume her mother's role when her mother was out drunk or high. And when her mother was killed, she believes she failed. Now she has to make it right."

"Like a do-over."

"Exactly like a do-over. She would see her mother as a failure, in life and death," Susan said. "Of course, I'm only making a guess based on what you've told me. But an educated guess. The most important thing to her right now is righting the past and keeping her family together."

I nodded.

"It has a lot to do with self-esteem." Susan shook her head. "So now you think Red and Moon will come for you instead."

"Yep."

I drank some bourbon. I heard it fortified courage and resourcefulness.

"You think they'll try to kill you?"

"I think they'll try to discourage me."

"And these are some pretty tough guys?"

"I have to say I was not impressed with Moon," I said. "I'll reserve judgment on Red Cahill. I heard he was pretty good with his fists and a gun."

"And Gerry Broz?"

"I don't think he's involved in this," I said. "This happened four years ago."

"But they work for him now."

"Yep."

"And he doesn't like you."

"Unbelievable, isn't it?"

"Absolutely."

"Aren't you going to tell me that I'm the toughest man alive and I do what I do because I'm a man among men?"

Susan rolled her eyes and took a sip of wine. "I don't think there are any esteem issues with you," she said. "Mushrooms and black olives?"

"Of course."

"So what's next?" she asked.

"We eat."

"And then?"

"We drink."

"And then?"

"And then I try to figure out why someone killed Julie Sullivan," I said. "I don't like any of the reasons I've been given. And I don't like Mickey Green for it anymore. Moon and those men who tried to scare Mattie made sure of that."

I lifted my glass to her. The ice rattled.

"You can't be sure, though. Maybe Moon just doesn't like other tough guys asking about him."

"Those guys ran a fourteen-year-old girl off the road."

"Mattie works like you," Susan said. "She annoys people until they trip up."

I nodded.

"And she's as tough as old boots."

"It's an act," Susan said.

"I'm not so sure."

"It's an act," Susan said. "Her toughness is like a callus on your hand."

"Calluses protect you."

"As they should."

"But not healthy for the psyche of a teenage girl?"

Susan shook her head. "She will seem much older and much younger to you at the same time."

"I caught her playing princess with her sisters the other day," I said. "It embarrassed her. But I think she was really enjoying it."

"She'll need more than revenge," Susan

said. "She'll need a good shrink."

"Don't we all?"

"Maybe not Pearl."

"I thought finding her mother's killer would make it all better."

"I'd love to tell you that it won't," she said. "But since it seems to be her compulsion, it would help some. It will get more complicated after that. She has to realize this is only part of her life story. From what you've told me, it's all she thinks about."

"What's my compulsion?"

"Maybe lost kids."

I nodded and took a deep breath. "She is completely unlike Paul, but somehow she makes me think of him. He had walled himself in complete apathy. Mattie has anything but apathy. She has the personality of a freight train."

"But both showed potential. Both abandoned by their parents. And both ignored by adults."

I finished the bourbon. The ice made empty rocky sounds in the bottom of the glass. I really had missed the bourbon.

"They're both extremes," Susan said. "You had to push Paul to engage, and you have to get Mattie to slow down."

"Maybe I understand Mattie more," I said. "She's reckless. I used to be reckless."

"And in other ways."

"Growing up without a mother," I said.

"You had your father and uncles," she said. "They taught you everything about being self-sufficient. She has nothing, so she's making up the rules as she goes along."

I nodded. The nodding made me grimace.

"Are you sore?" Susan asked.

"Of course not."

Susan smiled. She unwrapped the dress, placing a delicate hand on a hip. "Prove it."

And I did.

15

If I was going to go up against an entire
Southie crew, I figured I should keep in
fighting shape. The morning was cold and
gray, spitting sleet and rain, when I dressed
in my sweats, watch cap, and running shoes.
I walked over the footbridge to the Charles
River, jogging all the way to the Boston
University campus and back. The river was
still frozen but not frozen enough that
anyone dared to walk across. You could see
the hardened clumps breaking up, open
pockets of actual river that could swallow a
man. I thought of spring concerts at the
Shell, dogs frolicking in the Common, and
women in summer dresses.

At my apartment, I showered and carefully shaved. I chose a black turtleneck;
crisp, dark Levi's; and my peacoat to con-
ceal my .38. I decided on a knitted Sox cap
to complete the look. Business casual.

Feeling like a fine example of the American male, I drove south to Roxbury.

Mike's City Diner was on Washington Street, a couple miles from Boston Police headquarters. Although new, it boasted a retro look. There was an open stainless-steel kitchen fronting a long counter. The surrounding tables were covered in black-and-white gingham oilcloths. The waitresses wore little name tags.

"You Spenser?" asked a short black man.

"Most people say I resemble George Clooney."

"Quirk told me you looked like an old fighter."

"Quirk is jealous of my rugged good looks," I said.

"Alden Reid," he said.

Reid was neatly dressed in a silky black shirt and expensive-looking leather blazer. He had a thin trimmed mustache and close-cropped hair that showed a bit of gray at the temples. He had quick eyes, like most detectives I knew, and took in the room with discretion.

We shook hands and found a table looking out on Washington. There wasn't much to see on Washington besides an old brick apartment building and recently restored storefronts. A mailman toting a heavy canvas satchel passed the window. He wore a big fur hat.

A waitress brought menus and coffee.

"You been with the drug unit long?"

"Eight years."

"Like it?"

"Lots of job security," Reid said. "Shit isn't going away."

"Here's to crime." I raised my mug.

"And retirement," he said. "I have a time-share and a boat in Clearwater Beach."

"You won't miss shoveling snow?" I said. "My uncles said it built character."

"I won't miss shoveling shit," he said. He studied the menu and put it down just as quickly. He then studied my face, with subtle attention on the purplish mouse under my eye.

"Would you believe a champagne cork?" I asked.

"Nope."

"Had a run-in with a guy named Moon Murphy last night," I said. "Heard of him?"

"Sure," Reid said. He grinned. "You must be good. He usually breaks some bones."

"And his partner?"

"Red Cahill?" he said. "If you know the name, you know his rep."

"Hold that thought," I said. "Let's not talk hoodlums on an empty stomach."

I ordered the hash and eggs. Rye toast on

the side. Reid ordered the Mike's special, hand-carved ham and two over-easy eggs with toast.

"How'd you get to be a private cop?" Reid asked.

"I don't play well with others."

"Martin Quirk is first-class," Reid said. "He said to help you out in any way. He must like you. And Marty Quirk likes no one."

"What can I say?" I shrugged. "I make him laugh."

"Red Cahill," he said. Reid shook his head, deep in thought. "Small-time punk gone big-time. Lucked out now that heroin is back in style."

"Bell-bottoms and wide ties are next," I said.

"Heroin's rough, man," Reid said. "Junkies love that slow suicide. That's what it's all about. It's no fun if it don't kill you."

"Big business?"

"On Christmas Eve, we arrested two of Red's boys with six pounds of the shit."

I gave a low whistle.

"Street value of three million."

"Great Caesar's ghost," I said.

The waitress stopped and refilled our cups. She wore the classic waitress uniform, complete with a white apron and saddle shoes. Her hair was the color of cotton candy.

"What do you know about Cahill and Murphy working with Gerry Broz?" I asked.

"What I know and can prove are two different things."

"Story of my life."

"Last year, we had a hell of a case on Red," Reid said. "We got warrants to wiretap a garage where these guys hung out. It was a foreign-car place, fixed Porsches and Beemers, shit like that. This place was over on Old Colony, and for maybe four months, we saw these guys heading in and out of there like it was a beehive."

"What happened?"

"When we got the warrant, the activity stopped," he said. "You know Gerry Broz's old man?"

"We have a history."

"That garage was owned by him."

"He's been gone longer than that. Ten years."

"Yeah," Reid said. He nodded. "Him taking off is a whole other story. We figure he's got friends in the DA's office or with the Feds. They were coming for him when he decided to take an extended vacation."

"Joe Broz has to be dead by now," I said.

"I think he bunked with Al Capone in Alcatraz."

"His name still commands some respect," Reid said. "Even after all this time."

I nodded. The waitress arrived and slid warm plates in front of us. Hash and eggs on a cold morning was a national treasure. I took a bite of eggs, followed by a bite of rye toast. I drank coffee. Reid followed my lead.

"So Joe Broz really used to own this town?" Reid asked.

"Broz was the man."

"You go up against him?"

"Yep," I said.

"And?"

"In the end, we formed a mutual respect."

"And his son?"

"Gerry isn't cut from the same cloth," I said. "First time I met him, he was videotaping himself having sex with old ladies and blackmailing them."

"Class."

"With a capital *K*."

Reid drank some coffee. He cut into some ham and added a bite of egg to his fork. "He's shaking things up."

"So I've heard."

"For a while, there was an understanding between the Albanians on the North Shore

115

and the Italians on the North End. They kind of split Broz's old turf downtown and in Southie. And now the kid has come back wanting to reclaim his birthright or something."

"Gerry has always had something to prove."

"Maybe the old man is back and telling him what to do."

I stopped eating. I put my fork on the side of my plate. This was something I had not considered.

"So why'd you get into it with Moon Murphy last night?"

"There was a young woman in Southie who was killed four years ago," I said. "Her daughter was just a kid then but has just IDed Red and Moon as being in her mother's company shortly before she died."

"Addict?"

"Sure."

"Maybe she was just getting a fix."

"Maybe."

"How'd she die?"

"She was raped, stabbed, and run down with a car."

"Sounds like a message killing written in neon."

I nodded.

"But why?"

I shook my head.

Reid finished his breakfast. He reached for his cell phone and checked messages. He pulled out his chair and reached for his wallet.

I shook my head and laid down some cash.

"Watch your ass, Spenser," he said. "These aren't nice people."

"People keep telling me that."

"You got a plan?"

"Win them over with my dynamite personality?"

"You have a backup plan?" he asked.

"Working on it."

16

I knocked on seven different doors in the Mary Ellen McCormack Projects before I found the second-floor apartment of Genevive Zacconi. Zacconi was a hard thirtyish woman with bleached hair chopped up in a spiky bob. She was short and fat and wearing an XXL T-shirt that read MEAN GREEN DRINKING MACHINE. When I started to question her, she told me to hold on for a moment. She leaned back into her apartment and yelled for her kid to "please shut the fuck up."

When she turned back to me, she crossed her arms over her large breasts and frowned. "Yeah?"

"Did you win that shirt?" I asked.

"Whaddya mean?" she said, looking down to recall what she'd put on.

"I thought maybe it was a competition," I said. "Like you slam a half-dozen boilermakers and you get a shirt. You know, like a trophy?"

"Fuck, I don't know," she said. "It was clean. What the hell do you want?"

"Our book club is reading Dr. Spock this month," I said. "Would you like to join us?"

"Come on."

"Would it be too corny if I said I was a private eye?"

She looked at me with tired eyes and tried to slam the door. I smiled, wedged my foot in the threshold, and handed her my card. I knew my charisma would chip away at her hardened shell. She looked at the card and tapped the edge against an eyetooth. "Most people who knock on my door are trying to sell me something I don't need or religious nuts."

"The Lord works in thuggish ways."

"So whaddya want?"

"Did you know Julie Sullivan?"

"No."

"Woman was killed four years ago?"

"I know who she was," Genevive Zucconi said. "She lived downstairs. Her kids still do. With her crazy, drunk mother. But we weren't friends or nothin'. She was like ten years younger."

"Do you mind if I come inside?"

"Yeah," she said. "I got shit all over the

place, and I think my kid just crapped his pants."

"How nice for you."

"Did you just stop by to be funny, or did you want somethin'?"

I showed her the photograph of Julie Sullivan and the slick-haired man grabbing her breast.

"Know him?"

Even if she'd said no, the smile gave Genevive Zucconi away. She nodded and then shook her head. "Yeah," she said. "Yeah, sure. That's Touchie Kiley."

"Touchie?"

"Yeah."

"Where can I find Touchie?"

"Touchie's a riot." She laughed just thinking about him.

"Unwarranted groping is hilarious," I said.

"I don't know where he lives," she said. "He's just kind of always around. Did you check Four Green Fields? The pub?"

"Unfortunately, I'm persona non grata there."

"What's that mean?"

"It means they don't find me a riot."

"Try the deli on D Street," she said. "He used to work there. *Touchie Kiley.* Jesus H. I hadn't thought about him for a while. Tell him hello. What a fucking goofball."

"As much as I'd love to relive the glory days," I said, trying to dissuade more hilarity, "I could use some help. You remember anything about Julie Sullivan that might be of use? Anything around the time she was killed?"

"I don't know," she said. "Like I said, I was ten years older. She was playing with dolls and shit when I was in high school."

"You know she became an addict?"

"Sure," she said. "Everybody knew she was hooked. Her arms were all bruised up like a piece of old fruit. She was screwing every guy in the projects."

"Ever talk to her about it?"

"Do I look like a fucking counselor?" she said. "I'm real sorry about Jules, you know, God bless, but I got my own problems."

The child inside her apartment began to whine and cry out for his mother. Another kid joined in, screaming in tandem, yelling for the first kid to be quiet. Genevive held up her index finger to me again, turned, and yelled, "Shut up."

"Just one more minute," I said.

Genevive slammed the door in my face. Undeterred, I tucked the photo back into my peacoat and continued asking around. I followed sidewalks coated in snow and ice. Big bags of trash that sat waiting for pickup blocked paths. A notice had been taped to a lamppost looking for anyone needing rides to Walpole or Plymouth prisons. A carpool was only twenty bucks. I wondered if that's how Mattie had taken her visits with Mickey Green.

The project buildings stretched out like spokes from the common area, two and three stories of old red brick. Every unit the same. In a lone corner window, someone had pasted up colored drawings of Disney characters. Another had unicorns. It wasn't even one o'clock but felt like the end of the day. They sky was dark. Slush and icy puddles ran up to my ankles.

More doors slammed in my face. I found out a lot of Hispanics had moved into Mary Ellen McCormack in the last few years. A lot of Vietnamese, too. Most did not speak English.

An hour later, I met an old woman who spoke in a soft Irish lilt, telling me how lovely it had all once been. "Until they forced the blacks on us," she said.

"How unfortunate," I said.

"They brought drugs and crime," she said. She'd come to the door in a flowered house-coat and pushing a walker. Her eyes were faded blue with cataracts.

I did not point out that Southie's crime

rate was worse before the schools were integrated. I asked her about the Sullivan family.

She clucked and shook her head. She clutched her rosary on her withered old neck. "Have you spoken to the poor girl's mother?"

"No," I said. "But I'll try again with some coffee and smelling salts."

17

I figured Grandma Sullivan must be waiting for Mattie and the twins to come home from school. I bet she was making lemonade and baking sugar cookies. She may have taken up sewing or crochet to pass the time. Perhaps she would even invite me to dinner. Pot roast with new potatoes. A homemade apple pie for desert. Perry Como on the hi-fi.

I had to knock on the door for five minutes before she opened it.

Grandma had been sleeping one off. I was shocked. But I composed myself and gave another introduction, since she'd been comatose when we'd first met.

She didn't answer me. She walked back in the apartment and sat down on a ratty plaid chair. Grandma Sullivan lit a cigarette and fanned away the smoke. She didn't look quite as old and skinny today. She'd put on some makeup and wore a red camisole top that showed off some shapely freckled shoulders. Her nose was pert and her eyes a deep green. She was still in her forties, hard but not unattractive. Or maybe it was the dim light.

A little bit of light from the half-open curtains looked to be causing her some pain. I walked over, closed them, and sat down on a sofa. A television played a soap opera on mute. A man was in a hospital with a bandaged head. A woman appeared to be crying.

Grandma smoked some more. Strands of light bled from the curtains like thick fingers through the smoke. "You're the detective."

"I slay dragons, rescue maidens."

"Mattie talks about you a lot."

I nodded.

"She trusts you."

I nodded again. "She's a good kid."

"Stubborn," she said.

"What makes her so good."

"Mother was the same way," she said. "Couldn't tell her shit. She knew it all."

"People have said similar things about me," I said. "Can you tell me a bit about your daughter?"

"She was wild with boys and drinking, but she straightened it all out for Mattie," she said. "God bless that girl, she brought my

125

Julie back for a while."

"How long?"

"Few years."

Grandma walked over to the wall and the framed high-school photo of Julie. She held it in both hands and handed it to me with great care. Dust motes spun in a sliver of sunlight. The room had an attic-like quality, smelling of moth balls and old clothes. Toys and stuffed animals cluttered a rug in the center of the room. She stood over me as I studied the photo of Julie. She absently fingered her black-ink tattoo of her daughter's name.

"You know about the car wreck?" she asked.

I nodded.

"Mattie was four years old when Julie got hurt," Grandma said. "That wreck changed everything. Some stupid bastard T-boned her car as she was headed to work. That's how she got into pills, and from pills into coke. You go on from there."

"What about the guy who hit her?"

"We won ten grand in a settlement," Grandma said. "He was some jerk-off business guy from Revere. Never said he was sorry, hid behind his lawyer like a woman's skirt. Julie lost her job."

She tucked her unwashed hair behind her

ears. Her complexion was blotchy. She stubbed out the cigarette and started a new one. I learned her name was Colleen.

"And I guess the money did not provide a wealth of stability?"

"Money went straight into her arm," Colleen said. "I couldn't stop her. Then she started stealing shit. She sold all my dead ma's rings. She sold our TV. She'd moved in, and I had to kick her out. I kept Mattie. She didn't care about Mattie anymore. She didn't care about me until she got knocked up with the twins. That kept her clean for nearly a year. And then it was back to the stealing and lies."

"Who were her friends before she died?"

"Don't ever call those parasites friends. And don't get Mattie's hope up, either. How much is she paying you?"

"A dozen donuts."

"You're a funny one, aren't you," she said. She laughed as if I were being funny. "That how you got that eye?"

I placed my hands in my coat pockets. I shrugged. Grandma smiled at me in a hazy way. Maybe through the smoke and booze, the scar tissue around my eyes and busted nose wasn't as prominent.

"Ever see Julie with a guy named Red Cahill?" I asked.

She blew out some smoke and shook her head.

"Moon Murphy?"

She shook her head some more. She waved away the smoke.

"Touchie Kiley?"

She shook her head, not seeming to listen.

"You don't think much of me, do you?" she asked.

I didn't answer.

"You have kids?"

"Nope."

"You don't want to outlive a kid," she said. "I'd trade places with Julie any day."

I nodded.

"I'm doing the best I can," she said. "Mattie's strong. Stronger than me."

She'd started to cry, heavy with the booze, singing very softly a very old song. *" 'Oft, in dreams I wander to that cot again. I feel her arms a-hugging me. As when she held me then.' "*

"You know that old song?" she asked. "I used to sing it to Julie. I was just a kid myself when she was born. Isn't that some sentimental shit?"

"I heard Bing Crosby sing it in a movie once," I said. "I liked it."

She wiped her eyes with the back of her hand. "Hell, you want a drink?" she asked.

"It's pretty early."

"I didn't ask you for the tin[e]

I shrugged. She walked in[to] [the] kitchen and reached into a cup[board] the stove. She pulled out some Ol[d] and poured a generous shot into t[wo] jars featuring Bugs Bunny and Tweet[y] She handed me the glass as if it were n[o] of crystal.

"Ah, the good stuff," I said.

"Good enough for me."

"You know Mickey Green?" I asked.

"Whaddya you think," she said. "He's the rotten son of a bitch who killed my Julie."

"Did you know him before she was killed?"

"Yeah, I seen him around. Always acting like he was a good guy, doing little chores and crap to win favors."

"Mattie believes he's innocent."

"Kids need something to believe in," she said. She finished her drink in one gulp. "Like Santa Claus, the Easter Bunny, and all them saints. Me, I'm too old for that. So don't break my little doll's heart. Okay? Bad things happen in life. You swallow it and keep moving ahead."

I nodded. We just sat there for a while.

"You aren't half bad looking," she said.

"It's the other half that ruins it."

ou look like you've been in some aps."

Trouble is my business," I said.

I downed the Old Forester. Mattie's grandmother smiled at me for a while. It was a wavering, fuzzy smile. She leaned back in her chair, stretched, and let out a long, tired breath. An uncomfortable silence passed between us. I finished the booze, feeling it warm my stomach. I winked at her before I let myself out.

The wind in the common ground swirled in a bright, chilled vortex. Trash spun and danced, hitting brick walls and collapsing in a heap. I walked back to Kemp Street but could not find my car. If it had been a horse, I would have whistled.

I looked both ways. But my car had disappeared.

18

I saw two of them approach from Dorchester Avenue.

I walked in the opposite direction toward Monsignor O'Callaghan Way and north toward the T station. Two more met me halfway through the projects. I kept a bright, smiling clip. I could confront them, but I wanted to see what developed. I did not leer. I did not stick out my tongue. I did not wave around my .38. I walked with intent.

I nodded politely at an older Asian woman carrying groceries from her car. I waited on the sidewalk as a Hispanic boy played with a remote-control truck that jumped snow and trash. I turned up on a street called Logan, still within the brick maze of the Mary Ellen McCormack, and circled back toward Dorchester. I had not recognized any of the men. The first two looked like hard older guys, one with a beard, the other guy in an Army jacket. They looked like dopeheads, not toughs.

I stopped and glanced back. The third man was young and Hispanic. The man with him was white, with thinning black hair and a stubbled face. He wore a fake leather jacket advertising Marlboro cigarettes, the kind you win after collecting empty packs. Very stylish.

They all watched me. They nodded to one another, closing in.

I could stand and fight like Randolph Scott. But I did not figure a shootout near a playground was a good idea. I could turn back to them and give them the stink eye. The more I practiced, the more the stink eye worked. Practice made perfect. But I kept walking. I turned left on Devine.

The quartet followed. Perhaps they would assault me in song.

I reached for the .38 on my hip and slipped it into my peacoat pocket. I kept my hand there, walking. I began to whistle "Danny Boy."

After a few minutes, I decided I sounded pretty good. The street was very quiet at midday. There was a hush that came in the old snow piles and ice. Long rows of cars sat humpbacked and buried in snow. Someone had used a pink pen to write a eulogy to a dead friend on a mailbox. I made it to Dorchester and turned north again. I was out of the projects and headed into a grouping of haggard storefronts and a brand-new Dunkin' Donuts. The Dunkin' Donuts shone like a beacon in the distance.

I passed an auto-repair school, a liquor shop, a travel agent. The Andrew Station stood at the corner of Dorchester Avenue and Dorchester Street. I walked inside and paid two bucks for a pass.

The quartet was inside the station. The two old guys were conversing. I bet they were conversing about me. I did not take it to be complimentary.

I slipped the pass into the turnstile and headed down the stairwell. The young Latin guy and balding man in the faux-leather Marlboro jacket followed.

I stood at the T platform with maybe twenty other people headed inbound to the city. It had been some time since I'd taken the T. I could take the T from my apartment to Fenway. But on really nice days I chose to walk down Commonwealth. I worked in a driving profession. It was hard to tail a person on the T.

The men stood back. They conversed some more. They looked like schoolgirls gossiping. The two older guys joined them.

A subway poster advertised a new exhibit at the Museum of Fine Arts. A new exhibit called "Art of the Americas." George Washington stood proud on horseback. Washington wouldn't have retreated into a T station. George would've charged right for them.

I heard the rumble of the T. I glanced over at the two men. They did not try to approach me. They looked confused about what to do next. I wondered why Red or Moon hadn't come for me themselves.

I looked back at Washington. He had wooden teeth and a big set of brass balls. But muskets and swords were not .45s and .38s and Glocks. Four against one. Shooting it out on a crowded platform.

I stepped onto the T. The men stood deadfooted in the station. The doors closed with a hiss. Through the dirty glass, I smiled and waved to the quartet. They did not smile back.

I took the Red Line to South Station and got off. I walked upstairs to the large terminal where you could catch a bus to Logan or a train to New York. My cell phone was in my lost car. I found a bank of pay phones, glad to see they still existed.

I called Henry Cimoli's gym to find Hawk.

134

19

"You got it wrong, babe," Hawk said. "You suppose to follow bad guys. Bad guys don't follow you."

"Perhaps I should have explained the rules."

"Mighta shot you while you doin' the explainin'."

"That would've been poor form."

"Bein' a thug don't have no form," Hawk said. "Sometimes it got rules. Sometimes it don't."

Hawk and I sat at a corner table in the bar of the Long Wharf Marriott. The bar had a big bank of windows that looked onto a small marina dotted with sailboats covered up for the winter. Further out, you could see the choppy cold waters of the Atlantic and buoys being knocked to and fro. Hawk wore sunglasses.

"Never liked that car anyway," Hawk said.

"Whatever happened to your old convertible?"

"Susan said it was no longer practical."

"She says the same about my Jaguar."

I took a sip of Sam Adams. Hawk drank a glass of Iron Horse champagne. He topped himself off with the bottle.

"I could see you in a Mini Cooper," I said.

"Ain't nothin' mini about me, kemosabe."

Hawk was dressed like Johnny Cash today. Black boots, black pants, black shirt opened wide at the chest, and a black leather trench coat. A sterling-silver belt buckle with a turquoise center. Everyone in the bar turned to look at him when he made his entrance. Hawk was a pro at the entrance.

"This gonna be fun," Hawk said.

"Oh, yeah?"

"Been awhile."

"Since what?" I asked.

"Since we kicked some ass."

I nodded.

"You disappeared on me this winter," Hawk said, and sipped the champagne. "Me and you workin' out at Henry's was the first time I seen your white ass in a long time. Thought maybe you takin' it easy. Hangin' it up."

"Nope," I said.

"What else is there to do?" Hawk said.

"Yep."

"Glad you're back." Hawk nodded.

I toasted him with half my beer. I drank.

Hawk turned to study the choppy waters in the Atlantic. "Good ol' Gerry Broz. That motherfucker just don't know when to quit."

I signaled the bartender for another beer. Nothing against Southie, but I was happy to be on the waterfront. And I was happy to see Hawk. Although I never would admit I was happy to see Hawk. Nor would Hawk want me to admit the quartet had bothered me.

"If this boy Red or Broz sent four men for your Irish ass," Hawk said, "that's a compliment."

I nodded. I drank some beer and finished my last bite of club sandwich.

"Kinda respectful."

"I reported my car stolen," I said. "But it's gone. I'll need a car."

"Yep," Hawk said. "But I ain't no chauffeur. I got shit to do. Many high-class women to please. I can't be driving your ass around Southie."

"Red and Moon made their point," I said. "I don't know what Gerry's deal is in all this."

"What do you want with his boys?"

"Have a civil, polite conversation," I said.

137

"Ain't nothin' wrong with that."

"Julie Sullivan was last seen in their company."

"And knowing they're shitbag crackers makes you highly suspicious."

"Just a little."

"Man, you been making trouble for the Broz family since disco was cool."

I nodded. "Maybe I should just go and talk to Gerry. Patch things up between pals."

"He'd like that," Hawk said. "Talk about that time you shot him. You know, the good ol' days."

"You heard anything about his old man?"

"Ain't Joe dead?" Hawk poured the last bit of Iron Horse into his glass. Little bubbles rose to the top and spilled over the rim of the glass. He smiled with pleasure.

"If he is, they need to take down that picture of him in the post office."

"This little girl," Hawk said. "One who hired you?"

"Mattie."

"Mattie saw Red and Moon snatch up her momma."

I nodded.

"But they drug dealers and maybe shaking her down. How we know Mickey Green thing didn't happen after?"

"Mattie says he's not the type."

"And how we know Mickey Green ain't the type?"

"We don't."

"But you ain't so sure after that fat boy come and try to whip your ass."

"Yep."

"And you hoping if you keep pissin' people off, someone gonna slip up."

"Yep."

Hawk showed no expression behind the glasses. He took them off, neatly laid them on the table. "Notice I did not mention your eye."

"What's wrong with my eye?"

"Last time I saw your eye like that was after a warm-up bout with yours truly."

"You didn't fare so well yourself," I said.

"Bullshit," Hawk said.

"You have what they call a selective memory."

"I remember selectively whipping your butt," Hawk said, laughing.

I sipped some more Sam Adams. I wished the Marriott put out some nuts for you. The old Ritz put out nuts and snacks. You could count on it every happy hour. I'd been served so many times at that bar that my mouth began to water at five.

"You go with me to pick up Mattie at school," I said. "And then we stop by and see Broz."

"Little girl got some fair questions," Hawk said. "Deserves answers."

"You don't think it'll look like I had to bring my big, bad boyfriend along?"

"Nope," Hawk said. He finished his champagne and stood. He slipped back into the black leather trench and reached for his sunglasses. "I like you, white boy. But no one ever said I love you."

20

Hawk popped the trunk of his silver Jaguar. Grinning, he pulled away a heavy wool blanket, the kind used to cover furniture, and showed off four shotguns. Two Mossbergs, a Winchester, and a sawed-off Browning twelve-gauge.

We stood in the dim light of the Marriott's parking garage. Hawk was still wearing sunglasses.

"When one meets with the Broz family," Hawk said, "one should be prepared."

"One should."

"Joe's boy might need a lesson in etiquette with an ass full of buckshot."

"As Emily Post would recommend."

"Emily Post do know her shit."

"She do," I said.

He slammed the trunk closed.

We drove in style back to Southie and Gavin Middle School. We parked behind a row of school buses and sat there in the parents' line for about twenty minutes. When the final bell rang and the kids kicked open the doors, I was glad to be an adult. I would rather go up against any Southie tough than endure one more day of grade school, or any school, for that matter. Just the smell of the hallways induced instant dread. Kids passed Hawk's car and stared inside.

"Super nannies," Hawk said.

"Uncle Hawk," I said.

Hawk growled.

I stepped out of the passenger side and waited for Mattie.

I looked across the street. I looked to the other cars, studying faces of parents. I did not see Moon Murphy or my new friends from the Mary Ellen McCormack. Hawk stayed behind the wheel of the Jaguar with the engine running. I caught a bit of Tommy Flanagan's piano on the stereo. I believed the number was called "Cherokee."

Mattie emerged from the school. She was dressed as all the other kids were, in uniform. White shirt, blue sweater, khaki pants. She slid into her blue coat and her pink Sox cap outside the front doors.

I waved to her.

She said a few words to a young Asian girl in glasses. She walked cool and deliberate, not too excited to see me, down the front steps of the old brick building.

"Next time, I'll hold up a little sign with your name," I said.

"You don't have to pick me up anymore," she said. "I can walk."

"I prefer my clients not be run off the road."

"They were just screwing with me."

"Or that my clients are harassed."

"Where's your car?" she asked.

"Stolen."

"That sucks."

I nodded. "It does indeed."

"Your face looks like shit."

I shrugged.

We stood at the base of the school steps. Kids piled into the school buses, the diesel fumes adding an unpleasant smell to the air. The slush covering curbs was dark black. I walked her to the car. I let her sit up front with Hawk.

"Hawk, this is Mattie," I said. "Mattie, this is Hawk."

"Howdy," Hawk said. He cranked the ignition.

"He a detective, too?" Mattie asked.

"I just a simple thug," Hawk said. "Spenser the brains."

"Hawk is too modest," I said. "He's also

my fashion adviser."

She turned and studied him. She liked him. "Cool jacket."

Hawk checked his rearview mirror. He nodded in agreement.

"Where we going today?" she asked.

"You're going home," I said. "Hawk and I have an appointment."

"Bullshit."

"Lovely elocution," Hawk said.

"Bullshit," Mattie said.

"I work with Hawk today," I said. I leaned into the front seat. "Tomorrow may be different."

"You need me," she said. "Nobody's gonna talk to you. I got three more of my ma's friends I called last night."

"Why don't you let me handle this?"

"Nobody says they saw her before she was killed," she said. "But one of 'em saw Red this weekend at her cousin's wedding. He's goin' to parties, getting high, while Mickey Green lives in a cage."

"As your investigative consultant, I would advise you to quit running your mouth all over South Boston."

Mattie didn't respond.

"Hawk and I have a mutual friend," I said. "He will provide us with an introduction."

I saw Hawk grin in the rearview mirror.

"And then what?"

"We will have a talk with Red Cahill."

"The way you talked to Moon last night?"

"That's the way you speak to guys like Moon."

"By knocking them in the head."

"I knocked him on the chin," I said. "An uppercut."

Hawk nodded in appreciation.

"Nobody talks about those guys," Mattie said. "Nobody says jack shit. They're a bunch of cowards. They left her out there to die on The Point and don't have the guts to say anything about it."

I nodded. Hawk took a turn and joined up with Dorchester Avenue.

The music changed to Barry Harris. Or maybe it was Bud Powell. But it was that jazz piano that sounded playful and alive, cat and mouse with the rest of the band. Hawk's car smelled of fine leather and expensive perfume.

"Anyone ever tell you that your car smells like a French prostitute?" I said.

"What you know about French prostitutes?" Hawk asked.

"I knows one when I smells one."

Mattie didn't say anything. She did not laugh at our witty repartee. She just stared out the frosted window at the old storefronts

145

and apartment buildings. She wasn't listening to us. Perhaps a good thing. After a while, she spoke.

"Someone saw something," Mattie said.

She seemed to say it more to herself than to me. Or Hawk.

"Someone knows what happened," she said. "And they're too scared. Fucking cowards."

Hawk turned the steering wheel in an expert fashion. In the leather and shades, he blended into the Jaguar. Mattie just studied the long stretch of Dorchester before us. The dirty snowbanks, the covered cars, the battered road signs. SLOW. STOP. NO PARKING.

"You good at beating people up, too?" she asked.

"Oh, yes, ma'am," Hawk said.

21

Gerry Broz had opened a sports bar at the
edge of the Old Colony Housing Projects.
There wasn't much of Old Colony left; the
wrecking ball had taken out a good half of
the old brick buildings. What remained sat
in decay and dim light as we passed. I
remembered Old Colony being the kind of
place where kids filled Dumpsters with
water from fire hydrants to cool off in the
summer. It had been an infamous cove of
junkies and thieves, working-class fathers
and mothers, professional boxers and hoodlums. Almost everyone had been Irish, with
a few Italians tossed in.

"You remember that man from Southie,
tried to impale a brother with an American
flag?"

"During the busing."

"Now I see brothers all 'round here."

"We've been on the scene for a while," I
said. "Things change."

"Joe Broz had you shot back in the day."

I nodded.

"What was that about?"

"His son."

Hawk grinned.

We drank coffee and watched the parking lot in front of the sports bar. It was an old two-story industrial building slapped with a fresh coat of yellow paint and new plate-glass windows. The narrow point of the bar met at Dorchester Street and Old Colony. A large sign read PLAYMATES.

The bar was attracting a lot of business on a Tuesday night. Of course, I didn't think there was a hell of a lot to do on the south end of Southie. This section of the neighborhood wouldn't be reached by gentrification for another decade.

"How 'bout we kick in the door, grab Gerry by the neck, and say, 'Give it up, motherfucker.' "

"Or," I said, "we walk into the bar, ask to speak to Mr. Broz, and try to talk it out."

"Like I told the kid," Hawk said, "you the brains."

"God help us."

"Can I still say 'Give it up, motherfucker'?"

"Only if it makes you happy."

We dodged traffic and walked across Old

Colony. Hawk hid the shotgun under the edge of his trench as we made our way into the bar.

The bottom floor of the building was filled with dark wood booths, a long stretch of polished bar down the center. There were a lot of framed jerseys from the Sox, the Pats, the Celtics, and Bruins. Autographed pictures of sports stars and Boston actors who made movies about Boston hung on the walls. Throughout the bar, Gerry had rigged up a dozen flat-screen televisions, which glowed with dozens of different sports stations.

A sign at the hostess stand noted that tonight was MARGARITA MADNESS.

We bypassed the bar and found the stairwell leading upstairs. Both of us took two steps at a time to a metal door. The door was unlocked.

We found a hallway. And another door.

I went in first. Hawk covered me with the Mossberg pump.

Five nerdy-looking guys sat at a long conference table, studying laptop computers. I thought it a little shameful. Back in the day, we would have found five toughs with bazookas.

They squinted up at us like coal miners seeing the sun after a long absence. A large stack of cash sat on the edge of the table with two money counters. I waited for one to flick through its final count.

I asked, "Is this the Broz School of Business Management?"

Hawk put down the shotgun. He was disappointed, too.

Instead of thugs, we got the math club.

No one spoke. Two of the men snapped shut their computers. They looked to each other. One of the men, a young kid about twenty or so with slick hair and an off-the-rack suit, swept the cash off the table and into a gym bag. Another started for the door.

"Sit your ass down," Hawk said.

Hawk spoke with authority. The kid sat his ass back down.

"That goes for all you Gerry's kids," he said.

"Where is he?" I asked.

A fat kid in an XXXL T-shirt shot his eyes toward the back door. I walked to the door while Hawk covered the little conference table. Nearly out of earshot, I heard him ask, "So what's the line on Philadelphia?"

Through the door, in the back room, Gerry Broz was feeding his fish.

"Gerry, don't you know it's a cliché for bad guys to have a fish tank?" I said. "It's a metaphor for a guy who likes to be in

150

control. Power over his guppies."

He just stared at me. He put down the little green net and the fish food. He tilted his head at me like I was a hallucination.

"Spenser?"

Gerry had aged a hell of a lot in a decade. He looked beefy, like a guy who worked out with weights but still liked to eat and drink too much. His black hair was dyed, and he sported a spray tan that gave his face an orangey glow. He wore one of those slick dress shirts that middle-aged men wear untucked in an effort to be hip. His was purple. Gerry did not look hip.

"I'd hoped to find those guys you sent for me."

"Huh?"

"Well said."

"What the fuck do you want?"

"Even better."

"Christ," Gerry said. "Do you want me to call the cops?"

"For what?"

"Harassment," he said. "I'm a respected business owner."

"I think respect is on the Broz family crest."

"Fuck you, Spenser."

"I want to talk to a couple of your boys."

He studied me. He put his hands on his

hips. His shoes were black crocodile and very pointy. When I first met Gerry, his father had gotten him into Georgetown in an effort to class him up. Instead, he majored in coke dealing and blackmail.

"Moon Murphy and Red Cahill."

"What about them?"

"I want to have a sit-down," I said. "I want you to make that happen."

Gerry laughed. He reached for a pack of cigarettes and shook one loose. He smoked and studied me. He noticed the eye and smiled.

"You look like a raccoon."

"You look like an Oompa-Loompa."

Gerry stopped smiling.

With the same hand that held his cigarette, he scratched his cheek. He smiled. He smoked some more. "They don't work for me."

"C'mon, now," I said. "Don't lie to an old friend."

"Are you fuckin' nuts?" he said. "I missed you like a case of the piles."

"I guess that's why I hang out with assholes."

Broz shrugged, walked over to a big glass desk, and sat down. I pulled up a leather wingback chair and joined him. I put up my work boots on the edge of the desk. He did

152

not seem to appreciate my casual approach.

"That Hawk out there with you?"

"Yep."

"Jesus Christ," he said. "Can't believe nobody's killed you two yet."

"That's a hurtful thing to say, Ger. So much history. A lifetime of friendship."

He nodded as if considering the importance. He placed his hands behind his head and leaned back in his leather office chair.

Gerry looked at me. I looked at him.

He nodded some more.

"You think too much and you'll blow a gasket."

"Trying to figure why you want to shake me down."

"All I want is Red and Moon."

"To talk."

"To talk," I said.

"Or what?"

"Or I make some calls to the Boston police about your little betting operation."

"Go ahead," Gerry said. "Those dorks can run the operation from their mom's basement."

I shrugged. "Maybe not."

"I can ask," Gerry said. "But they don't work for me."

"Sure, Gerry."

"You still at that craphole at Berkeley and

Boylston?"

"The sign says 'luxury office space.' "

"We see the world different, you and me."

"Thank God."

"Let me give you some advice, Spenser."

"I'm breathless."

"Don't bust a man's nuts when you come asking for a favor."

"This isn't a favor," I said. "It's a request with muscle."

I did not hear Hawk. But I felt him standing over my shoulder. Gerry's eyes raised from me to above my head.

"And I's the muscle."

"You fucking guys make me laugh," Gerry said. "My dad used to call you Deano and Sammy. Okay. Okay. I'll make some calls."

I stood. Hawk had the shotgun hanging loose by his leg.

"Which one of us is Sammy?" I asked.

We walked out past the dorks and their laptops and the big stacks of cash. I looked at my watch and told them curfew was coming up.

"Kids today," I said.

We made our way out of Playmates and across Old Colony and back to Hawk's Jaguar. Our coffee was still warm.

"He playin' nice guy?" Hawk asked.

"Yep."

"You believe it?"

"Nope."

"You think those boys will meet with you?"

"I would request neutral ground."

"We could call Vinnie in on this."

I shook my head. Hawk cranked the engine. The stereo played Brubeck, "Take Five."

"Vinnie won't be a part of anything to do with that family," I said. "Joe Broz raised Vinnie like a son."

"Like the son he never had."

"He won't go against Joe's kid."

"So it's little ole me and the Great White Hope."

"Everybody's got to have a dream."

Hawk drove north. He dropped me on Marlborough Street.

I dropped my useless car keys on the kitchen counter and poured out a thick measure of Wild Turkey over ice. The streetlamps cast the slick street in a fine yellow glow. I studied the patterns of shadow and light as I drank.

I turned in to sleep.

I knew I'd need my rest.

22

The next morning I rented a car, drove Mattie to school in Southie, and then headed back to Back Bay. I bought two oat-bran muffins and a large coffee, and ate at my desk while listing witnesses on a yellow legal pad. I leaned back into my office chair and stared at the ceiling. I stared at a collection of framed Van Meer prints Susan had given me. I turned to my window and stared out at the new office building across Berkeley. Staring was on the agenda today.

I would follow with more coffee. The second muffin wasn't long for this world.

I circled the name Touchie Kiley. I opened up a phone book and was paging through it when a paunchy man in a designer suit walked into my office.

He did not knock.

He loomed in front of my desk. I put down the phone book.

I pointed to my client chair. He sat down

as if he paid the rent. He leaned forward with a small grin. "You Spenser?"

"Is the nature of the question existential?"

The grin faded. "It's a fucking question."

"Oh," I said. "One of those."

He leaned forward and pulled out a badge from the jacket of the designer suit. The suit was navy and tailored. He wore a crisp white shirt underneath with cuff links. His tie was a bright yellow, and he had a yellow show hankie in the breast pocket. The badge said he was a special agent for the Federal Bureau of Investigation.

"Hey, I've heard of you guys," I said.

"Good for you."

"I watch a lot of TV."

He rubbed his jaw the way dumb guys do trying to think of what to say next. Suddenly it came to him. "Epstein said you were a smart-ass."

"Epstein is a great judge of character."

"He's been reassigned to Miami."

"Lucky him."

"He said to tell you hello."

I nodded. I offered him an oat-bran muffin, telling him that fiber would make him less cranky. He declined. He had a beefy, florid Irish face. Jowly. His hands were short and thick, with squared nails that looked to be the work of a manicurist. His thick

brown hair, shot with gray, had been bar-
bered into a glossy helmet.

"Tom Connor," he said. He said it like I
should have heard of him and shake from
excitement.

I drank some coffee.

"You paid a visit to Gerry Broz last night."

I nodded. I noticed my coffee needed
more sugar. I added some from the little
packets I kept in my right-hand desk drawer,
next to my .357.

"I came to you as a courtesy to Epstein,"
he said. "He's a good guy."

"He is."

"We have operations going on in South
Boston," Connor said. "You buzzing around
Mr. Broz could fuck up two years of work."

"That would be a shame."

"You bet it would."

"Aren't you going to ask me what I'm up
to?"

He shook his jowls and grinned again.
"Don't want to and don't need to."

"Would you like to study my Van Meer
prints?"

"It's a simple request."

"Just lay off?"

Connor smiled. "Say, you got the idea,
Spense."

I let that one go and said, "I'm a quick study."

He put his squared-off little hand across my desk. He offered a shake. I did not shake. He frowned and retracted his hand.

"We can make life difficult for you," Connor said.

I nodded. He had a point.

I turned my chair on the swivel and looked out across Berkeley. "There used to be a woman who worked in the office opposite mine. She'd dazzle me every day with her figure. In the spring and summer, I got almost no work done."

"So?"

"So now the building is gone," I said. "The new building kind of looks like the old one. But now I look across at a bald guy who cleans teeth."

He shrugged and stood up. He self-consciously ran his tie between his fingers and buttoned up his coat. I noted the service revolver under his arm.

"Thanks for dropping by."

"I got my eye on you."

"*Your attitude has been noted,*" I said. "Someone once said that to Omar Sharif. I think it was Alec Guinness. Or was it Rod Steiger?"

Connor looked back from the door frame.

"You can't be a hot dog forever," he said.

He left. He did not shut the door.

I drank some more coffee. I pulled out the phone book and went back to searching for Touchie Kiley. Sometimes being a hot dog took persistence.

23

I found Touchie Kiley parking cars outside the Four Seasons Hotel on Boylston Street. I made my introductions and waited twenty minutes before he took a break. I sat on a park bench outside the hotel, where I could look out on the frozen tundra of the Common. My peacoat was large and thick, and I'd planned ahead with double socks. I also wore a nice pair of cashmere-lined gloves Susan picked out for me at Neiman Marcus.

There were a lot of dogs in the Common today. My prediction called for a lot of yellow snow.

Touchie took a seat beside me. He was eating a hamburger from McDonald's and absently reaching into a greasy sack for his fries. He was a good-looking twentysomething guy with dimples who wore too much grease in his hair. It may have been gel or mousse or some kind of styling product. I

161

did not touch it. I took it to be grease.

"Julie's kid really hire you?" he asked.

"She really did."

"How old is she now?"

"Fourteen."

"Wow. In a few years, Jules could've been like a grandmother or somethin'."

"Fingers crossed."

"Jules and I went to high school together before I dropped out," Touchie said. "Her and me were in English together."

"And learned much."

I showed him the photograph of him with Julie Sullivan. He shook his head as he worked on a wad of hamburger. He nearly choked getting it down. He pointed to the photo and smiled, nodding a lot.

"She was a lot of fun," he said. "Great tits. But she wasn't my girlfriend or anything. More of just a fuck buddy."

"How nice of her."

He grinned and shrugged. "Fuck buddies are the best kind of buddies."

"A friend in need," I said.

He nodded with understanding. He ate some more fries. Touchie Kiley was probably coming up on thirty but was one of those guys who didn't want to go much beyond nineteen. He would dress the part, wear his hair in a certain style, and keep playing young until it didn't work anymore. Most guys like that never did know when they passed that point. Today he was dressed in the spiffy greens of a parking attendant. Tonight he'd be a rock star.

"Were you still buddies when she got killed?" I asked.

"I didn't have shit to do with that, man."

"Didn't say you did," I said. "Just trying to figure out who was in her circle. What her life was like. Find people who may know more about her death."

"Mickey Green killed her."

"Mickey Green was convicted of killing her," I said. "Julie's daughter thinks he's innocent."

"Mickey Green is a fuck-up piece of shit."

"That may be the case," I said. "But it doesn't mean he killed her."

Touchie Kiley finished off the burger, wadded up the wrapper, and sized up a trash can with gold trim. He took the shot. And missed. He walked over and placed the wrapper and the fries bag into the can. He sat back down. Conscientious.

"So," I said, "besides Mickey Green, who else would've been in Julie's company?"

"Shit, I don't know."

"Think, Touchie," I said. "Try it. You'll like it."

"We just kind of hooked up sometimes."

"As fuck buddies should."

An older black man in a red-and-gold uniform and matching hat called out for Touchie and pointed to his watch. Touchie held up his hand, acknowledging he'd heard him. The man shook his head in annoyance and walked back to the valet stand. He opened the door for a silver-haired woman exiting a silver Lexus.

"There was this chick."

"And what was this chick's name?"

"Shit," he said. "This was, like, four years ago."

"It was four years ago."

"And it's hard to remember," he said. "I was kind of fucked up myself."

"But Julie had this friend."

"Yeah, she went to Southie High, too. Shit, she was always with Julie. You didn't see one without the other. Frick and fucking Frack."

"Was she spotted in the company of a Thin Man?"

"I don't know," Touchie said. "I don't remember him."

"Never mind," I said. "Would this girl's name happen to be Theresa?"

"Yeah, Theresa Donovan," he said. "She had great tits, too. I wonder if she's still around? I bet we're into the same shit, knowing the same people and all."

"What are you into, Touchie?"

"Having a good time before my dick quits working."

"A noble goal."

"You got a wife?"

"Sort of," I said.

"What's that mean?"

"It means I've got total commitment but don't need a piece of paper to make it so."

"You been married?"

"Nope."

"Then what makes you different than me?" he said. "If you get the milk for free, then why buy the cow?"

" *'Soul and body have no bounds,'* " I said. " *'To lovers as they lie upon.'* "

"What is that, Bon Jovi?"

"Auden."

"Some old-school shit."

"Yep."

Touchie took out a pocket comb and slicked back his dark hair. Damn if it wasn't old-fashioned grease. I wondered if he carried a switchblade, too. He stood and shook my hand.

"Anything else you recall?" I asked. You always ended the interview like that. *One more question, ma'am.* Over the years, I'd perfected it.

"You didn't ask me about the old guy."

"And I say, 'What old guy?' "

"Older 'an you," Touchie said. "I seen him with Julie a lot before Mickey killed her. I figured you'd be all over that."

"Name?"

"Don't know," Touchie said. "He was somebody. You know, like a guy who thought he was top dog or used to be one. I was in the pub and kind of trashed when I met him."

"I'm sensing a pattern."

"One night, I go up to Jules and say, 'How's the kids, how's your ma, how you doin' in the McCormack?' and all that shit. I guess we was talking a little too close, and this old guy comes up and nearly takes my fucking head off. Just for talking to her."

"What'd he say?"

"Didn't say nothin'," Touchie said. "He just reached over, grabbed my hand, and pulled my arm off Jules. He had a grip like a gorilla. Strong as an ape. A big crazy mick. A couple old guys pulled him away and tried to calm him down 'cause he'd just gotten out of the joint."

"What'd you do?"

"Not shit," he said. "Guy was nuts. Old men get a piece of young tail and they lose their mind. Fuckin' nuts. People were grabbing me and telling me to get lost, that he'd kill me or something. A lot of drunk shit. Pub stuff. Me? I like to joke around. Have a drink. Have a smoke. Have fun."

"People tell me you're a riot," I said.

"What can I say? It's a gift."

Touchie smiled. He was very pleased with himself.

"You know anyone who'd recognize the old guy?"

"Nah," he said. "Like I said, my memory ain't so good. I mean, the big guy coulda been you."

"Wasn't me."

"Shit, I don't know," he said. "He was a big old tough guy."

"You remember any detail about him?"

"He was a mean bastard."

"Would it help if I brought some photos?"

He shook his head. "I was pretty trashed."

I nodded. I made a mental note. I would ask around.

"Jules was a sweet girl." He looked out into the Common and smiled, thinking some sweet and faraway thought. Wind kicked up flecks of snow and scattered bits along twisting paths. The smile was frozen on his face. "Real sweet. She was a mess, but she sure loved her kids."

I gave him a card. And twenty bucks. "Ask around about the old guy," I said.

Touchie Kiley thanked me before running off to park a Cadillac. He waved in the shiny new car as it passed me on the half-circle drive. He looked very at home behind the wheel.

24

Peter Contini, attorney at law, kept an office on Washington Street, not far from Kneeland. I once had an office in the same neighborhood, when it was known as the Combat Zone. I still recalled the Teddy Bare Lounge, the Two O'clock Club, and the Naked I with great fondness. The Naked I had a terrific sign with a neon eye flashing over a woman's crotch. There were dancers like Princess Cheyenne and Fanne Foxe, the Argentine Firecracker. Dozens and dozens of peep shows and burlesque clubs and dirty movie houses.

But then came redevelopment and home video. Men could watch naked women on their computers. No need for a raincoat and sunglasses. Now most of the old Combat Zone was filled with electronics stores and Vietnamese restaurants.

There was a cold rain that afternoon, and I had my collar turned up on my coat. The rain slickened the neon streets, signs shining in Asian symbols and letters.

My Sox hat was soaked by the time I knocked on Contini's office door.

When he opened it, I could tell he was slightly drunk.

"I'd like to talk to you about Mickey Green," I said brightly.

Contini looked at me like I was the Ghost of Christmas Past. I smiled reassuringly at him. He did not smile back. He just walked back into his small office, which was cluttered in papers and thick bound files.

He sat at his desk and took a sip from a coffee mug. Contini was a small, skeletal man with very white, very bad skin. His suit had probably been purchased at a warehouse sale. And even ten years ago it must've been just as ugly.

He face was pockmarked. He was in need of a shave.

"How's the coffee?" I asked.

"I don't drink coffee," Contini said.

I smiled.

"Mickey Green?" he said. "Sorry. I think he fired me. Someone else is doing his appeals."

"Can't imagine why," I said. "Top legal beagle like you."

"Hey, what the hell?"

"Do you have a chair?"

Contini pointed one out under an avalanche of documents and bills. I moved the pile to the floor, careful not to dismantle his ornate filing system.

"Do I know you?" he asked.

I gave my name and profession.

He wrote it out on a pad.

"With an *S*," I said. "Like the English poet."

Contini scratched out what he'd written. He nodded as if he were a great fan of Elizabethan poetry.

"Mickey Green told me you were a lousy lawyer."

"Mickey Green's family still owes me money."

"He said you missed several hearings."

"I don't recall that."

"He said you failed to consult forensic experts."

"Hiring your own experts costs money."

"And that you never presented a single alibi witness."

"Because he didn't have any."

"Tiffany Royce," I said. I crossed my legs. My jacket was flecked with rain.

"Who's that?"

"Alibi witness," I said. "Manicurist. Woman Mickey slept with at her house that

171

night. Very nice body. Butterfly tattoo on her lower back."

"Mickey lied to me so many times I didn't know what was what."

"Did you know Julie Sullivan had a boyfriend at the time of her murder?"

Contini's left eye twitched. How I'd love to take his money at poker. I leaned into the chair, placing my elbows across my knees.

"She was also seen in the company of a pair of Southie shitbags hours before the killing."

"Says who?" Contini asked. The legal mind was awake. Ready to fence.

"Julie Sullivan's daughter," I said. "She hired me to find out who killed her mother."

"You work for a kid?" Contini asked. "Jesus Christ."

He placed a pair of big unpolished black shoes on his windowsill. He laughed. "What's she pay you in? Girl Scout cookies?"

"Nope," I said. "Chocolate-glazed."

"You ever worked a criminal investigation before?"

"One or two."

"You're welcome to look at his file," he said. "See if you can make chickenshit into chicken salad."

"People do say I am a wonderful cook."

He rummaged around in his office for several minutes. A bottle of Scope sat on a tall file cabinet. He had framed a print of the Paul Revere statue behind his desk. *"One if by land, and two if by sea."* A framed diploma from Suffolk Law School had yellowed and bubbled behind the glass.

I sat in the chair and studied the rain slanting along Washington Street. I missed the hookers and pimps. At least they were honest.

He handed me the file.

"Can I ask you a question?"

He nodded.

"What do you keep in that cup?"

"Fighting Cock whiskey and Sprite."

"Good God."

He shrugged.

I stood. "I'll have copies made."

"Keep it," Contini said, before taking a swig of hooch. "I flushed the toilet on that turd a long time ago."

"Well, you did everything humanly possible."

"Let me give you some free advice, Spenser," Contini said. I figured we were old buddies now, as he rubbed the shadow on his jaw. "You know, since you're such a nice guy."

"Ah, shucks."

"You're wasting your fucking time."

"So I've been told."

"But you think he's innocent."

"I think Julie Sullivan's daughter has a lot questions," I said. "I think Mickey Green never got a fair shot."

"What would you think of me if I said not everyone deserves one?" Contini asked.

"Not very much."

25

I had skipped lunch. Sensing this might be a sign of the Apocalypse, I invited Mattie to an early dinner in Cambridge. Susan joined us.

We ate at a little place on the square called Flat Patties. The shoestring fries were excellent. The burgers were indeed flat. Sadly, though, they did not serve beer.

"You can't have beer with every meal," Susan said.

"But with a burger and fries?" I said. "There should be a law."

Outside the plate-glass window, a group of students gathered on Brattle Street. They were protesting something in carefully chosen ragged-looking clothes and bright ski hats. I chose not to listen. It was hard to imagine an oppressed Harvard student.

Mattie watched the students chant and began to furtively wrap the uneaten burger in some wax paper.

"Not good?" Susan asked.

"I'm not hungry," Mattie said. "I'll bring it home for my sisters."

"Go ahead and eat," I said. "We'll get a couple burgers to go."

Mattie looked to Susan. Susan nodded. Mattie shrugged. Her reddish hair had been braided and looped through the back of her cap.

"So you have twin sisters?" Susan asked.

Mattie nodded and took a bite.

"What are their names?"

Mattie told her. Susan picked at her salad.

"And you live with your grandmother?"

Mattie took a larger bite. She nodded with her mouth full. I felt Susan's hand on my knee. I took this as a sign to keep my mouth shut. I promptly filled it with more burger and a couple of fries. The burger was top shelf. The BBQ Blue. Blue cheese, barbecue sauce, and bacon. It was easy to keep my mouth at work.

Susan had ordered an Asian salad with scallions, toasted almonds, and noodles.

"So what do you do for fun?" Susan asked.

"I don't know. Watch TV and stuff."

"I mean, if you could do anything for a day, what would you do?"

"Who has a day like that?"

"What if you could take a little vacation

from life?"

"But I can't."

"If you could," Susan said. She said it sweetly, smiling as she nibbled on a Chinese noodle. Just a couple ladies shooting the breeze. Susan had a wonderful ability to coax in the gentle pauses. But Mattie was one very tough nut.

"The weather sucks," Mattie said. "You can't do crap outside. If you do go outside, people screw with you. I guess go see a movie."

"Is that fun?"

"I guess."

"What did you used to do for fun?" Susan asked.

"When I was a kid?"

"Yes," Susan said. "Back when you were the same age as your sisters?"

"I don't remember," Mattie said. "What did you do?"

Susan took a sip of tea and smiled. I continued to eat. Susan's hand had yet to leave my knee. It was not at all unpleasant.

"I liked to play dress-up," Susan said. "I liked old dresses. I had dolls. I know it's not original, but I loved dolls when I was six."

"She was the princess of Swampscott," I said. "Sometimes she'll still play dress-up."

Susan gently kicked me.

"What about your sisters?" Susan asked. "What do they like to do?"

"They like the cartoons. They watch a ton of freakin' cartoons. All that Japanese crap. Dora. SpongeBob. They like to go to the playground when you don't freeze your ass off. They have friends at school. I don't know. Kid stuff."

"Do you enjoy playing with them?"

"I don't play," Mattie said. "I'm fourteen."

I almost mentioned the tiara at the princess party but did not care to be kicked under the table twice.

"That's not too old to play."

"I got stuff to do."

"Like what?" Susan asked.

"Get my sisters ready for bed," she said. "Make sure they have clean clothes for school. All that. Sometimes my grandma helps. Sometimes she can't."

Mattie finished her cheeseburger in record time. She sat back. She eyed Susan. And then she eyed me. She smiled slightly and took a deep breath. "What about you, Susan?"

Susan widened her eyes. "Me?"

"Yeah," Mattie said. "You got kids?"

"No."

"How come?" Mattie asked. She crossed her arms across her chest and leaned back.

Susan smiled slowly, admiring Mattie's tactic, and nodded. "I wanted children when I was younger, but after my divorce, it wasn't practical."

"Why'd you get a divorce?"

"Her husband was an asshole," I said.

Mattie smiled. Susan did not. She grasped my knee firmly.

"We became different people."

"That's me," Mattie said. "You're asking me about bein' a kid and all that. It's not the same. I don't even remember things before my ma died."

"But you realize you are the same person," Susan said. "That kid is you. It's your life history. Past, present, and future."

Mattie shrugged.

"You can't stop your life while you search for what happened," Susan said. "Unhappiness won't bring back the dead. That's something hard to understand for many of my patients."

"You ever lost a parent?"

"No," Susan said. "Not like you have. You've gone through a horrific event."

"This is what I do," she said. "I'll see it through."

"But it will grind you down."

"Nah." Mattie shook her head. She looked

at Susan with very old eyes. "It keeps me going."

Susan nodded. Mattie nodded back at her.

I took a breath. Susan let go of my leg. There was a sliver of tension at the table. It was up to Mr. Personality to cut through it.

"Who'd like a malt?" I asked. "You know I skipped lunch? Something I haven't done in twenty years. My dedication is unwavering."

I ordered two malts.

The protest broke up and some of the protestors filtered into the restaurant. I detected the protest had not been about eating red meat. A few of the coeds removed their heavy winter jackets and scarves to reveal some very tight T-shirts. The T-shirts protested the war. I took note as the malts arrived.

"You ever thought about what you'd like to do when you graduate?" Susan asked.

"That's a long time," Mattie said. "Like in four years."

"Four years goes quick," Susan said.

"You'll have to excuse my friend," I said. "In a previous life, she worked as a guidance counselor."

"I don't know," Mattie said. "Maybe be like him."

I jabbed a thumb at my chest in surprise.

I raised my eyebrows in triumph.

"Yeah," Mattie said. "All you do is go around and ask questions. Bother people till they give you answers. I figure I could do the same thing. You basically act like an asshole and don't let people lie."

Susan grinned. "The young lady makes an excellent point."

"Sometimes I do have to shoot people."

"I could do that," Mattie said. She sipped her milkshake. Her pink ball cap was slightly askew. Her winter coat had been buttoned all wrong.

I looked to Susan. Susan watched Mattie.

"Shooting people is not the highlight of my work," I said.

"If I got a gun," Mattie said, "I'd shoot down Red Cahill and Moon Murphy in two seconds."

I didn't say anything.

"I'd kill 'em both and go to prison for the rest of my life with a smile on my face. That'd be my freakin' vacation."

Susan's face showed concern. I nodded.

I understood.

26

After dropping off Mattie in the projects, I made two phone calls. I checked in with Bobby Barrett, the patrol officer I'd met. I told him about my run-in with Moon and the thugs who'd stolen my car and escorted me away from the Mary Ellen McCormack. He said he'd been checking on the Sullivans and would continue. He didn't offer much hope for my car.

I thanked him anyway.

I then called my answering service to learn that a Mr. Red Cahill had called that afternoon. He would like to arrange for a meeting tonight.

"Jeepers," I said to the service operator.

"Excuse me, sir?"

"It's an expression I use when filled with both anticipation and dread."

I called Red's number. He answered on the second ring.

"Where?" he asked.

"No fond greeting?" I asked.

"Where?"

"Quincy Market."

"Sure," he said. He had a gravelly voice. Subdued. "What time?"

"An hour?"

"Come alone or I ain't sayin' shit."

I agreed.

Then I called Hawk.

"You want me to make my presence known?" Hawk asked.

"No."

"My step will be as stealthy as the catamount's."

"You and Natty Bumppo."

I drove back to my office and slipped into a leather rig for my .357. I placed the loaded .38 in my side pocket. I searched my drawers for some grenades but came out with nothing more than a handful of bullets.

I placed those in my jeans pocket.

I zipped up my leather jacket, fixed my Braves cap down over my eyes, and drove toward the Quincy Market in the rental car.

A light snow had started to fall. The snow drifted so fine and light, it could be detected only in the streetlights on Boylston.

27

I liked the Quincy Market despite itself. You had to look beyond such authentic Boston staples as the Cheers Bar and Ned Devine's Irish Pub to appreciate the charm. But inside the old brick building you could find some decent fast food and a hot cup of coffee. At night, white festival lights shone off icy brick pathways.

I bought a cup of coffee and found a seat inside the center of the market, under the rotunda.

A group of Japanese tourists was posing next to a pushcart that sold Boston T-shirts and Sox hats. All the pushcarts had cute little names: A Hat for Every Head. Happy Hangups. Every Bead of My Heart. In spring, the carts would move outside and the open space between buildings would be filled with tables topped with umbrellas. Women with very long legs would be sipping wine and smoking cigarettes.

I looked forward to that time. But now it was too cold.

I warmed my hands with the coffee cup. I looked out for thugs with red hair.

I didn't have to wait long.

Halfway through the coffee, a man with the lean, muscular build of a welterweight walked through the side door to the market. He scanned faces.

I raised my cup. He caught my eye.

Red Cahill crossed the rotunda and slid into the seat on the other side of me. Less than half of the tables were filled with tourists dining on pizza, chicken fingers, or teriyaki chicken. I wondered if every food court in America served teriyaki chicken.

I asked Red.

"How the fuck do I know?"

"You always find hot pretzels, too."

"So the fuck what?"

I drank some coffee. I waited.

"Mr. Broz said you want to talk."

I nodded.

Red wore a black leather blazer and a black skully cap. His nose was red and growing bulbous. His eyes were so blue they looked almost transparent. He seemed fidgety as he waited to get down to it. He had big, thick hands and hard, round knuckles. I detected the bulge of a gun under his left arm. I expected nothing less.

I drank some more coffee. His knee pumped up and down like a piston.

I watched faces in the rotunda. Businessmen and -women out in Beantown. A few families.

Hawk was out there somewhere, moving as a catamount.

"Julie Sullivan," I said.

"Who?"

I groaned and worked a crick out of my neck. I shook my head.

"Can we get to it?" I asked. "Or do you want to play Abbott and Costello?"

"Who?"

I smiled. I noted calcium deposits over his brow. I figured it must impair brain activity.

"You fight long?" I asked.

He nodded. "Mr. Broz said you fought, too."

I nodded.

"You go pro?"

"I did."

"What happened?"

"An ex-champ derailed my aspirations."

"I went out west," Red said. "I found a manager, but he didn't do jack. He took me to a queer bar and wanted to suck my cock."

"He must have had great faith in your talent."

"I came back and tried to get on with some promoters," he said. "They talked a lot of shit but could never get me a decent fight. I had to eat. You know?"

"So you started selling drugs?"

"It's a living."

"It is."

"Who was your trainer?" Red asked.

"Henry Cimoli."

"Holy shit," he said. "Get the fuck out of here."

"Nope."

"He's famous."

"He'd agree."

"You must've been pretty good."

I smiled. I finished the coffee.

"You still think about it?" Red asked. "Things you could've done different?"

"Not so much anymore."

"But you loved the life," he said. "Being a fighter. The training and all."

"I did."

I scanned more faces. Two large men walked through a side door. The two men did not look at us. They walked over to a pizza kiosk and debated pepperoni or anchovies.

"Let's say I knew this woman," Red said.

"Julie Sullivan."

"Yeah, Julie," Red said. He rubbed his

hands together. The skin was cracked and chapped. He blew his breath into a fist and nodded. "So what?"

"So it seems she was in the company of you and Moon Murphy before she got killed."

"You know what I do for a living?"

"Yes."

"So maybe she just wanted a score."

"Maybe she did."

"And maybe I'm not responsible for dumb whores who get hooked and get killed," he said. "I sell dope. Sue me. What she does when she's fucked up is her business."

I rubbed my jaw. I listened.

"Why'd you send those guys for me?" I asked.

Red screwed up his face. "I don't know what you're talking about."

"You sent a welcome wagon out to the projects to steal my car and chase me out of Southie."

"If I wanted you out of Southie, I woulda done it myself."

"Or tried."

He looked at me and snorted.

I tilted my head.

He met my eye. He nodded.

I nodded back.

"I don't want trouble," Red said. "I come

188

here because Mr. Broz asked me to. He don't want trouble, either. You want to know about that broad, and I told you. I sold her dope. But I didn't kill her."

"And Moon?"

"Moon doesn't like nosy guys from Beacon Hill asking questions about him at his favorite pub."

"Why does everyone think I'm from Beacon Hill?" I asked. "You're starting to give me a complex."

"You ain't from Southie."

"The Man from Laramie."

"Where's that?"

"West of Pittsfield."

"We done?" Red placed his scarred hands on the table and began to stand.

"How about I buy you some coffee?"

"Nope."

"Cinnabon?"

"Nope."

"You must've heard what really happened to Julie Sullivan, and why," I said. "Word gets out in the neighborhood when something like that goes down. Your cousin's doing life for it, but did he do it?"

He turned his light eyes away from me. "Mick always found trouble whether it was his fault or not. Since we were kids, he was the unluckiest bastard I ever met. Julie only came to me for drugs through Mickey."

"Did you ever see her with a guy, maybe twice as old as her?"

"The boxing must've fucked up your hearing," he said. "I barely knew her."

"What time did you see Julie that night?"

He snorted again. "Man, that was four years ago."

"After midnight?"

"Probably," he said. "Yeah, it wouldn'a been till real late. I don't start work till after midnight. I sleep in the day."

"You see her with Mickey earlier?"

He turned and faced me full-on. His blue eyes took me in. Appraised me.

"I sold her drugs."

"You have to throw her in the car to sell her drugs?"

"She tried to stiff us."

"Good motive."

"If I say I fucking killed her, what does it matter now?"

"Matters to Mickey. Don't you care that he's in jail?"

"Of course. Mickey is family."

"So?"

"So I don't fucking rat on family," he said. "I don't rat on no one."

"Um, he's been convicted and is currently incarcerated at Walpole. He can't do worse."

He nodded.

"Did he do it?" I asked.

He did not break his stare. Red scratched his face.

"You asked me if I did it," he said. "I said no. You asked if Moon did it, and I said no. Isn't that what you wanted?"

"Did Mickey do it?"

"I'm sorry what happened to Mickey," Red said. "He got mixed up in somethin' that wasn't his business."

"Whose business was it?"

"I didn't kill her," Red said. "Moon didn't kill her."

"Who did?" I asked. "Why was Julie Sullivan killed?"

Red stood up. He offered his hand.

"Me and you through?"

"Probably not," I said.

"You know if you don't leave this alone, you're gonna have big problems with Mr. Broz."

"I just call him Ger. And yes, the thought had crossed my mind."

"That don't bother you?"

I shrugged. "Why does Gerry give a crap what I do?" I asked. "What's he have to do with all this?"

"You're causing him headaches," he said. "Me and Moon take care of Mr. Broz's headaches."

"Does Gerry know what happened?"

"No."

"And you don't either?"

"Didn't I give you my fucking word?"

"You *are* a street thug," I said.

"And what are you?" Red asked me.

He turned and waded into a group of tourists gathering by a side door. As Red Cahill headed toward Faneuil Hall, I spotted glittering light against a shiny black head following.

28

"I had a visit from a federal agent this morning," I said to Hawk.

"You don't say."

"He told me he was making a case against Gerry Broz and his crew," I said. "He wanted us to quit bothering poor Gerry."

"What happened to your buddy, that Fed Epstein?"

"Miami."

"Jew heaven."

"He would agree with you," I said. "New agent's name is Connor. He was not enthusiastic about a joint investigative effort."

"So why are we staking out Broz's boys?"

"You got anything better to do?" I asked.

"Got me a new woman," he said. "Keeps silk sheets warm. Iron Horse chilled."

"I brought coffee."

"Ain't the same, babe."

"Simple pleasures are the best pleasures."

"Best pleasures come in black lace with

193

garters."

"You have a point."

We sat in the front seats of Hawk's Jaguar, watching a two-story house on East Third Street, not far from Dorchester Bay. The house seemed like a midget among the three-deckers, pulled away from the other buildings and ringed by an actual front and backyard. In the backyard, there was a small metal shed. Christmas lights still hung on the front railing of the house. They looked pretty in the lightly falling snow, although we were a couple months past the season.

It was nearing midnight and no one had come from the house. Red's green Range Rover sat parked up on a curb across the street. I'd parked on G Street before joining Hawk.

"You find out who owns the house?" Hawk asked.

"I'll run it at my office."

"You learn how to use the computer?"

"I subscribe to a service."

"Progress, Spenser. Progress."

We spent the next hour talking about spring training for the Sox. Talk of baseball led to the downfall of boxing. And the downfall of boxing led to a lively discussion of the good old days of boxing. We recalled the lead-up to the Clay and Liston fight in

Miami. We laughed at Clay calling Liston a big ugly bear.

"Liston never got up after being beat twice," Hawk said.

"Died a few years later."

"Heroin," Hawk said. "Never cared for that shit."

"Killed a lot of good people."

"Coltrane."

"Billie Holiday."

"Chet Baker."

"Liston," Hawk said. "That big ugly bear."

"Not every big black man is as pretty as you."

"Ain't it a shame?"

I finished my coffee, now cold.

"You think maybe we follow Red and Moon to their stash?" Hawk asked.

"Then we steal their stash?"

"Make 'em more willing to talk."

"It could work."

"You thinkin' you made Red nervous and he might tip off who really killed Mattie's momma?"

"Yep."

"Or maybe he just call 'im on his cell and say what's up."

"Sure."

"But you also interested in the new shake-up in Southie," Hawk said. "You want to know about Gerry's new operation."

"Never thought the Broz family celebrated Saint Patrick's Day."

"But now they're in with a mick crew."

"*Mick* is a derogatory word for my people."

"Okay," Hawk said. "Makes you wonder why a Polack would throw in with all these potato-eaters."

"Broz is a Slavic name."

"Y'all look the same to me."

We stayed on the small house till three in the morning. At three-ish, Red and Moon walked out of the two-story and to the Range Rover. I was pleased to see Moon sported two black eyes and several bruises on his face.

"You give him that?" Hawk asked.

"I did."

"Spenser," he said in appreciation.

Red finished a cigarette and ground it underfoot before climbing inside. The tail-lights clicked on, and he backed up before going forward. Hawk cranked the Jaguar and followed them to Marine Park and then south on Farragut Road. Farragut joined up with Columbia, and we followed the crook of the harbor down to Old Colony.

"Gerry's place," Hawk said.

"Kind of late for a sports bar."

"After hours."

"Wonder if they'd still pour me a beer?"

"How's beer set with bad coffee?"

"My stomach is iron," I said.

"How 'bout we just hang and see what happens?"

"Instead of just busting in?"

"Yeah."

"Gerry would appreciate that."

"Glad to make Gerry happy," Hawk said.

We parked alongside a chain-link fence by a laundry service. The air smelled of strong, hot detergent. The little side road had a nice view of the front of Playmates. The bar downstairs was closed and dark. The second floor was brightly lit with shadows of men crossing by windows.

"Wonder what they up to?" Hawk asked.

"Maybe it's a book-of-the-month club."

"Crime and Punishment?" Hawk said.

"Lil' Abner," I said.

Red and Moon walked out of the side door thirty minutes later. Moon carried two black duffel bags. Red opened the rear hatch, and Moon tossed them both inside. Red lit a cigarette. He finished and they both climbed back in the car.

Hawk cranked the Jaguar.

"Hold on," I said.

The Range Rover made a quick U-turn on Old Colony and headed north. The tail-lights disappeared.

"They got the shit with 'em," Hawk said. "Now or never."

"Stick with Broz."

Hawk shook his head and switched off the ignition. Snow continued to fall, light and shiftless. I stretched my legs.

We did not talk for some time.

Hawk had no need to fill the silence. We had nothing more to discuss.

A half hour later, Gerry Broz came out wearing a black satin baseball jacket and a matching Kangol hat. He kept his right hand in his pocket and held a lit cigarette with his left. From across the street, I could see the smoke leaking from his mouth.

He must've pressed the button on his keychain. The lights of a black Lexus flicked twice. Broz stood there smoking, his head tilting to the door, waiting for a man to join him on the street.

He locked up behind the man. And the two men stood there talking for a second.

The other man was a good head taller that Gerry. He was much older, with a ruddy face and thick, curly blond hair. His eyes were small and closely set, his face pale and deeply weathered. He wore a long black overcoat with the collar up. He smoked a cigar, his hands covered with fingerless gloves.

The man nodded at Gerry's words while checking out the bottom of his shoe.

We were parked in shadow. But the larger man turned and stared into the straight shot of alley. Hawk placed his hands on the key-chain.

"Man sees us," Hawk said.

"He can't."

"He do."

"Okay."

Hawk started the engine and turned north on Old Colony. The Jaguar purred. Hawk started to laugh.

"The Irish Connection," I said.

"Jumpin' Jack Flynn."

"Maybe Gerry's boy isn't the boss."

"Nope."

"I thought Flynn got life."

"Guess they didn't expect him to live so long," Hawk said. "Evil don't die."

I nodded.

"And now he's doing business with Gerry and your boys, Red and Moon," he said. *"Hmm."*

"Would you call that a clue?"

"Yas-suh."

"Interesting."

"You want to talk to Vinnie about this

thing?" Hawk asked, steering the car with two fingers.

"Yep."

"Vinnie don't like Flynn," Hawk said. "Hate him the way Gerry Broz hates you."

"Curiouser and curiouser."

"Plain fucked up," Hawk said.

"That, too."

29

I met Vinnie Morris early the next morning at a Starbucks across Boylston. I felt slightly guilty for not supporting my hometown Dunkin' Donuts. But it was within a baseball toss from my office, and at last count, Dunkin' Donuts still outnumbered the boys from Seattle in the greater Boston area. I added a lot of milk and sugar to combat the bitter taste.

"You see the tatas on that coffee girl?" Vinnie asked.

"I believe the proper term in *barista*."

"She got a great set of tits in any language," he said. "So what's up?"

Vinnie wore a navy cashmere topcoat with a glen plaid suit underneath. His dress shirt was a blue-and-white stripe, and his tie a light purple. He carried an umbrella, and his cordovan wingtips were protected by a pair of black rubbers.

We stood at a small counter against the

window facing Boylston.

"I saw Gerry Broz last night," I said.

"Sorry to hear that."

"He was conversing with Jack Flynn."

"Oh, shit."

"That's all you have to say?"

" 'Oh, shit' pretty much says it all."

"Can you enlighten me?" I asked.

Vinnie nodded.

He took a sip of coffee. I think he needed a moment to think. He was a medium-sized guy of dark complexion, his dark hair swept back in executive style. But I didn't know many executives who could shoot a hole through a nickel at a hundred yards.

"I'd heard some rumors," Vinnie said. "But I thought it was bullshit. I don't like this picture. Not at all. You've just fucked up my morning, Spenser."

"Glad to be of service."

The office workers walking down Boylston were bright-eyed and bushy-tailed. The sidewalks had been swept and salted. The banks of snow were dwindling just a bit but were still high enough to cover the parking meters. Parking meters were best covered. I had tickets going back a few decades.

"You know about Joe Broz and Flynn?" Vinnie asked.

"I know they used to be in cahoots."

202

" 'Cahoots'?"

"Technical term," I said.

"If *cahoots* means shaking down loan sharks, busting up bookies, and killing people that got in their way, then yeah, I'd say they was in cahoots."

"How long was he part of Joe's crew?"

"He was never part of Joe's operation," Vinnie said. "He wasn't really part of no one's operation. Jack Flynn did for Jack Flynn. If working with Joe meant more for Jack, then, well, good for everyone. They had kind of a, I don't know what."

"Mutual admiration society?"

"Yeah."

I drank some coffee. I watched a young lady stroll in front of the big plate-glass window facing my office building. She must've been nearly six feet tall in her high-heeled riding boots and a smart wool coat. Her hair was in a neat bun, and she wore big Holly Golightly sunglasses. She was very put together.

"You see that?" Vinnie asked.

"Yep."

"Nice."

"Well groomed."

"So, yeah. Jack and Joe were tight before my time," Vinnie said. "Back during the gang wars, they took out a lot of people who tried to buck the system. I know personally that Jack took out two boys from his own crew to keep the peace."

"That was mighty big of him."

"Last man standing," Vinnie said.

Another woman passed by the window. She wore a bright red coat and walked a small rat terrier on a long leather leash. She also was wearing tall riding boots and wearing large sunglasses. I sensed a trend. Her ears were plugged with buds to an iPod.

"What about during the Vinnie era?" I asked.

"He did jobs for us," Vinnie said. "But Joe never trusted him. Said that Flynn liked killing too much. Like he'd send Jack to take care of something, you know, just to scare the shit out of someone, and the fucking guy would end up dead. Kind of screwed up the extortion process."

"A man who loves his work."

"He's a fucking sociopath."

"You've killed a lot of people."

"Yeah, sure. But I don't get off on it or anything. It's a goddamn job same as any other. Lots of guys in Southie were last seen in the company of Jumpin' Jack Flynn."

"Women?"

"I don't think he'd kill a woman," Vinnie said. "You don't just whack a broad. Unless it's business. I mean, it's got to be a real good reason. You kill a woman and your reputation goes in the shitter."

I rubbed my jaw. I turned back to the barista. She was serving up a couple of scones. I contemplated returning to my office with more coffee and scones. I wondered if they were blueberry. Vinnie joined me in staring. But I don't think he was looking at the scones.

"Can you see what's what?"

"I can talk to the kid," he said.

"Gerry is a middle-aged man."

"In the head, he's still a fuckin' kid," Vinnie said. "Joe wouldn't like him bringing in Flynn for anything. The kid should know that."

I finished my coffee. I decided to get one to go, with scones on the side.

I reached for my gloves and my ball cap.

"Vinnie, you mind me asking what ever happened to your previous employer?"

"You mean like where'd Joe go? Is he still alive? Is he still active in the life?"

"Yeah," I said. "That."

Vinnie grinned and tucked his umbrella under one arm. He put his index finger to his lips and smiled.

30

I returned to my second-floor office, opened the blinds, and kicked my feet up on my desk. I pulled out the file on Mickey Green I'd gotten from his tireless attorney. It was thick and daunting. But I had a tall cup of coffee and blueberry scones. I would prevail.

Today called for cold rain, not snow, and the first signs of it began to tap at my glass. Coffee and scones just tasted better on a cold day. While I ate, I made a few notes on a yellow legal pad.

I noted Mickey Green had spent the night of the killing with Tiffany Royce. Royce was never interviewed by the cops or by Green's attorney. Tiffany was also an addict at the time and might not have been the most reliable witness. Mattie Sullivan saw her mother that same night with Red and Moon. But that fact wasn't in the case file, despite Mattie telling the detectives. Legally, she wasn't reliable, either — she was ten.

Of course, Red Cahill said he was only selling Julie drugs. Red's word not exactly the gold standard.

Touchie Kiley said Julie Sullivan had a new man in her life. An older guy. The jealous type who'd tried to toss Touchie onto his caboose for chatting Julie up at the pub and scared the piss out of everyone else.

Now there was an older thug in the picture. Still, it seemed like Touchie would've recognized a guy as known as Jumpin' Jack Flynn.

Or maybe all the oil in Touchie's hair had impaired his brain.

I circled Flynn's name.

I wondered if he'd been in or out of the pokey four years ago. I wondered if he worked for Gerry Broz or if Gerry Broz worked for him. I wondered why they'd aced five guys in Dorchester last month. I wondered if I'd just walked into a new gang war that didn't have jack to do with the death of a twenty-six-year-old mother of three four years ago.

I picked up the phone to call a woman I knew in the Department of Correction. She was there, and we chatted for a moment. She said she'd fax me what she had.

I thanked her and hung up.

I ate some more scone. I read several more

pages of the report, careful not to leave grease prints on the documents.

There was the standard page after page of preliminary hearings and motions. All cases generate a lot of paperwork. And a murder case generates more than most.

A fat third of the way into the file, I spotted a list of evidence. I tilted my chair forward.

Prints and blood taken off Mickey Green's car. Crime scene photographs and castings of tire tracks taken at the crime scene. Julie Sullivan's torn and bloodied clothes. And nail clippings taken from the deceased.

"Oh, ho," I said.

"Oh, ho" usually signaled a discovery. I read on.

I read through another scone, and the rest of my coffee.

"That son of a bitch never requested lab results on the nail clippings," I said.

I wished someone had been there in the office to hear my discovery. I think it would have merited applause. Even Pearl would have at least lapped at my hand. If Julie Sullivan had time to fight back, the nail clippings could produce DNA.

I stacked the papers and tucked them back into the file. I stood and placed the file in one of my two cabinets and walked back to my window.

This was something.

Just as I was feeling pretty damn good about myself, a black SUV parked next to a hydrant on Berkeley.

Two men in dark suits got out and stepped onto the curb. Both men were white and youngish, with identically cropped hair. Their ugly ties flapped in the wind and rain. The wind knocked open one of their suit jackets, and I clearly spotted a gun and holster.

One of the men reached into the SUV for a couple of Windbreakers. As they slid into them, I noted the brand name on the jacket. FBI.

"Yikes."

I left my office door open and sat down at my desk to wait.

I heard their shoes in my hallway. I leaned back in my chair.

The two young men stepped inside.

"You Mr. Spenser?"

"If not, I should fire the guy who painted the name on the door."

"We'd like you to come with us."

I stood up. I was wearing a gun. My jacket hung on the tree by the door.

"To whom do I owe the honor?"

"Your vehicle was impounded in Buffalo

last night," one of the men said. They were hard to tell apart, sort of like Tweedledee and Tweedledum.

"Goody," I said. "How I love Buffalo."

"A couple pounds of heroin were discovered in the trunk," Tweedledum said.

"Ouch."

"You mind leaving the weapon?" Tweedledee said.

"I have a permit."

"Not for long," Tweedledum said. He grinned.

"You do realize my vehicle was reported stolen several days ago?"

The agents did not respond.

"And you do realize I am a respected Bostonian with numerous law enforcement contacts who can vouch for my stellar reputation?"

"Tell your attorney," Tweedledee said. "We got you on interstate trafficking."

"Wonderful," I said. I slipped into my leather jacket and followed them out.

31

Tom Connor had a whole different hairstyle than his brethren. He went more for the big-hair, helmet-head look. Obviously, he spent a lot of time with it, the thick salt-and-pepper swept back from his florid Irish face. He wore a double-breasted pin-striped suit that had a light sheen to it. And an honest-to-God ruby pinkie ring.

"Pinkie ring," I said. "Nice touch. Haven't seen one of those in a while."

Connor did not respond.

He walked through the interview room on the sixth floor of Government Center. The small room had a nice view of the North End and the waterfront. If it had been a hotel, they could've charged a hefty price.

As I sat, Connor made a big show of taking off his slick suit coat and hanging it on a hanger by the door. He flattened a black-and-silver tie over his protruding belly and took a seat at the table. He opened a folder, took a deep breath, and flipped through several pages.

"You know, some people are able to read without moving their lips," I said.

His eyes flicked up to mine and then down at the file. "Kind of cocky for a guy whose car was loaded with all that dope and impounded."

"That car was stolen in the Mary Ellen McCormack Housing Projects on Tuesday," I said. "Call the Boston police."

"Smart guy like you would've reported it stolen just in case."

"Yeah, sure," I said. "I called the cops before heading up to Buffalo to score some heroin."

"Your vehicle was picked up as part of an ongoing drug investigation of a Puerto Rican drug syndicate."

"Okay," I said. I spread my palms wide. "You got me. I'm a member of the Tito Puente cartel."

Connor continued to read, slowly flipping through the pages. The pages sounded crisp and loud in the small white room.

"Are you charging me with anything?" I asked. "Because if not, there's a sale at Filene's Basement."

"I'm getting to that."

"You know about the sale, too?"

"The goddamn report."

I nodded. I stood up and looked down at the waterfront. I stared out at all the moored and covered boats in the bright morning. Large broken sheets of ice drifted toward the shore. Seagulls rode waves of brisk wind. I started to whistle "I've Heard That Song Before."

"Sit down," he said.

"I asked if you were going to charge me."

"I said, 'Sit down.' "

I smiled. "Ask nicely."

"What the fuck does it matter how I ask?"

"Ask nicely," I said, dropping the smile. "It matters."

"Please sit the fuck down so I can ask you some questions about your dope car."

Connor looked up from the papers. His cheeks were full of ruddy bluster. His eyes simmered with violence as they roamed over my face. His hands stayed steady on the file as he took in a slow breath and said, "This don't look good for you."

"It *doesn't* look good," I said, sitting. "If you're going to be an asshole, use good grammar."

Connor tilted his thick head. "Pretty fucking stupid to throw in with these bad guys."

"Me and Tito."

He nodded and shook his head. Connor

213

drummed his fingers on the report.

"You want to tell me how you got involved?"

I shrugged. "Well, it first started with a mambo and then developed into a salsa," I said. "Before I knew it, I had engaged in an entire cha-cha."

Connor nodded. He did not smile.

"Are you gonna charge me?" I said. "Because I'd kind of like to call my lawyer. She'd find the whole thing pretty funny at first, but then she might get kind of pissed about it. You don't have a damn thing."

"We have jail cells here," he said. "You can rest up while we figure it out."

"You have no cause," I said. "If you wanted to scare me, you're doing a shitty job."

"I try to not take an offense at two-bit thugs who make a living out of staring into peepholes."

"Is that Nat Pendleton or Ward Bond?"

Connor studied me. He shook his head in disgust.

"Let me recount how this will play out," I said. "You know this is all crapola, but you'll keep me here as long as humanly possible. I will call my ball-busting yet gorgeous personal attorney, and I'll be drinking a cold beer by happy hour."

Connor closed the file, leaned back into the office chair, and smiled. He was very pleased with himself.

"I will continue to investigate," I said. "I don't care if the people involved are the people you want to bust."

"I can make your life hell."

"You offered me coffee," I said.

"Your car was full of dope."

"And not the first stolen car to be used in a crime."

He shrugged. "How much money you make staring into peepholes?"

"More than you get plugging your little pecker into them."

Connor pushed back the chair and stood up fast. His face was the color of a fire engine. He breathed hard through his nose.

"Eek," I said.

"We got a hell of a case."

"I bet."

"You'll lose your license."

"I doubt it."

"You'll lose your gun permit."

"I doubt it."

"I don't know how you and Epstein worked things out," Connor said. "But I ain't Epstein."

"No," I said. "You're not. He was much smarter. And had a better sense of style."

Connor thundered to the door and slammed it shut. Touchy.

I stood and took in the view. I continued to watch the seagulls flutter and ride the cold wind, searching for morsels on the shore.

They looked like they were having a hell of a time.

32

"How is it that you make friends so damn fast, Spenser?" Rita Fiore asked.

"I don't know," I said. "I guess I am truly blessed."

"You're lucky I'm on good terms with the U.S. attorney."

"Or maybe he just likes hearing your sexy voice."

"I didn't sound sexy when I called him," she said. "They had absolutely no probable cause. I've never seen such a heinous arrest in my life. What the hell did you do to this agent? Screw his daughter?"

"If I were ever to step out on Susan, it would be with you, Rita."

"I certainly hope so."

"Besides, if this guy had a daughter, she would resemble a gorilla."

Rita and I walked down the big steps of Government Center in the late blustery afternoon. She had covered up a very form-

217

fitting emerald green belted dress with a winter-weight Burberry trench. She wore take-no-prisoners black boots that gave her impressive legs at least another four inches.

Rita Fiore was redheaded and built. Not only did she reek of distilled sexuality, she happened to be a pit bull in the courtroom.

"May I ask what you did to piss him off?"

"I'm looking into a couple street soldiers who work for Gerry Broz."

"Joe's son?"

"One and the same."

"What'd they do?"

"My client thinks they killed her mother."

"Any proof?"

"She saw them push her mother into a car a few hours before her death."

"What are you going to do next?" Rita asked. A gust of cold wind shot down Congress Street and threw a slash of red hair across her eyes and mouth.

"Eat."

"You always eat."

"It helps me think," I said. "Would you believe this is the second day in a row that I've skipped lunch?"

"No, I would not," Rita said. "Would you like some company?"

"Will you keep your hands to yourself?"

"Maybe."

"Okay, then," I said. "I'll buy."

"Where?"

"Let's walk over to Union Oyster House," I said.

Union Oyster House was the oldest restaurant in Boston, the kind of place that bragged that they had routinely served Daniel Webster. It was in the section of original storefronts by the harbor and had that kind of touristy, nautical feel that was more pleasant than annoying.

Rita and I sat at the horseshoe bar facing Union. I ordered a large bowl of chowder and some Sam Adams Brick Red. They only served Brick Red at restaurants along the Freedom Trail. I always felt patriotic when I drank it.

Rita ordered a martini.

The bartender served her first, then poured my beer.

With the first sip, I was pretty sure I heard the sound of angels.

"So how have you been?" Rita asked. "Besides having your car stolen, packed with drugs, and being threatened by lawman and hood alike?"

I waffled my hand over the bar.

"I figured you would have cashed that check from the firm and taken Susan to someplace very sunny."

"I like to work."

"Who's your client?"

"A fourteen-year-old kid from Southie."

"Pro bono?"

"Nope," said, sipping some beer. "I'm adequately paid."

"Good for you," she said. Rita turned on the barstool and crossed her legs. There was a lot of leg to cross. And so artfully done.

"Are you staring at my legs?" she asked.

"Didn't you want me to?"

She offered a sly smile.

I told her about Mattie. I told her about Julie Sullivan. We talked about Red and Moon. Gerry Broz, too. Mainly I told her what I'd read in Mickey Green's file earlier in the day.

"Who was his attorney?"

"Peter Contini," I said. "Heard of him?"

"No," she said. Rita removed an olive and popped it into her mouth. "And I hope I never do."

A big steaming bowl of clam chowder arrived with a thick wedge of cornbread. The heavens opened up. The angels reappeared.

"Poor baby," Rita said. "Didn't they have a chow line in the big house?"

"They had Zagnut bars and cheese crackers in a vending machine."

"Snob," Rita said.

I shrugged.

"So let me guess," she said. "You want me to call in a favor and have me file some motions for this poor schlub, Mr. Green?"

"You would be a credit to your profession."

"If I got him off —"

"Poor choice of words."

"If his case was tossed."

"Even worse."

"Eat your cornbread and be quiet," Rita said.

I did.

"If what you say is true," she said, eyeing me.

I listened. I kept quiet.

"Then we need a judge to grant us a hearing to test those nail clippings," she said. "But the DNA could go either way for us. Do we really want to find out who she scratched that night?"

"I have a pretty good idea."

"Those two hoodlums?"

"Maybe."

"Or someone else," Rita said. "I see it in your eyes."

"One step at a time."

"You were going to call me on this case anyway," she said. "Play toward my liberal guilt."

I drank the second half of my beer. The bartender brought me a second Brick Red without me asking. Professionalism.

"Having me bust you out of jail was just fortuitous," she said.

"You did get lunch in pleasant company."

"Dinner," Rita said. "Dinner is much more intimate."

"Aren't you going to eat?"

Rita uncrossed her legs and smoothed down her skirt over her thighs. "I have a date."

"Lucky man."

Rita finished her martini and stood. "You better believe it," she said. "And if you weren't so damn pussy-whipped, you'd find out how lucky."

She slipped into her trench, knotted it, and strutted away. I watched her until she disappeared on Union.

I made a low wolf whistle.

33

I had forgotten about Mattie. I'd been spending some quality time with Agent Connor and his pinkie ring when I was supposed to pick her up. And now it was nearly six p.m. and dark. I called her four times from my apartment without an answer. So I decided to drive back to Southie in the rental.

It was nearly seven by the time I knocked on her door in the projects. She came to the door, looked me over, and walked back inside. The apartment seemed as cold as the hallway.

The twins were curled up on the sofa under a knitted blanket, watching a reality show. They turned in unison, bright light flicking over them in darkness, as I took a seat at the kitchen table. Not interested, they returned to the woman in a bikini eating a bowl of hog entrails.

"Where's Grandma?" I asked.

Mattie shrugged.

"PTA?" I asked. "Confession?"

Mattie shrugged again. She took a seat in a chair facing the television and tucked her legs up into her arms.

"You mad?"

"I waited around for like two hours."

"I was unforeseeably detained."

"No biggie," she said. "But if you ain't comin', you coulda let me know. I felt like a fucking idiot standing there."

"You walk?"

"My math teacher gave me a ride," she said. "Her car smelled like cat pee."

"A hazard of being a math teacher."

I smiled at her. Mattie looked at the television.

The bikini woman retched. The redheaded twins laughed. Vomiting was obviously comedy gold. Mattie craned her head to look at me. "Ain't like I'm payin' you. You don't owe me nothin', okay?"

"I got arrested."

"No shit."

"No shit," I said.

She looked impressed. "You beat up someone?"

"No."

"Shoot 'em?"

"No." I shook my head. "Sorry. Long story."

Mattie sprung off the chair and walked back to the kitchen. She was wearing a black Mickey Mouse sweatshirt beneath an old Army jacket, blue jeans, and thick wool socks with holes at the heel. More eye makeup, poorly drawn, outlined her eyes. If the goal was to make her look older, it had failed. She looked like a kid playing dress-up.

"I think I got Mickey Green a new lawyer," I said. My hands were deep in my peacoat pockets.

"He any good?" she asked.

"She is."

"The lawyer is a lady?"

"You have a problem with lady lawyers?"

"She tough?"

"When she was a prosecutor, she made hardened criminals suck their thumbs."

"Mickey wants us to come out to Walpole and see him again."

"He have something new to say?" I asked.

Mattie shrugged and sat on top of the table. She played with a St. Christopher's medal, sliding it back and forth on a silver chain. I felt very foreign in the kitchen. The room smelled of cheap fried food and harsh disinfectants. There was something vaguely institutional about it.

"There may be some DNA evidence," I said.

"What?"

I took a breath. I could hear a cold wind shoot around the edges of the old apartment house. One of the twins yelled out to Mattie from the sofa.

"Shut up," Mattie yelled. She turned back to me. "What evidence?"

"Some blood," I said. "Fingernails."

"Mickey's fingernails?"

"Your mom."

She nodded. Her face tightened a bit.

"Don't they test all that shit before the trial?"

"They should," I said.

"Will it tell us who did it?"

"Maybe, maybe not," I said. "Just more stuff to check out. A good lawyer will help."

"Is this gonna take forever?"

"Maybe."

"I'm getting sick of it."

"This is how it works."

Mattie shook her head with disgust. Her legs kicked back and forth under the table like a pendulum. "Sometimes I think I should just leave it alone," she said. "My grandma says all the women at church think I've gone nuts. People sayin' I should be on

226

medication."

"People say I'm nuts," I said. "Then I realize it's just me, talking to myself."

I smiled at her. She stared at me.

"You know it's okay to laugh," I said. "It won't go to my head."

"Say something funny."

"You're a hard woman to please, Mattie Sullivan."

She rolled her eyes and shrugged. The universal communication of the teenager. When I'd first met Paul Giacomin, he'd been a champion shrugger.

"Is there anything that pleases you?" I asked.

"I know what you were trying to do last night with your friend Susan," she said. "She wanted me to start crying and say that my life is all a mess."

"That wasn't really the plan."

"But talking about my feelings and crap doesn't do jack."

"Does for some people."

"I'm not the one who got killed," she said. "I'm not crazy for wanting to know what happened."

"Why don't you let me handle the gumshoe work and you handle just being a kid," I said. "I'm a professional. You did the right thing finding me."

She stopped playing with the medal.

"You can take some pride in that," I said.

"I'm not unhappy, you know," she said. "Just 'cause you only see me when I'm talking about my mother."

"So what does make you happy?"

"That's a real corny question, Spenser."

"Okay, then. What's your favorite food?"

"I don't know. I like pizza. I got a birthday cake one time at Tedeschi's. That was pretty good."

"When life is tough, take pleasure where you find it," I said. "That doesn't make you soft. It means you're taking care of yourself."

She shook her head.

"Don't make life tougher than it already is," I said. "You could not stop what happened to your mother. You couldn't stand up for Mickey. But you're doing everything possible to make that right. Like it or not, you're a kid, and you need some practice at being a kid."

"This is what I got."

"What about a ball game?" I asked. "You like the Sox, right? Would you go to Fenway with me sometime?"

She eyed me. There was strength there, something very solid. The twins called out again.

"Yeah?" she asked.

"Yep."

She nodded. I nodded back. One of the twins cried out that they were hungry, really stretching out the last word for emphasis.

"Yeah, yeah, yeah," she said, yelling back. "They get grouchy if I'm late on dinner."

"You mind if I help you cook?" I asked.

"You cook?"

"Like a bastard," I said. "And I promise to clean up."

"Okay." She shrugged. "But we ain't got much. Grandma was supposed to bring some things home two days ago."

"I've been known to perform miracles."

She tilted her head, keeping her place on the kitchen table. Her pendulum legs continued to rock and swing. She stopped playing with the medal.

I opened the refrigerator to find a nearly empty milk carton, a foam box with stale french fries, half an onion, an opened bag of very old carrots, and an open roll of cookie dough. The dough was so old it looked like wood putty.

A sharp odor emanated from inside. I closed the door.

"See?"

"I'm not done yet," I said.

"How come you cook? What about your

girlfriend?"

"Susan burns coffee," I said. "Sets toast on fire. And I grew up in a house with just my old man and two uncles. We all cooked."

"I bet you lived like pigs," she said. "A bunch of nasty guys."

"Just the opposite," I said. "Maybe because we knew what people would expect."

"People expect us not to get by," she said. "Social worker's always on my grandma's ass."

"But you find a way to get by," I said.

Mattie nodded.

I checked the cupboards. Half a box of oatmeal. An empty box of Frosted Flakes. Stale saltine crackers and a can of chicken noodle soup.

"Okay, you got me beat," I said. "Suit up the twins. Time to stock the house."

34

Hawk would have paid handsomely to see me push a wobbly cart down aisle six of Tedeschi's with three small girls in tow. The cart was already packed, even with Mattie returning most of what the twins handed us. She kept several boxes of junk cereal and cookies and jugs of fruit juice and milk. She put back the packs of chewing gum, barrettes, and pink cupcakes.

I wondered if I was the only shopper packing a .38. In Southie, I doubted it.

I tried for fresh produce, but Mattie wanted cans. I reached for ground round. She looked at the price and reached for the chuck.

"It's on me," I said.

"We got an EBT card."

"No good," I said.

"We're doing fine."

"If you buy smart, it will last," I said. "Growing up, we didn't have money, either.

We bought quality stuff and used every ounce. There was a small grocery in Wyoming where we bought cuts of beef. Bacon and Borax."

"What's Borax?"

"Detergent with the power of a twenty-mule team," I said. "We made it last."

"So do we."

"How about you let me buy some food without a cartoon on the label?"

"We got meat and stuff."

"Breakfast?"

"We don't have time."

"You can make breakfast whenever you want," I said. "I always make sure I keep a dozen eggs, some bacon, and a loaf of bread. You won't go hungry if you got that."

"The girls like scrambled eggs."

"My scrambling skills are the stuff of legend," I said. "All in the wrist."

One of the twins dropped a box of Pop-Tarts into the cart. The other dropped a pink-headed doll. Mattie didn't see them. I winked at them both.

"I don't suppose the twins would care for eggs with cream and chives?"

"Nope."

"Maybe just cheese?"

"Sure."

"Havarti?" I asked.

"Cheddar."

"Dark rye?"

"Wonder Bread."

We compromised on a cheap loaf of whole-wheat, and I insisted on a couple pounds of sliced smoked turkey from the deli. I extolled the virtues of Havarti cheese with caraway seeds, halfway joking. And the need to have a jar of kalamata olives and feta.

"What's that?"

"Aged goat cheese."

The twins said "Yuck" in unison.

"Goes nice with some Syrian flatbread."

"You been hanging out in Cambridge too much."

We added in a box of laundry detergent, a pack of Ivory soap, four packs of luncheon meat, two thick slabs of hoop cheese, two loaves of wheat bread, apples and pears, some bananas, a tub of oatmeal, pasta, tomato sauce, dry beans, cans of green beans and peas, a bag of frozen chicken breasts, and a pound of coffee for Grandma.

"She likes coffee," one of the twins said.

"I bet," I said. "You think she's home yet?"

"Nope," Mattie said.

"You don't rely on her," I said, "do you?"

Mattie snorted.

"You rely on anyone?"

Mattie slowed the cart and looked up at me with great thought. She nodded. "Yeah," she said. "Myself."

"Me, too. But you won't give yourself a break," I said.

"Give it a rest," she said. "I enjoy stuff."

I smiled. "Sometimes having fun is pretty hard work."

"Where'd you learn that?"

"The esteemed philosophers Calvin and Hobbes."

Mattie pushed the cart into the checkout lane. I took out my wallet. Seeing the cash in my hand made her uncomfortable. She wasn't in control. Being in control was total for her.

"Are you ready for the meal of your life?"

"I can cook," Mattie said.

"No," I said. "You'll cook food. There's a difference."

"I appreciate this, but it's not going to change anything."

"What am I trying to change?"

"Me," she said. "You want me to act like someone I'm not. You want me to cry it out and let you be the grown-up. You want me to wear a dress and say my prayers and say everything is all right. But it doesn't happen that way. Not now."

The twins had their small hands clutched

on the grocery cart. Their eyes had grown very big.

"I don't want to change you," I said. "I like you as you. But I do want to help."

Mattie clenched her jaw. But soon it worked free, and she said, quite unexpectedly, "Okay."

35

I didn't get back to my apartment until late. I had stayed parked along a side street with a good view of the Sullivans' apartment for several hours after the dishes were put away. When Grandma stumbled home from the pub at eleven-thirty and the last light clicked out, I headed back to Marlborough Street. I decided to cancel my order for a WORLD'S BEST GRANDMA coffee mug.

I took off my leather rig and placed it on my kitchen counter. I uncorked some bourbon and doused a healthy splash over ice. I thought about adding a bit of water. Real aficionados called it "opening up the whiskey." It seemed like a waste to me.

I stood at the counter while I drank. I checked messages.

I added some more bourbon to the ice. Marlborough Street was a still life in hushed snow and ice. The piked fence at the Public Garden stood defiant. The soft yellow glow of the streetlamps burned smooth and pleasant.

In my wallet, I found Epstein's card. A long time ago, he'd handwritten his personal cell phone under the FBI insignia. I knew it was late, but I called anyway. He picked up on the third ring.

"What?" Epstein asked. "You want me to talk dirty to you?"

"Is the bingo game over already?"

"If it wasn't for bingo and a trip to the deli, I wouldn't know what to do with myself."

"If only there was crime in Miami."

"If only," he said.

"Still at the office?"

"I've taken a cot by my desk."

"Got a problem."

Epstein laughed. I heard the squeak of a desk chair as he settled in to hear the problem. "Name it."

"Tom Connor."

Epstein didn't say anything. I heard him let out a long, uneasy breath.

"He accused me this morning of being a mule for a Puerto Rican drug-smuggling ring."

Epstein laughed. He laughed so hard he nearly choked.

"I'm honored to have brightened your day."

"How in the hell did that happen?"

"Connor says they found two pounds of heroin in my car."

"And you don't usually keep two pounds of heroin in your car?"

"I keep it under my bed, like normal people."

Epstein laughed some more. "Have you been fucking with him?"

"He stopped by my office yesterday to tell me to back off an operation in Southie."

"Mmm."

"You sound like you agree?" I asked.

"I don't agree, but it sounds like Connor," Epstein said. "He was in the Boston field office a long time before I got there. Passed over many a moon for promotion. He's the kind of agent who uses the policy memos for coasters."

"Or perhaps toilet paper."

"You want me to call the new SAC?" Epstein asked. "I can help you through the complaint process."

"Maybe later," I said. "Right now, I just want to pick your brain. I haven't seen a Fed this crazed since J. Edgar bought his first training bra."

"So tell me about what you're up to in

Southie."

"Apparently there's a new crew working near the Old Colony projects run by Gerry Broz."

"The kid."

"The kid," I said.

"Oy vey."

"Just when I try to lift you from certain stereotypes, you throw me a fastball right down the center."

"You know the old man Broz used to be only a few notches below Bin Laden on our most-wanted list."

"And now he's jumped a slot," I said. "What an accomplishment."

"Connor has been gunning for Joe Broz for decades," Epstein said. "He's obsessed. Nuts over it. He once had to meet with the Bureau shrink because it was interfering with other assignments."

"I don't like Joe Broz, either," I said. "But I never lost much sleep over him."

"Connor is the kind of guy who wants to be like that old sheriff in *Gunsmoke.* You know, what's-his-name."

"Matt Dillon."

"Right, Matt Dillon," Epstein said. "Jesus, he must have something solid to try and jam you up. Five-to-one, this is all about him finding Joe Broz."

"I always figured Joe Broz for Miami," I said.

"Maybe," Epstein said. "Or South America or Europe or fucking China. We've been looking for the bastard for ten years."

"Sorry if I get the feeling that Connor is dirty."

"He may be an asshole, but he's a good agent," Epstein said. "If I thought different, I would have shit-canned his ass when I was SAC."

"You coming back?" I asked.

"Yeah," Epstein said. "I really miss the fucking sludge. Every time I see a girl in a bikini Rollerblade by my window."

"But don't you miss me?"

"I miss season tickets to Fenway."

"You never asked me to join you."

"Conflict of interest."

"What conflict?"

"You being a Puerto Rican gangster and all," he said. "I'll make some calls."

"Not necessary," I said. "I can handle it."

"I'll make some calls."

Epstein hung up.

I picked up my bourbon and sat in the darkness on my sofa. On the mantel, I had placed a half-finished block of cherry wood. I had started carving it years ago and had left it whittled down to the form of an unknown animal. I figured I was going to find the first Pearl the Wonder Dog in that hunk of wood. Or maybe it would be a horse. Or a lobster. I didn't know, and so I'd left the block of wood on my mantel for years. Lots of dust had gathered.

My apartment was very quiet without Pearl or Susan. You could hear a car coming down Marlborough from a long way off. I walked to my window and looked down on the street. I saw no assassins.

I thought about Mattie and Julie Sullivan. Joe Broz and Gerry. Jumpin' Jack Flynn.

I walked back to the mantel and found the block of wood and my carving knife. I pulled up a chair to the dull streetlamp glow that bled off Marlborough Street. I dug into the old wood, just chipping away a little nick at a time.

36

Neat, clean-shaven, and fresh as a daisy, I dropped Mattie at school and bought a tall coffee and a sack of corn muffins at a Dunkin' Donuts. I felt vaguely domestic as I hopped the expressway south. I soon turned south on Interstate 95 toward Providence and took the exit to Walpole and the prison.

Walpole had a nice little brick downtown. The rep probably played hell with the folks from the chamber of commerce.

There was a sign for a seasonal farmers' market, a quilting club, and a handful of fine-looking restaurants, including one called the Raven's Nest. A sandwich board outside boasted a daily special of fish-and-chips with a side of Guinness. I made a mental note for lunch and downed the last of my coffee.

At Cedar Junction, I parked and went through the prison mechanizations I knew so well. My permit was shown, gun was taken, and I was ushered back to the visitors' room to wait for Mickey Green.

I wondered if Mickey would note that I had shaved and brushed my teeth. Probably not. The Plexiglas between us was very thick.

After a few minutes, a heavyset female guard walked Mickey into his slot.

He picked up the phone.

I picked up my phone.

I smiled.

Mickey did not smile back.

"Good morning," I said.

"Where the fuck is Mattie?"

"And to think I shaved so carefully."

"I ain't meeting without Mattie."

"It's Friday," I said. "Mattie is in school."

"Come back tomorrow," he said. Mickey started to stand.

"Sit down." My voice didn't sound friendly.

"What?"

"That kid thinks you got a raw deal and that you're a good guy," I said. "Go against your instincts and be smart."

"What's that mean?"

"It means I have some questions, Mickey," I said. "I've been slugged and threatened and arrested all over Southie on account of

243

you. I'm pretty sure you're sharing just a sliver of what you know with me."

"If I knew who killed Julie, you think I wouldn'a said something?"

"You're holding out."

Mickey blew out his breath. I was glad there was Plexiglas. He did not look neat, clean, and shaven. He looked like he'd brushed his teeth with a toilet scrubber.

I reached into my leather jacket for a folded piece of yellow legal paper. I held it against the glass. Mickey turned his head to read it.

"What?"

"Say the names."

"Theresa Donovan, Tiffany Royce, Touchie Kiley," he said. "Moon and Red. Yeah, so what?"

"Who am I missing?"

"Missing from what?"

"Who goes into that list?"

"I dunno."

"Gerry Broz?"

"Who's that?"

He kept the same dumb expression. An expression he must have mastered long ago.

"Jack Flynn?"

"Nope."

His eyes flicked away from mine and then scattered back. "What?"

"Everybody in Southie knows Jack Flynn," I said.

"I mean, I know who he is, but I don't know why you were asking."

"No," I said. "You said you didn't recognize the name."

He shrugged and slunked back into his hard plastic seat. He just looked at me, phone against his ear, and then studied his dirty fingernails.

"I don't like you, Mickey," I said.

"So."

"I think Mattie Sullivan can do a hell of a lot better than wasting her time in your company," I said. "But like it or not, you're wrapped up in this. To find out who killed her mother, I might just have to get you freed. So if you have just a sliver of sense in your thick head, listen up and give me the truth."

"I never met Jack Flynn."

"What's he have to do with Julie's murder?"

"I don't know. I don't know shit about that."

I studied his face as he tried to look tough. His cheeks had grown red. He narrowed his eyes and clenched his fists.

"Okay," I said. "From the top. Did you see Julie that night?"

245

"I said I ran into her at the pub," he said. "So fucking what?"

"At any time did you touch her?'

"Fuck, no."

"Did she have any reason to scratch you?"

"Scratch me?" Mickey laughed. He leaned into the glass and said a firm "No."

"I fired your lawyer for you," I said.

"He was a turd."

"Yep," I said.

"Didn't do jack crap."

"I got you a new lawyer," I said. "Better than you deserve. You'll have to sign some paperwork, but she will make sure some DNA evidence is processed."

"What evidence?"

I explained it. I had to go very slow to make sure he understood. I thought about explaining that DNA was a kind of science. Or maybe I should've just told him it was magic. He might've gotten the magic part easier.

"I'm gonna ask you one more time about Jack Flynn."

"Jack Flynn wouldn't know me," he said. "I wasn't nobody."

I nodded. "What about Red?"

"I don't know," Mickey said, scratching his paltry beard. "Ask him."

I nodded.

"I can't find anyone who will talk about that night."

"You see Theresa Donovan?"

"Sure," I said. "Works at a convenience store near Columbus Park."

"I told Mattie that Red didn't do it," he said. "That's her own crazy idea. What did Theresa tell you?"

"She said she believed the police got the right man."

"She fucking said that?"

I leaned back into my seat. I rolled my shoulder and took a breath. Talking to Mickey Green was not a pleasant experience. I kept the phone to my ear against my better judgment.

"I can't believe that," Mickey said, shaking his head to himself. "She fucking said I did it, and here I was trying to be a good guy and not pull her into this shit."

I leaned forward. "Pull her into what?"

Mickey kept shaking his head with great disappointment. "Jesus Christ. Jesus. That bitch."

"Pull her into what, Mickey?"

"Theresa left Four Green Fields that night with Julie," he said. "She was fucking with her that night. What in the hell did she say?"

"Not much," I said. "She said she stopped hanging out with Julie since she got hooked."

"That bitch."

"You already said that."

"Well, I'll say it fifty more times, shit."
Mickey shook his head. For good measure,
he shook it some more. "Shit. Shit. Shit.
Fuck."

At least he was trying to switch it up.

I raised my eyebrows at him. He shook his
head. Mickey slammed the receiver down
on the counter twice before him and called
for the guard.

There was the buzz of a dial tone. The
heavyset woman returned to lead him back
to his cell. I hung up the phone.

I looked at the time. And to think I had
planned the day so well.

37

I stopped off on Old Colony on my way
back downtown. I checked in at the convenience store where Theresa Donovan
worked to ask a few more questions. Instead, I found an old woman behind the
register. She was short and fat, and wore a
sparkly sweater vest. Her hair was white.
The sweater vest featured a pair of teddy
bears raking autumn leaves.

The woman said Theresa hadn't shown
up for the last week. She kept the long
pauses alive by smacking gum.

I asked if she knew where Theresa lived.

She smacked her gum some more. She
said she didn't.

I didn't believe her.

"Has she picked up her check?"

She frowned and told me to call the
manager. I didn't bother. I called a cute
paralegal at Cone, Oaks who helped me out
in such matters. Cute paralegals could not

resist me.

It turned out a Theresa Donovan, a white female of that age and general neighborhood, lived up by Dorchester Heights. The paralegal called me back after a few minutes and confirmed it was the same Theresa Donovan who'd graduated from South Boston High School the same year Julie Sullivan graduated.

It was early afternoon when I parked my rental beside a hydrant. Rita had started the process of getting my car back from Buffalo. But I had grown used to the rental in the way a cowboy gets used to a new horse.

I got out of the car and stretched, looking down upon Carson Beach and Old Harbor. Dorchester Heights, as the name implied, was a long way up. A good place to watch if the British ever decided to invade again.

Theresa's apartment was in a boxy, four-story brick building at the foot of Thomas Park. She lived on the first floor. I buzzed her apartment five times. She did not answer. I checked her mail slot. The bills were plentiful and crammed inside.

I walked back to my rental and drove around until I found a Subway. Properly equipped with a foot-long turkey sub on wheat and a cup of coffee, I returned and parked in a nice spot with a view of Theresa's building and her apartment. If Theresa came home, I'd see her. If she walked in front of her windows, I'd see her.

The watching part of the job always made you feel like a pervert. Maybe eating a sandwich while watching windows made you less of a pervert. Or maybe it just made you a gluttonous pervert.

I ate and thought of such matters. I drank a little coffee. I listened to the news. In keeping with the spirit of perversion, I recalled great sexual adventures with Susan. I tried to control myself with thoughts of the 2004 Red Sox and Margaret Hamilton naked. I recalled more great sexual adventures with Susan. One in particular caused me to blush.

I ate the first half of the sandwich and wisely saved the next half for later. If I'd known I'd be on watch, I would have brought a thermos of coffee. Subway should not go into the coffee business.

But it was coffee and fully caffeinated. It would keep me focused.

I turned the radio to WGBH. The Ray Brown Trio was playing "Bye, Bye, Blackbird." This was followed by an upbeat Sonny Rollins tune, "Blues for Philly Joe."

The hours passed. I recalled the great WBUR shows of the late Tony Cennamo.

How I missed Tony.

I tapped the steering wheel. Soon it was time to pick up Mattie, and I pulled out and headed back to Gavin Middle School. I had gotten pretty good at the pickup process. The crossing guard smiled at me and waved me in front of the school. I smiled back and wheeled up.

I unlocked the passenger door.

She slung in her backpack and climbed aboard with a heavy sigh.

"Eighth grade is a bitch," I said.

"You went to see Mickey Green," she said.

"I did."

"And didn't take me."

"I didn't know I needed permission."

I waited for the crossing guard to wave me into the flow of traffic.

"Mickey left me a message," she said. "He was pissed."

"Pissed at me?"

"Pissed at me," she said. "Mickey said he didn't want you coming around unless I was there."

"Did I hurt his feelings?"

"He said you asked a bunch of useless questions," she said. "Said you and Theresa Donovan wanted to make sure he was locked up for good."

"You believe that?"

"Shit." She hugged the backpack in her lap like a stuffed animal. "I don't know what to believe."

"Does Mickey Green take you grocery shopping?"

"He's a good guy," she said. "He loved my ma."

I shrugged. It was the best I could come up with at the moment. When in doubt, follow a trend.

"Where we going?" she said as we passed the Andrew T station, looping back down to the Mary Ellen McCormack.

"Home again, home again."

Mattie didn't speak for a while. She leaned into the door frame, head resting against the window.

"I can't take you everywhere."

"It's not what you promised," she said.

"I have been up front with you," I said. "To do what I do best, sometimes I got to go at it alone."

"Or with Hawk."

"If the situation calls for it."

"Does it call for it today?" Mattie asked.

"No."

"Then why can't I come?"

"You would find it very boring."

"And I should wash behind my ears and do my homework?"

"Your ears look pretty clean," I said.

I slowed on Kemp Street. Other children with backpacks were shuffling their way home from school. Some stopped to share a smoke in slanting shadows of the old brick buildings. Other kids walked alone down icy paths, letting themselves into their empty apartments. Many of the children reminded me of Mattie. Self-sufficient.

"This is bullshit."

"So you have told me."

"But you don't care?" she asked.

"Take care of your sisters," I said. "Your grandma."

"You're a real jerk."

She blew out a long breath and opened the door in a hard, violent way. She stomped off down the path to her apartment. She left the car door open. The car chirped to alert me until I closed it.

At least I had half a sandwich.

38

I watched a couple teenage boys racing up the long, icy steps to the Revolutionary War monument in Thomas Park. One slipped on the ice and fell. The other laughed and kept running. The other shouted to his buddy that he was "a real piece of crap." That amused me for a good two minutes.

Every thirty minutes, I cranked the car and let the heat run. Not much happened here in the dead of winter. Cars circled Thomas Park. Old ladies walked their dogs. I recalled a Fourth of July long ago when I'd watched a fireworks display high on the hill with a woman named Brenda Loring. I wondered what ever became of her as I ate the second half of my sandwich.

Night came early. It grew quite cold. I watched some other tenants enter the building. I waited another hour.

By ten, I was pretty sure Theresa wasn't coming home. So I buzzed her door again.

And then I buzzed a few neighbors.

I finally got the "Yeah" I needed.

"Bill Lee," I said. "Spaceman Products."

The door buzzed and unlocked. I walked inside. My next trick would be pitching the World Series while under the influence.

I knocked on Theresa's door. Nothing.

I knocked again.

I kept an eight-piece lock-picking set in my jacket. It was so easy to pick a lock, I wondered at the use in locking doors at all. Within ten seconds, I was inside her apartment, a studio unit with a pull-out sofa and a small kitchen.

Art on the walls was of the discount-store variety, framed prints of Paris, Picasso, and one of a monkey drinking some kind of Italian dessert wine. In the kitchen, someone had left a half-eaten Lean Cuisine lasagna next to a saucer filled with cigarette ashes. A bottle of Sprite had been left open. The lasagna had congealed into a solid mass. The Sprite had gone flat.

A dirty fork had fallen on the floor, along with a glass. There was a puddle around the broken glass. I searched for more signs of a struggle but saw none. No telltale smears of blood or bullet holes. No scuffed heel marks on the vinyl floor. I sniffed the air for the sweet smell of chloroform.

The food on the counter had not started to mold, but it probably had a shelf life of a hundred years. I checked the phone for a voice-mail service, but the line was dead. So few use actual landlines these days. Theresa would rely only on her cell.

A suitcase lay open on the unmade sofa bed. The suitcase was half filled with jeans, sweatshirts, wool socks, and underthings. I checked a chest of drawers, finding mainly clothes. Theresa had a collection of maybe thirty CDs of singers and groups I didn't know or care to know. She had magazines that told about the private lives of celebrities. One was open to a page of Hollywood weight-loss tips.

I found her bathroom cabinet fully stocked with makeup, lipstick, and other women's products.

I walked back into the studio. The light was weak from an imitation Tiffany lamp. On the wall hung a shellacked picture of Saint Jude with the words PRAY FOR US. On top of a small chest was a collection of pictures in cheap plastic frames. One snapshot showed a young man in a Marines uniform before an American flag. Another was of a frail old woman in a large recliner. The other was of Theresa and Julie Sullivan at their high school graduation, smiles full of optimism and hope. Faces unmarked by living hard lives.

I read some mail and went through her bills. She owed more than five grand to a cut-rate credit card company. She had been offered many other credit cards. Another letter offered her good luck and prayers if she'd give a donation. I turned off the lights to the bathroom and studio.

I cracked open the door to the hall, listening for neighbors. Not a creature stirred.

I let myself out and walked back to the street facing Thomas Park. The wind blew harder and colder up in the Heights. I pulled my Braves ball cap down over my eyes. I wore no gloves and sank my hands deep into my pockets.

I did not like where this was heading.

39

A light was visible at the sill of my apartment door. I thought it was perhaps karma. Someone was creeping me while I was creeping Theresa Donovan.

I pulled the .38 from under my leather jacket and lightly felt the knob.

The door was unlocked. I heard shuffling inside. It sounded as if someone was going through my papers and drawers. I wondered if they'd find my autograph of Hank Aaron tucked inside Zane Grey's *Code of the West.* Or my sexy pictures of Lotte Lenya.

I opened the door fast, gun in hand.

Pearl tilted her head. She'd been drinking from a bowl of water and slobber dripped from her jowls.

I put away the gun and closed the door behind me.

Susan had made a fire and sat on the couch, drinking a glass of wine and reading a Charles Portis novel. She looked up from the book for a moment to smile at me. She took another sip and dog-eared the page.

"I might have shot Pearl."

"Pearl was unarmed," Susan said.

Pearl trotted up and offered her head for me to pat. I patted her head.

"Been here long?"

"Oh, since five," she said. "Last appointment canceled. He's the commitment-phobe."

I nodded.

"I brought takeout from Chez Henri."

"Cuban sandwich?"

"Also got you that selection of cheeses you like. That thingy with the fruit and toasted nuts."

I opened the refrigerator and found a bottle of Amstel. I pulled out the containers from Chez Henri. I placed the Cuban sandwich in my toaster oven and set it to warm. I cracked open the beer and picked at the fruit and cheese.

"I ever tell you that you are a saint?" I asked.

"Not as often as you should," she said. "I hoped you'd come home tonight."

"You could have called."

"I knew you'd be home when you were ready."

"Like a stray cat."

"Exactly."

Susan stood and finished her wine. She was wearing an old gray Boston College sweatshirt given to me by the football weight coach, and not much else.

"I like your style," I said.

"This old thing?" Susan asked. She opened the refrigerator and poured herself more wine. Chateau Ste. Michelle Riesling. "Why, I only wear it when I don't care how I look."

I studied her butt as she bent over to replace the wine in the low section of the fridge. I smiled. I sipped some more beer.

"I spent the night looking into a young woman's windows and checking out her drawers."

"Creepy."

"A chest of drawers."

"Oh."

Susan sipped her wine. I found a cookie for Pearl in the cookie jar. Pearl nearly took my fingers off chomping it down.

I hung up my leather jacket on a rack by the front door. I unclipped the holster from my belt and put away the gun.

"Wyatt Earp," she said.

"You ever get used to what I do?"

"Nope," Susan said.

"Does it excite you?"

"Not really."

"You eat?"

"I had the paella. Would you rather have had the paella?"

"No," I said. I removed the Cuban sandwich from the toaster oven. The cheese was again the proper gooeyness. The slow-roasted pork inside the pressed bread was very good. Citrusy.

"How's Mattie?"

"As she'd say, she's 'royally pissed.' "

"What did you do?"

"I did not take her for another field trip to Cedar Junction state prison."

"To see the man who may have killed her mother."

"We're beyond that," I said. "She actually likes the goober."

I ate more of the sandwich, properly chased with the Amstel.

"She would," Susan said. "She'll see paternal traits in him no matter how horrid he seems to you."

"Come again?"

"His conviction feels like an injustice to her. She's built him up in her head — with a little prompting from him — as the only man who cared about her mother. She could identify with his plight, and in turn as a father."

"I would hope she'd pick a better role model."

"She may be pissed at you because you're challenging that," she said. "You are probably very different from Mickey Green."

"God, I hope so."

"Does he stand a chance?"

"I got Rita to take his case."

"That's a hell of a favor for someone you don't like," Susan said.

I shrugged. I ate more of the sandwich. I found another bottle of Amstel.

"The kid's damn sure Green didn't do it," I said. "Cops never asked her what she saw that night."

"At this point, are we sure he's innocent?"

I sighed. "Not really. He knows more than he's telling. And he's definitely no heroic father figure. Mattie deserves a lot more than Mickey Green."

Susan nodded. I stood there and drank and ate. I studied her long, shapely legs and was quiet for a moment.

"Oh, God," Susan said. "You don't have plans to take her in? The way you did with Paul?"

"Nope."

"Or mentor her."

"Mattie doesn't need anyone to teach her how to fight," I said. "She could bring Mike

Tyson to tears."

"Or be self-sufficient."

"Nope."

"Is that frustrating?"

"That she's so damn self-sufficient?"

"That you can't teach her anything the way you taught Paul how to dress and how to act and how to be a man? Or what you did for Z."

"Perhaps," I said. "She can't see anything beyond freeing Mickey Green and nailing her mom's killers."

"You may not be able to make it all better," she said.

"The thought had crossed my mind."

"You understand, her unhappiness is a form of self-flagellation," she said. "That doesn't just go away."

"I figured that," I said. "I told her I'd take her to a ball game this spring. Hard to flagellate at Fenway. You'd get arrested."

"Momentary happiness, enjoyment of life, may be the only thing you can teach her."

"Tall order, but I'm trying."

"Who better?" Susan said. "You choose to work in an ugly, violent world yet find enjoyment."

"Sometimes I whistle while I beat people up."

"Even if you free Mickey Green and put

264

those men in jail, Mattie will continue to beat herself up."

I nodded.

"It could help initially," she said. "But she'll need some help. And a lot of time."

I nodded again.

"You ready for that?" Susan asked.

"A work in progress?"

"Yes."

"She's worth it."

"Why?"

"I respect her sense of justice."

"And you will teach her how to live until she finds it."

I nodded.

Both of us found a place on my couch to watch the fire. Pearl ambled into the room and jumped between us.

"She missed you," Susan said.

"She tell you that?"

"Doesn't she talk to you?"

"Depends on how much I drink."

"I suppose you're going to keep at this all weekend?" Susan asked. She tucked her bare feet up under her.

"Yep."

"What are you going to do?"

"Start from the beginning," I said. "Follow Red and Moon."

"Can you take Hawk with you?"

"If Hawk is available."

"Hawk will make time," she said. "As always."

I nodded.

"You made time for him when he was shot."

I nodded.

"Take Hawk."

"Yes, ma'am."

My old sweatshirt rode up above Susan's taut waist and very tasteful panties.

"I like those panties," I said.

"I don't think they'd fit you."

"Lace isn't my thing."

"What is your thing?"

"Extra-large boxers with red hearts."

"Sexy."

"In some cultures."

"So I've waited around for you long enough," Susan said. She sipped at her wine. "Disrobe."

"Twist my arm."

40

Susan and I breakfasted at the Paramount in Beacon Hill. I had hash and eggs and black coffee. She had an egg-white omelet with fruit on the side. The pain in my ass was gone. I had a spring in my step as we followed the Public Garden back to my apartment. Susan and Pearl headed to Cambridge. I went back to work.

I parked, bought another cup of coffee across Boylston, and opened up my office.

A stack of mail had spilled through the slot and onto the floor. I threw away all but a rent notice and a card from Paris. Paul was touring with his dance troupe. He wrote me in French. Paul was very aware I did not speak French.

He was a grown man now, and a successful human. But when he'd been Mattie's age, he had no one. His existence centered on soap operas and game shows. I'd taken him up to Maine to work on a cabin. I taught him to lift weights, box, and drink beer. I was afraid if I taught Mattie how to box, I would unleash a loaded weapon on Gavin Middle School. I wondered if trying to think of an equivalent plan for a girl was sexist. Probably. And Mattie was not the typical girl. In the movies, teen girls solved all their problems through a makeover. I could only do what Mattie had asked of me. I could offer shrinkage from Susan, but she would probably wholeheartedly decline. What I wanted more than anything was to return some sense of childhood to her. Finding her mom's killer was the first step. A makeover was lower on the list.

I sat at my desk and used my computer to check the weather and play Ella singing "Angel Eyes." I called my answering service. And then I called Hawk.

Hawk said to give him fifteen minutes.

"I got to say goodbye to the lady."

"The woman with the silk sheets?"

"Don't know what kinda sheets this one got," Hawk said. "Didn't make it to the bed."

I sipped some more coffee and looked down at the building across Berkeley. The lights were off in the insurance offices. It seemed I was the only one who enjoyed working Saturdays. At street level, Shreve,

Crump & Low enjoyed a brisk business. They sold fancy jewelry, and for a long while had a display for something they called The Gurgling Cod. It was a fancy pitcher shaped like a fish. New England chic.

I was halfway done with the coffee when I heard Hawk's heavy footsteps. You always know when it is Hawk walking. He walks with authority.

"For your troubles, I'll buy you a gurgling cod."

"What the fuck's that?" Hawk asked.

I told him.

"White people got more money than sense," Hawk said.

"No arguments here."

"What's for breakfast?" Hawk asked.

"I ate with Susan."

"Didn't bring me nothin'?"

"I didn't know you'd be available."

"Am I not a faithful sidekick?"

"I consider myself a first among equals."

"No shit," Hawk said, pondering the statement. "I just consider myself first."

"They got scones across the street."

"I don't want no doorstop," Hawk said. "I said breakfast."

Hawk was wearing a brown suede sport coat and a black silk shirt opened wide at the neck. His jeans were properly faded and frayed in the current style, and his cowboy boots were made from ostrich hides.

He caught me staring at his boots.

"What'd an ostrich ever do to you?" I asked.

"Bird died with pride knowin' it be on my feet."

I grabbed my peacoat, and the .357 out of my desk drawer.

"Double gunnin'?" Hawk asked.

"Always be prepared," I said brightly.

"Boy Scouts?"

"Genghis Khan," I said.

I locked the door behind us. We walked side by side down the flight of steps in a pattern and rhythm we'd developed running Harvard Stadium.

"You did notice the suits parked by the Arlington Street Church?" Hawk asked.

"I didn't walk that way," I said. "I walked from my place. I had a spring in my step."

"Well, Easter Bunny," Hawk said, "since people are looking to do you in, you might want to be more vigilant."

"Why be vigilant when I have you?"

" 'Cause if you ain't, you be dead."

I stopped at the landing outside my office building. "You do have a point."

"Where to?" Hawk asked.

"Did the car have a federal plate?" I asked.

"Yes, suh."

"A little joyride around town," I said. "After we lose them, I figured we might want to see what Moon and Red are up to."

"Not Gerry and ole Jumpin' Jack?"

"Nope," I said. "Foot soldiers do the work. They'll trip up while Broz and Flynn pick their teeth and count their money."

"And my breakfast?"

"You work up an appetite?"

"You bet," Hawk said. He grinned very wide.

"Lunch at Legal?" I asked.

Hawk nodded.

I pulled out into traffic. Two lights down Boylston, I made the Feds' car behind me. I kept my eyes on the rearview mirror.

"On a full stomach, we ditch these turkeys."

I nodded and headed downtown.

41

We played cat and mouse with the Feds for a while. We ate oysters and drank draft Sam Adams at Legal Sea Foods by the Custom House Tower. Afterward, we indeed ditched the Feds in the South End and looped up to Fenway just to make sure. We drove around for a long while until we headed into Southie and Gerry Broz's sports bar.

On the way, I told him about Theresa Donovan.

"She dead," Hawk said.

"You don't know that."

"Woman don't show up for work, leave a plate of food half eaten, and clothes half packed," Hawk said. "Don't need to be Sherlock Holmes to figure that shit out. Larry Holmes coulda figured that shit out."

"The Easton Assassin," I said.

"Only man to defend the belt more was Joe Louis."

"Doesn't mean he'd make a good detective," I said.

Hawk agreed.

We parked in another alley with a good view of Playmates and the wrecking ball facing the Old Colony Housing Projects. A chain-link fence surrounded the property. The day was cold and colorless, the trees bare and stark against gray skies.

"They supposed to tear down all this shit last year," Hawk said.

"Takes a long time to break it down," I said. "Built with quality."

"Lot a bad shit happened in those walls."

I nodded.

" *'Go, nigger, go,'* " Hawk said. "I can still hear them shouts."

"That was not good for Boston."

"No," Hawk said. "Irish got some hard heads. Must be all the potatoes you eat."

"Or the beer we drink."

Hawk grinned.

"You think Broz did the shooting in Dorchester?" I asked.

"Yep," Hawk said. "Course, he didn't pull the trigger. You think Gerry knows one end of the gun from the other?"

"Probably not."

"Leaves us with Red and Moon."

"Bad guys," I said.

"We been up against much badder," Hawk

273

said. "Those boys still minor-league."

"And Jack Flynn?"

"Jack Flynn is on the thug all-star team."

Hawk reclined in the passenger seat. His eyes were half closed. He'd always been able to calm himself. I'd known him since we were seventeen and remembered how he'd nearly fall asleep before he'd step into the ring. He could come alive with violence as fast as he could nap. He was on shut-down mode now, waiting for Red or Moon. Or both.

"Heard Red was a good fighter," Hawk said. "Trained down at McDonough's."

"Not much future for old fighters."

"Man makes his way with his fists got few options."

"You ever think about selling insurance?" I asked.

"I am the reason for insurance, babe."

At five, I cranked the car engine. Hawk lifted up the passenger seat.

We watched as Red Cahill and Moon Murphy piled into a green Range Rover and made a series of turns before cutting onto Broadway. Hawk and I did not speak as we drove.

I watched my tail in the rearview. No suits.

Red stopped off at a dry cleaner. We had to park too far away to see what was going on inside. We didn't want Moon to spot us.

Red climbed back in the Range Rover and headed west. We passed over D Street and a Catholic Charities Labor Center. Red circled into a Burger King parking lot. A black Chevy Blazer pulled alongside, headed the opposite way.

Something passed between the cars.

"Pay that piper," Hawk said.

I nodded. Red wheeled back onto Broadway and stopped in at a liquor store and a gas station. He cut up Dorchester Avenue at the T station.

"Since when they got a goddamn yoga studio in Southie?"

"World's going to hell," I said.

We followed Red north toward downtown on Dorchester Avenue, passing the old Gillette plant. We crossed over the channel bridge and passed the post office distribution site. We turned north on Summer Street, near the bridge, and made our way up the waterfront.

Red turned into the Boston Harbor Hotel. He and Moon both got out.

He tossed the keys to the valet.

"Red gone upscale," Hawk said. "Shall I?"

"Please do."

Hawk got out and walked inside the Boston Harbor Hotel. I stayed on the street for about twenty minutes.

I watched the valet stand until Red and Moon reappeared. Hawk opened the passenger door and got back inside.

"Taking a piece of the book from the bartender?"

"Passing some drugs off to some preppie kids," he said. "Drugs ain't got no social class."

I nodded.

"Vinnie know about all this?" Hawk asked. "Gettin' close to Gino's turf."

I nodded, careful to keep about four cars back. Red and Moon turned into the city.

For the next two hours, Hawk and I counted twelve more shakedowns. Mostly bookies. They also visited two strip clubs just off the Common. Hawk volunteered twice for surveillance inside the clubs.

My stomach told me dinnertime approached as Red dipped south again and headed back over the Summer Street Bridge and to the three-decker off G Street.

They parked and went inside.

"You thinkin' what I'm thinkin'?"

"On my last stakeout, I enjoyed a sub sandwich downed with a pot of motor oil."

"We can do better," Hawk said.

"One would hope."

"How long we wait?"

"I don't know," I said. "Kind of hoped something would come to me."

"How's that workin'?"

"Give it time. Give it time."

A sedan headed toward us on G Street. I slowed to a stop nearly nose to nose. The headlights clicked to bright, blinding us.

Hawk was out of the car. I was out of the car.

I had my .357, and Hawk had a Mossberg pump.

Two figures crawled out. The two young agents who arrested me two days ago.

They put their hands up. But they did not smile as they did it.

Hawk dropped the shotgun to his side. I lowered the .357.

"Nice night," one of the men said. I believe it was Tweedledee. In the dark, it was hard to tell. "You looking for something?" said Tweedledum. His breath was a cloud.

"Looking for a couple pencil-dick motherfuckers," Hawk said.

"Oh, look," I said. "We're in luck."

"Get lost," Tweedledee said.

"Public street," I said. "Or do you want to arrest me again?"

One agent looked to the other. They got back into the car. They dimmed their lights.

They just sat there for a while.

"You still call it a Mexican standoff if we in Southie?" Hawk asked.

"If Red and Moon come out, we're blown," I said. "They know it. Doesn't do us any good. They probably know the Feds, but they don't know my car."

Hawk tilted his head from side to side. His neck popped.

"You want to start fresh tomorrow?" he asked. "Woman with the sheets just shot me a text message."

"Two-timer," I said.

"Who say they just two?"

"Hawk, you give us all hope," I said.

"Yeah," he said. "I sure as hell do."

42

Sunday morning started off the same. I had spent the night with Susan in Cambridge and again had a fine spring in my step. I hit the stairs to my office with a bounce and a smile. Hawk arrived a short time later. He brought donuts and two large coffees.

He did not say a word. He opened the box and sat in my client chair. He sipped and grinned.

"You burn a hole in those sheets yet?" I asked.

"At the height of passion, Teddy Pendergrass on the stereo, she gone and tell me she love me."

"Hazard of the job."

"Can you believe that shit?"

"And Hawk loves no one."

"I love myself," he said.

"How could you not?" I said. "And you loved Cecile."

Hawk did not speak. He sipped some cof-

279

fee. He leaned my client's chair back on two legs and crossed his boots onto my desk.

Then he said, "You gonna eat or go all Dr. Phil this morning?"

I shrugged before choosing a cinnamon. I thought it a bold yet solid decision.

"We gonna drive around again today?" Hawk asked. "Follow Red and Fat Boy to hell and back?"

"You have a better idea?"

"I do."

"And?"

"You wanna find out what's what," Hawk said. "We go see Tony. Tony will know."

I nodded.

"Does Tony work Sundays?" I asked.

"After church," Hawk said. "Somebody got to run the whores."

"I like a man with priorities."

We both polished off three more donuts and walked down the steps to Berkeley with the rest of our coffee. We agreed to take my rental again.

"You think a black man in a Jag is conspicuous?"

"Only in Southie," I said. "South End is another story."

We drove to the bottom of the South End to Tony's bar. The parking lot across the street was empty, as were many of the storefronts that lined it.

A few years ago Tony had a marketing consultant rename the bar Ebony and Ivory. Hawk and I had a lot of fun with the name. Not a lot of ivory drank at Tony's bar. But since I'd last seen him, he'd gone back to the original name, Buddy's Fox.

A new neon sign spelled it out in neat cursive letters. We crossed the street and found the front door open.

Junior and Ty-Bop, Tony's muscle, looked up from a game of pool in the barren bar.

Ty-Bop nodded to us. Junior ignored us. Ty-Bop hammered off a shot that sounded like bones cracking.

Red vinyl booths lined each side of the room, with a bar at the far end. A door beside the bar led to Tony's back office. The bar had not changed in decades. In a strange way, I liked that.

Had we not been so well respected by Tony, Ty-Bop and Junior might have stalled us. But they kept playing. We kept walking.

The door to Tony's office was open. He sat behind his desk.

Tony was dressed in an immaculate gray pin-striped suit with a purple tie. Boston's most successful pimp looked just like an aging CEO, down to the soft neck and graying temples. His mustache was neatly trimmed.

"Look what the motherfuckin' cat dragged in."

"Tony," I said.

"Spenser," he said. "Hawk, my man."

Hawk nodded at Tony. Tony grinned and rubbed his chin. He smiled, taking us both in like we were auditioning for a comedy act. I was not sure if I was Martin or Lewis.

"What y'all want?"

"Information," Hawk said.

"I should start chargin' for that shit," Tony said. "Do I look like goddamn four-one-one?"

"You owe me," I said.

"How long till that tab run out?"

"Long time," Hawk said.

Tony nodded. He knew Hawk was correct.

Tony lit a fat dark cigar and leaned into the padded leather desk chair. His lighter was bright gold. He smoked the cigar in an expert fashion as he snapped the lighter shut.

"Y'all want a drink?"

"I don't drink on Sunday," I said.

"Now, I know that's some bullshit."

Tony pressed a button on his desk and told Junior to bring in three glasses of Crown Royal. In a few moments, Junior lumbered in with three glasses of whiskey rattling on a tray. He left the whiskeys on Tony's desk without a word.

Hawk and I drank. Tony left his on his desk while he smoked.

"Y'all want to sit?"

Both of us shook our heads.

"Okay," Tony said. "Tell me what you want to know."

"What's Gerry Broz doing with Jumpin' Jack Flynn?" I asked.

"Oh, shit."

" 'Oh, shit'?" I asked.

Tony smoothed down his neatly trimmed mustache. "Seems like me and you have a similar pain in the ass."

"They cutting in on your turf?" I asked.

"Just starting," Tony said. "Joe's kid got some kind of ambition."

"You know Gerry's in his forties," I said. "Why's everyone call him a kid?"

"That motherfucker got back into it last year," Tony said. "I thought it was a joke. Don't think it's a joke no more. Especially now he thrown in with Flynn."

"Dorchester."

"Five people dead."

"What was it over?" I asked.

"What the hell you think?" Tony asked. "Drugs."

I nodded and Hawk nodded. He removed his sunglasses.

"What's Flynn's deal in this?" Hawk asked.

"You know Jack Flynn?" Tony asked.

I nodded.

"He been out of the joint a few years," Tony said. "Figure he out of the life till I heard about him openin' that bar in Southie with Broz's kid. One got more money than sense. Other bring a lifetime of respect and fear."

"Partners?"

"You got to ask them that," Tony said. "Didn't study their got-damn business plan. And I don't give a shit. I just know I can't have any of you Irish motherfuckers thinkin' you gonna run some skin, too. You see?"

"Jack Flynn is not my people," I said.

Tony leaned in. He threw back his whiskey. "How long I been in the life?"

"Long time," Hawk said.

"Yep," Tony said. "And I'll say this. Jumpin' Jack Flynn is the craziest, most fucked-up son of a bitch I ever known. That a thing, ain't it?"

Hawk nodded.

"Your problems may be over soon," I said. "The Feds are all over Broz and Flynn."

"They been all over me for years. Doesn't

change shit. Whores need to be run. I know how to do the runnin'."

"They want to shut down Broz," I said. "And close the case on the old man."

"That what you heard?" Tony asked. His mouth pursed into a tight smile.

I nodded.

"Well, you wrong," Tony said. "They ain't after Broz. They after the Italians and Gino Fish."

I looked to Hawk. Hawk looked back to me. He lifted his eyebrows.

"Jack Flynn did five years for one murder," Tony said. "I know for a fact that sociopath killed at least fifty. I ain't shittin' you, man."

"You think he cut a deal?" I asked.

"What's it look like to you, Irish?"

"You got proof?"

"Man, I just counting my money and taking it day by day," Tony said. "God willing."

I nodded.

"What if they come for you next, Tony?" Hawk asked.

"Reason I got Ty-Bop and Junior," Tony said. "Nobody likes no gang war. But they happen from time to time. I got other people, too. I hold my fucking ground."

"Gino know about this?" I asked.

"Since that shooting, the territory's been up for grabs," Tony said. "You better believe ole Gino is holding on to his nuts. Or having someone hold them for him."

I nodded. Hawk looked to me. He put his sunglasses back on.

"I'm glad you got back the bar's original name," I said. "It's what kids today call retro."

"Glad you like it, man," Tony said. "Ain't nothin' like the real thing."

Tony did not stand. He did not shake hands with us. He just kept that look of humor on his face as we exited from the darkness of Buddy's Fox.

43

"Since when does Tony go to church?" I asked.

"Tony always go to church."

I nodded.

"Even pimps got faith."

"You think Junior and Ty-Bop go with him?" I asked.

"Nah, man," Hawk said. "Probably steal the collection plate."

My cell rang in my coat pocket. I answered.

"We got to talk," Mattie said.

"Okay, talk."

"Right now," she said. "In person."

"I'm with Hawk."

"Meet me at the playground at the Mc-Cormack."

"Hawk will like that."

I made a U-turn and headed toward the bridge.

"Southie?" Hawk said.

"Yep."

"Mattie?"

"Yep."

"What she want?"

I shrugged and headed that way. It had started to rain, but it felt warm and pleasant inside the car. I turned on the windshield wipers as Southie passed in the washed-out hues of an old Polaroid. Old brick and chain-link fences. Churches and donut shops. Abandoned storefronts and renovated condos. The road was slick but not yet iced.

We parked in front of the small playground. There was a swing set with heavy chains and thick rubber seats laden with wet snow. Small metal animals with handles for ears and springs for feet poked from the white ground.

Cold rain pelted the windshield. We got out and stood with Mattie.

"You want to sit in the car?" I asked.

"Theresa Donovan is fucking missing," Mattie said. "It was all people were talkin' about at Mass. People tried to shut up when I was around. I guess they thought it might freak me out."

"What did you hear?"

"That she's gone," Mattie said. "You know she about shit a brick when you started ask-

288

ing about my ma. And I know Mickey is saying she was with my ma the night she died."

"You spoke to Mickey?"

Mattie nodded.

Hawk stood close on the sidewalk and leaned against a wrought-iron fence. Rain beaded down his bald head. His arms folded across his chest. He looked completely at home.

"You know it was Red and Moon," Mattie said. "You got to do somethin'. Her little sister is my age. She puked her guts out this morning."

"If she's with those two," I said, "we'll know."

"Let's go," Mattie said. "Come on."

"I love a spunky kid," I said.

"I wanna watch you guys stomp those animals," Mattie said.

"We good at the stompin'," Hawk said.

"Years of practice."

The rain turned to sleet and felt like tiny needles on my face. The expanse of the housing projects seemed to grow quiet and still. It felt as if we were the only three present.

"You don't go off half cocked," I said. "You move when the time is right, not when you're mad. You go clearheaded and with a plan."

Hawk nodded. "If they got this girl, we get her."

Mattie shook her head. "Must be easy for you two to be cool," she said. "How can you? You just stand around and move slow and make jokes. How can you joke around? What are you thinking?"

"Hawk and I have been up against a lot worse," I said. "We watch and wait. We rush in and scare them, we'll never find her."

"She's fucking gone," Mattie said. "They'll kill her."

"If they wanted to shut her up," I said, "she's already dead."

Mattie's face had grown red. Her hands balled into fists. She was doing that biting thing with her cheek again. "Jesus. Neither of you know what it's like. I lost my mother."

"I lost my mother, too," I said.

"It's not the same," Mattie said. "Your mother died. Mine was killed. You don't know what that feels like. It fucking hurts."

The air seemed to drop a few degrees. Sleet fell harder than rain. We all stood there, stubborn. Two cars passed, rolling slow, down the road through the projects.

Hawk turned to Mattie. "I know."

I had known Hawk most of my adult life. He'd never mentioned a family. For all I knew, he'd just appeared fully formed like a Greek god.

"I was older than you," Hawk said. "A bad man killed her."

"What happened?" Mattie said. She dropped her fists and stood in the sleet in her misshapen coat and ridiculous cap. She studied Hawk with an open mouth. She breathed as if just finishing a marathon.

"Doesn't matter," Hawk said.

"Did you find him?"

Hawk nodded.

"Did you get even?"

"Oh, yes."

Mattie wet her mouth. Her face had gone from bright red to colorless. Sleet salted the shoveled pathways, crooking in broken mazes. I kept quiet.

"How'd that feel?" she asked.

Hawk moved from the fence toward us. He looked down a few feet at Mattie. Without much emotion, he said, "Perfect."

44

Mattie sat in the backseat. Hawk rode shot-gun.

She had removed her soaked Sox cap. Her jacket was weatherproof and slick. She chewed gum and smiled, leaning into the seat between us. "Where we headed?"

"We goin' on a stakeout, missy," Hawk said. "Sit back and enjoy the excitement."

I turned on the car's heat. The sleet pinged off the road ahead. Bringing Mattie along contradicted every microfiber of good judgment I had. But she'd asked to watch us work. And watching and waiting wasn't a dangerous gig. And since I wasn't going to teach her how to box or build a house, maybe this was something.

"This is fun to you?" I asked.

"Yeah," she said.

"Why?"

"Because it feels like I'm doing some-thing," she said. "They're not making the rules. Feels like we're in charge."

I nodded.

"So why don't you just snatch up those two bastards and beat their ass?" Mattie said.

"That's what I keep on telling Spenser," Hawk said.

"You should listen to Hawk more," Mattie said.

Hawk smiled.

I followed Dorchester Avenue up to West Broadway and took the main thoroughfare over to G Street and Red Cahill's three-decker. I parked down the street in a neat, unobtrusive spot between two cars still blanketed in snow. The rain and sleet had done little but pockmark the mounds of snow and ice. The sleet prattled on the windshield as I turned off the ignition. Hawk leaned back in the passenger seat. The rental felt warm and somewhat homey on a winter day.

"Did Theresa's family have any ideas about where she might have gone?" I asked.

"Nope," Mattie said. "Finished up her shift and was gone."

Mattie leaned in again. She blew a large pink bubble. "She and her kid sister are real close. They were really freaked out."

Mattie was quiet for several moments.

Hawk shut his eyes.

"So what do you two do on stakeouts?" she asked.

"Sometimes Parcheesi," I said. "Sometimes Hawk likes to sing to me."

Hawk did not open his eyes as he hummed a few bars from "Old Man River."

"So you sit around, drink coffee, and bullshit."

"Kid's good," Hawk said.

Thirty minutes later, Red and Moon were on the move. I started the car.

I waited a beat and then followed the Range Rover out of Southie and over the Summer Street Bridge. When Red took Atlantic toward the North End, I half expected to learn of some kind of Irish-Italian collaboration. But Red kept on driving north over the Charlestown Bridge, past the Garden and up over Old Ironsides. They parked in Charlestown across from a stretch of public housing and walked into a pool room cleverly named A-1 Billiards. In a few minutes, they walked back to their car and drove off.

I hoped Mattie was getting bored.

She wasn't.

She studied how I drove. I lagged far behind on straightaways but followed close at lights. If Red stopped at a business, I kept going. I'd circle the block, make sure they were off the street, and find a place. We blended in. We flowed with traffic.

At one point, Mattie thought we'd lost them. I jockeyed for position on a bridge and came up two cars behind them.

I smiled with satisfaction.

"Not bad," she said.

We weaved in and out of traffic along the JFK. I would slow to five, six, eight cars behind Red's Range Rover. I would speed up and pass them and fall back behind.

"He just showin' off," Hawk said. "Besides, those two wouldn't know if they was bein' followed by the Oscar Mayer Wienermobile."

"You saying they're dumb?" Mattie asked.

"If those boys any dumber, someone need to water 'em," Hawk said.

We followed them onto Storrow Drive along the river. Red left Storrow and headed south, back to the Fenway. He slowed in the neighborhood around Boston University. I was caught at a stoplight as he turned onto Kenmore Square. The huge Citgo sign stood proud over the red-brick bookstore on Beacon.

Pedestrians navigated the ankle-deep mess, umbrellas in hand, huddled under their hoods and ball caps. The light turned.

I followed and caught up.

"Lovely day," Hawk said.

"Just why do we live here?"

"To appreciate the full beauty of the seasons," Hawk said. "But if they hoof it, you follow. Can't ruin my new boots."

"That may be the most unthuggish thing you've ever said."

"Shit," Hawk said. "These boots cost more than everything you got in your closet."

"Over there," Mattie said.

The Range Rover U-turned on Beacon and pulled in front of a sad-looking bar advertising two-for-one chicken wings. Green paint molted from the old wooden façade. A half-dozen neon beer signs blazed from the window. Busted-up metal garbage cans sat on the curb.

Red and Moon got out of the car. Moon stretched and scratched his fat butt.

We parked off Yawkey Way near the big Sox team store that was larger than the stadium. Hawk had his eyes closed. Mattie leaned up between us, and I heard her breathing against my neck.

She was popping her gum. The windshield wipers swiped every few seconds.

I folded my arms over my chest and watched the bar. I left the car running. After ten minutes, I killed the engine.

Everything grew very quiet. Sleet and rain tapped at the windows.

"I can take you home if you like," I said.

"No, this is cool."

"Got school tomorrow."

"You trying to get rid of me?" she asked.

"Nope," I said.

Hawk grinned.

A few minutes later, Red and Moon hustled out of the old bar. They dragged a very short, very skinny gray-haired man behind them. I thought I knew him. I elbowed Hawk to confirm.

Hawk leaned up to the windshield. He did not speak. He stared and then nodded.

"Right?" I asked.

"It's him."

"It's who?" Mattie asked. "You two always speak in code?"

"Chico Hirsch."

"Who the hell is Chico Hirsch?" she asked.

"Big-time bookie," I said. "Been around since the Braves were in Boston. Jesus. How old is Chico?"

"Got to be around ninety," Hawk said. "I thought that motherfucker was long dead."

Moon gripped Chico's upper arm and shoved him roughly into the back of the

Range Rover. He said something harsh and unpleasant, and then slammed the door. Red and Moon piled into the Range Rover and took off.

We followed. Mattie was absolutely hooked.

In the rearview, I saw an honest-to-God smile.

Good judgment be damned.

45

They didn't drive back to Red's three-decker. Red and Moon hustled Chico Hirsch into a pleasant two-story house on Third Street in Southie. It was getting dark and very cold. Sleet fell in the failing light.

"Shoulda got some of them chicken wings," Hawk said.

"Two for one," I said.

"I could go for food," Mattie said. "There's a corner store close across the street."

She pointed to a convenience store within sight, so I gave her some money for some sandwiches and coffee. The sleet tapped harder against the windshield. Streets were icing. Melting snow banks solidified.

"What you think they doin' with Chico?" Hawk asked.

"Asking him about the good ole days," I said. "They want to learn from the wealth of his experience."

"Bullshit pickin' on an old man," Hawk said.

"It is."

"What we gonna do?"

"I could knock on the door and shame them to death."

"Or we could bust in the front door and say, 'Give it up, motherfuckers.' "

"You're dying to try that out, aren't you?"

Hawk grinned. "Yep."

Mattie returned with the coffee and sandwiches. The sandwiches were the premade kind, wrapped tightly in cellophane for long life. I think King Tut was wrapped in the same manner. The mustard pack was the only nourishing part of the meal.

"You owe me," Hawk said, checking out what was between the bread.

"You are not enjoying the bounty we have provided for you?" I asked.

"Sitting in a Ford sedan, drinkin' bad coffee, and eating a shit sandwich ain't exactly my idea of heaven."

"Where's Chico?" Mattie asked.

We didn't answer. Hawk leaned forward and rolled his shoulders. He lolled his neck until it cracked. His Mossberg pump lay against his right leg.

"Where is he?" Mattie asked.

"Hasn't come out," I said.

"What are we gonna do?"

"Natural selection," Hawk said. "Chico is a bookie. Bookies got to play the game."

"He's an old man," Mattie said. "They're gonna kill him."

"Chico know what it's about," Hawk said. "This ain't his first shakedown."

"Well, you got to do something," Mattie said. "Call the cops. Or something."

I took a deep breath. I wadded up the rest of my sandwich. I opened the door and tossed out the remaining coffee onto the street. Steam rose from the asphalt. I closed the door and looked to Hawk.

"We take you home," I said to Mattie. "Then we'll do something."

"That'll take too much time," she said.

We didn't say anything.

"I won't get out of the car," she said. "I swear. If something happens, I'll call the cops. Can't you just check? Please just check."

"This isn't why we're here," I said. "We check on some bookie, we might not find Theresa."

I turned around and looked at Mattie. She said please again. The please wasn't something that came naturally to her.

Hawk and I climbed out of the car. Mattie moved into the front passenger seat and

301

closed the door. I checked the load on the .357. I absently felt for the .38 clipped to my belt.

We walked side by side down the street, empty except for the cars and trucks packed tight against the curbs. No people, just the quiet and stillness of sleet. The air felt thin, with a silent patter of the tiny ice pellets.

"Can't say no to the kid," Hawk said.

"It's part of her therapy," I said. "Watching masters at their trade."

"Uh-huh."

"Don't you miss having hair in this weather?" I asked.

"I am bulletproof."

"Able to leap tall buildings in a single bound?"

"Yeah," Hawk said. "All that shit."

Hawk moved ahead, Mossberg in his right hand, and skirted the edge of the pleasant two-story house. The house was painted a light green, with black shutters. From the driveway, you could see a picket fence surrounding a small backyard.

I watched the street. Mattie watched us from the car.

Hawk looped back around the house and met me out front.

"Got Chico in the kitchen," he said. "Lot of blood in that old man."

"Any others?"

"Only see the two."

"Back door?"

"It's one of those wrought-iron security jobs," he said. "Locked."

I nodded. We walked to the front door.

I tried the knob, and it turned loose in my hands.

"Shit. I wanted to kick it in," Hawk said. He peered in a side window and moved close to my shoulder.

With the .357 extended, I turned the knob and Hawk pushed in the door. I moved into the room fast. Hawk followed and scanned the corners and staircase. We hit the kitchen within three seconds of getting in the house.

Red was screaming at Chico. Chico was telling Red to go fuck himself.

I had the .357 on them. Hawk stood at my side with the pump.

There was a lot of blood on the front of Chico's wrinkled dress shirt. On a nearby table, I spotted several Baggies of what looked like drugs and a small digital scale.

"Give it up," Hawk said. "Motherfuckers."

Hawk grinned.

"Shit, shit, shit," Red said.

"Hello, Red," I said. "So how you been?"

Moon was standing. He stared at us with bovine eyes. Two handguns sat on a kitchen counter. Moon and Red were maybe three feet from the counter. Miles.

"Put your hands up," I said.

No one moved. Moon inched himself toward the guns.

Hawk bolted forward and rammed the muzzle of the shotgun into Moon's sternum. He was down. I trained my gun on Red.

His hands went up.

Chico put his hands up, too. He wore an ill-fitting wool suit. His right eye was swollen. The bulging eye made him look like a frog. He squinted at me. His thick glasses lay broken on the kitchen floor.

Hawk checked the boys for weapons. He found a .45 stuck in Red's belt. Moon wasn't armed except for a folding knife. Moon started to get to his feet.

He came for Hawk.

Hawk rammed the stock of the Mossberg into his gut. Moon was down on his knees. I figured Moon must suffer some type of learning disability.

"Where's Theresa Donovan?" I asked. I tossed Chico a few napkins for his nose. I kept staring at Red as I bent down and picked up Chico's glasses. One of the lenses was cracked.

"Who?" Red said.

"Playing dumb suits you to a T, Red," I

said. "Theresa Donovan?"

He shook his head. "I'm not fucking lying. What the hell?"

"How about Jack Flynn? Does he know?"

This time Red smiled and took one step back. "Don't know him," Red said. "You, Moon?"

Moon made a sound like a deflating blimp.

"Moon don't know him, either," Red said. He shrugged. "Guess you're fucked now."

"That's a unique perspective."

Chico got to his feet. He shook his head and spit on the vinyl floor. The spitting was very theatrical but very appropriate. The old man stood next to me and put on his glasses.

"You tell Jack and Gerry to go and have intercourse with each other."

"Chico," I said. "So polite."

"I'm old," Chico said. "I got to make peace with this shit."

Hawk smiled. The Mossberg still trained on Moon. I had the gun on Red.

I walked to the table and laid the .357 before me. I took a breath and leaned in. I smiled. Spenser, professional mediator.

"Who's in charge?" I asked. "Jack or Gerry Broz?"

Red shrugged.

"Easy question, Red," I said. "Shall I

305

speak more slowly?"

Moon wavered to his feet. He wiped the blood off his doughy face. He had the expression of a beaten man.

I nodded. "Lots of dope on this table," I said. "Got a ninety-year-old man ready to press charges."

"No," Red said. "He won't. We were just playing. Right, Chico?"

Chico's eyes shifted from me to Red. From Red to Hawk and Moon.

He didn't say anything.

"Still a lot of dope," I said. I pulled a cell phone from the inside of my coat. I laid it by the .357. "One call."

Red's eyes flicked over me. He kept a tough-guy stare.

"What do you want?" Moon asked.

I raised my eyebrows. I turned to Moon.

"Did you take Theresa Donovan?"

He shook his head. His breath was labored. He'd thrown in the towel.

"Okay," I said. "Let's try this. We just want to know what happened to Julie Sullivan. You answer that and we're gone."

"Chico goes, too," Chico said.

"Yeah," I said. "Right. Chico is with us."

Red shook his head at Moon. Moon looked over to Hawk and then me. He leaned against the table. He looked to Red.

"I can't go back to prison, man," Moon said. "I'd rather fucking die."

"Shut up, Moon," Red said.

"We took the girl to see Flynn."

"Shut up, Moon," Red said. "Shut the fuck up."

"This ain't business," Moon said. "You talk to Flynn. He had us snatch her."

"Why?" I asked.

"Shut the fuck up, Moon."

"Because —"

I had been studying Moon's face and body language. I had been waiting for a telltale sign he was lying. I watched his eyes. The way he breathed.

I broke eye contact with Moon.

Red snatched up my .357 and shot Moon right in the head. Moon toppled.

Hawk blasted a large hole in Red Cahill's chest. There was a lot of noise and blood with the smell of smoke and gunpowder. My ears rang.

And then silence. The silence amplified the sleet against the roof and windows. To punctuate the violence, Red's body slipped from the chair and onto the floor beside Moon's.

"Holy Christ," Chico Hirsch said. He walked over to Red and kicked him hard in the head. "Holy Christ."

"A fine mess you've gotten me into," Hawk said.

Hawk was not smiling. I took a deep breath.

I left my .357 on the floor beside Red. The crime scene techs could later lecture about the setup. At least that was something.

"Crapola," Chico said. "That kid's chest looks like a plate of spaghetti."

Death was very ugly, even among ugly people.

"You want to call Quirk?" Hawk said. "He gonna love this."

I nodded.

46

Quirk was not pleased. He walked from the kitchen into the living room, where I'd been going over the story with Frank Belson. Hawk was outside, talking to a young female detective I didn't know. The front door was left open, with crime scene techs and detectives going in and out. The room had grown very cold.

"What a mess," Quirk said. "What a fucking mess."

"Spenser says he was just being a Good Samaritan," Belson said.

"Just happened to be tooling around Southie and ran across Chico Hirsch getting the crap kicked out of him?"

"He and Hawk had been tailing those guys and saw them abduct Mr. Hirsch," Belson said.

"Oh, goody," Quirk said.

"I knew how much you missed seeing me," I said.

"I was in my easy chair, watching the game," Quirk said. "I had about this much Johnnie Walker poured into my glass."

He spaced his thumb and index finger very far apart.

"I can see you're still in your house clothes," I said.

Quirk wore a stiff-collared white dress shirt under a navy V-neck cashmere sweater. His charcoal pants sported a sharp crease. His wingtips gleamed from a recent shine. The trench coat had been expertly folded under his right arm.

"We got your gun for Moon Murphy and Hawk's shotgun on Red," Quirk said.

"Red took my gun," I said.

"That's embarrassing," Quirk said.

"It is."

"That's the part I don't get," Quirk said. "Why would he shoot his partner?"

"We were going to call the police," I said. "And Moon Murphy, being a recent parolee, was not excited about returning to the pokey."

"And he was about to rat on Red?"

"Something like that."

Quirk shook his head. He looked to Belson. Belson shook his head.

Belson reached into his coat pocket for a cigar and stepped outside for a smoke. I

310

recalled a time when he'd light up standing over a dead body.

"I'm getting the feeling I'm going to be x-ed from the Citizen of the Year Award by the Boston police."

"Yeah," Quirk said. He nodded as he appraised me. "But you're number one on our shit list."

"Was the Johnnie Walker Red or Blue?"

"Blue," Quirk said.

"Ouch," I said.

"Shit list," Quirk said.

"On the other hand, Chico Hirsch wants to name his great-grandson Hawk."

"Explain that at Hebrew school."

"Chico is an old man," I said. "They could've killed him."

"Spenser, patron saint to bookies, con men, and thieves."

I shrugged. We walked outside to join Belson. From the stoop, I saw Mattie standing with a patrol officer. The officer was a young black woman. Mattie was talking, and she was taking down notes.

"We hadn't even talked about the kid yet," Quirk said. "What the hell? You gone nuts?"

"You hadn't heard?" Belson said. "Business is so bad, Spenser babysits for beer money."

"That's Julie Sullivan's kid," Quirk said.

I nodded.

"Why'd you bring her into this mess?" Quirk asked.

Belson smoked the cigar. I was glad the cold wind scattered the smoke. Belson liked them cheap.

"You get a dozen for a quarter, Frank?" I said.

"Nah," Belson said. "Are you kidding? These are a whole dollar apiece."

"Red and Moon kill her mom?" Quirk asked.

I shook my head. "We were getting to that when Moon met his early demise."

Quirk nodded. "We'll be taking your gun."

"I figured."

"And Hawk's gun, too."

"Hawk won't be pleased."

"Do I look like I give a shit?"

"Stand a little more in the light."

"You mind a little off-the-record advice?" Quirk said.

I waited.

"You may want to rearm," Quirk said.

I nodded.

"Yep," Belson said. "You want to tell him? Or you want me to?"

"Tell me what?" I asked.

The two cops grinned at each other.

"House is owned by none other than Mr.

Jack Flynn," Quirk said. "We're going to talk to him next."

"He'll probably be a little pissed about you guys redecorating the kitchen," Belson said. "And acing a couple of his people." He plugged the cigar into the corner of his mouth. The stubble on his face had grown thick since shaving that morning.

"You want to tell us what the fuck is going on with Jumpin' Jack?" Quirk said. "I know that's not your way and all. And obviously you have the matter well in hand."

"We didn't plan this," I said. "It happened."

"Shit happens?" Quirk said. "You might want to put that on your business card."

47

Rita met me at Boston police headquarters, and after a long while of her reading forms and me signing them, we had breakfast. We sat at the counter at Mike's City Diner, and the same pink-haired waitress who waited on me the other day poured us each a cup of coffee. I smiled at her. She didn't return the smile. I think my rugged but handsome appearance flummoxed her.

"She's flummoxed," I said to Rita.

"If I were in my early twenties with pink hair, you'd flummox me, too."

"Are you saying I'm an acquired taste?"

"Like a single-barrel scotch," she said. "A little bitter to all but the discerning palate."

"Swell."

Rita wrapped her fingers around the thick coffee mug. She added some cream and sugar.

"You did the right thing."

"Losing my gun?"

"Calling me," she said. "There could be civil suits. Family members would raise hell if they knew you were such close friends with Quirk."

"I think Quirk would run me out of town on a greased rail if I did something wrong."

"I disagree," Rita said. She sipped coffee. She left the imprint of her very red lipstick on the edge of the mug.

"You haven't known Quirk as long as I have."

Mike's was bustling at six a.m. Plenty of young professionals and grizzled retirees packed the tables, reading fresh copies of the *Globe* or reading the *Globe* on their iPhones. I did not have an iPhone. Strangely, I used my phone to make phone calls. Simpler times.

"So now that your suspects are dead," Rita asked, "how does that leave Mr. Green?"

"No worse than yesterday."

"So let me get this straight," she said. "Now we believe the distinguished misters Murphy and Cahill didn't kill Julie Sullivan?"

Rita sipped coffee. She looked at me with her big green eyes over the mug.

"They played a role in her killing," I said. "But there's more. Others. They were following orders."

"I know a good psychic if you'd like to go that route."

"I have a working theory."

"So let's say the real killer's two accomplices are now dead," she said. "How do I make a case to exonerate Mr. Green? Those nail clippings are a long shot. It'll take months to return from the lab, and that doesn't necessarily clear him. A judge won't care if his DNA is absent. We'll need more."

"You ever hear of Jack Flynn?"

"Sure."

"What do you know?"

Rita shrugged. "I don't know. Typical Southie hood. I once prosecuted some guys in his crew. They'd hijacked a cigarette truck and were selling their spoils out back of a supermarket in Quincy. Wasn't he convicted of some killings sometime back?"

"I'm being told he worked out a deal with the Feds."

"With your friend Agent Connor?" Rita raised her eyebrows. "Sticky. Sticky."

"Yep."

"And now the Feds' ace in the hole may have killed your client's mom."

"I've known Jack Flynn since about as long as I've been in this business," I said. "He used to be a shooter for a bookie in Charlestown named Frank Doerr."

"Doerr still in business?" Rita asked.

"Let's say he took an early retirement," I said. "From there, Flynn worked a little for Joe Broz. But Broz never trusted him. Flynn's mainly freelance. He's really the only guy in the city who could work his own people without getting squeezed by the Italians. He's sort of been grandfathered into the criminal system."

"Hoodlums and their complex codes," Rita said. "Endlessly tiresome."

She set down the coffee and picked up a laminated menu. She crossed her legs as she read. Her heavy wool coat lay on the stool next to her.

"Hash and eggs are highly recommended," I said.

"If I ate hash and eggs for breakfast, I'd need more sex to burn the calories."

"If you were any more sexed up, you'd spontaneously combust."

Rita raised an eyebrow. "So how certain are we that Flynn killed Julie Sullivan?"

"Fairly," I said.

"Why?"

"That's where it gets tricky."

"Did Red Cahill and Moon Murphy know?"

"Yes," I said. "Flynn sent them for her. I think he was her boyfriend."

Rita nodded. "Now we'll never know."

The waitress stopped at our table, refilled our coffee, and took our orders. Rita decided on a Greek omelet, no toast, with a small OJ. I had hash and eggs. I wanted to underscore my point.

I again smiled at the pink-haired waitress. She narrowed her eyes at me and walked off.

"Maybe she thinks you're nuts," Rita said.

"You think I've lost it?"

"You still got it," Rita said. "And I got it, too. If you were smart, we could join a mutual admiration society."

"If only my heart did not belong to another."

"Your loss," Rita said.

I grinned. We were quiet for a moment. My ears still rang from hearing gunshots at very close range. I took comfort in the diner activity. The pouring of coffee, orders barked back to the chef, and the clang of silverware were much nicer than Jack Flynn's kitchen.

"How bad was it?" Rita asked.

"To quote Quirk, 'It was a royal clusterfuck.' "

"Does Hawk need help?"

"He has a good lawyer."

"Not as good as me."

318

"No one is as good as you."

"Hawk's reputation will make this a pain in the ass for Quirk."

"Hawk puts Quirk in a tough position," I said. "Hawk's reputation is the stuff of legend. Even when Hawk does right, it puts Quirk in a tough position."

"It's not easy being a professional thug."

"I resent that remark."

"What will you do now?" Rita asked.

"As you know, Mattie saw her mother with Mr. Murphy and Mr. Cahill the night she died."

"That's not enough."

"Did I mention there may be an eyewitness to the killing?"

Rita tilted her chin downward. *"Hmm,"* she said. "Must have slipped your mind."

"I have reason to believe there is a woman who witnessed the murder."

"Someone the cops didn't know about?"

"This wasn't exactly a high-priority case for them," I said. "And the witness seemed to value her life a little too much to come forward."

"That's fantastic," Rita said. "She'll talk now?"

"It would be fantastic," I said. "But she's disappeared."

"Disappeared as in dead, or disappeared

as in flown the coop?"

"Excellent question," I said. "I have good reason to believe she may have left her apartment in some disarray. Not that I creeped her apartment or anything."

"Lots of people live in disarray."

"True," I said. "But it looked like she'd left her dinner on the kitchen floor."

"Maybe she's messy."

"She left a half-filled suitcase," I said. "And she had a pretty good supply of makeup left in the bathroom."

"Men are endlessly fascinated by makeup," Rita said.

"And underthingies."

Rita smiled slowly at me and flipped her red hair.

"Our witness may have a huge cache of makeup, who knows?"

"What about leaving her luggage?" I asked.

"Did she leave her purse?" Rita asked. She raised her eyebrows.

"I didn't see a purse."

"Sounds like she made a run for it."

"Or someone took her purse, too."

"Maybe," Rita said. "Maybe not. Maybe something scared her so bad, she grabbed the only thing she could and took off. Does she have a car?"

"I couldn't find one registered to her."

Rita nodded.

"She's pretty broke," I said. "I don't think she could run far."

"If she knows what you think she knows, it wouldn't matter much," Rita said. "I bet she has credit cards."

I nodded. "She does, but I can't track her credit cards," I said. "Only the cops can do that."

The waitress slid the plates before us. Steam rose from the hash and eggs. More coffee was poured. Rita ate and crossed her legs. She noticed me staring at her knees and smiled.

"Jeez," she said. "If only you knew some cops to help out."

48

"You owe me," Belson said. "Quirk doesn't know I'm doing this."

"You think he'd disapprove?" I asked.

"I think he'd have my ass."

"You mind if I send you a box of decent cigars?" I asked.

"I like 'em cheap," Belson said. "You send me the good stuff and my lungs might revolt."

"Point taken," I said. "What do you have?"

I cradled the cell phone to my ear as I headed north on Arlington toward my apartment. I needed a hot shower, a shave, and maybe a twenty-four-hour nap.

"Theresa Donovan has four credit cards," Belson said. "Only one that isn't maxed out. She's run up about six hundred in charges this week."

"Where?"

"Gas station in Quincy, six trips to a Mc-Donald's, and, oh, I see a hotel, too."

"Gee," I said. "You think you might want to share that information?"

"You really worried this girl is in danger?"

"I am," I said.

"Holiday Inn in Worcester," Belson said. "You want me to draw you a fucking map?"

"I believe purgatory is a lot like a Holiday Inn in Worcester."

"Don't screw me on those cigars," Belson said. He hung up.

I parked right off the Public Garden on Marlborough and walked up to my apartment.

I was careful unlocking the door. For the last several hours, I'd felt a sharp tension in my trapezius muscles. I was not at ease until I checked the bedroom and closets.

I took a long, hot shower and shaved. I made another pot of coffee. I loaded a .40 caliber Smith & Wesson that I'd grown quite fond of. In my line of work, it was good to have a spare.

I dressed in a black fisherman's sweater, dark jeans, and my peacoat. Before I closed and locked the door, I reached for my Boston Braves cap.

I was dressed to impress. When calling on the scared shitless, it's important to make a good appearance. Spenser Crime-fighting Tip #111.

I really should write all of this down.

The sun broke through the gray clouds as I hit the I-90 ramp at Huntington Avenue. I drove west, thinking of Mattie and her mom. I thought of Theresa Donovan and hoped I'd get to her first.

I thought about Jack Flynn. The tension in my back returned.

49

The Holiday Inn in Worcester was not the Ritz-Carlton or the Four Seasons. It really wasn't much of anything but a place for business travelers to lay their weary heads. A honeycomb of rooms, a business center, a coin laundry, and a sterile little restaurant decorated with black-and-white photos of Massachusetts town squares. If you stared long enough, maybe you'd feel quaint through osmosis.

I did not bother to try to shine on the woman at the front desk. I did not try to bribe a bellman with a twenty, which was for the best, since there were no bellmen at the Holiday Inn in Worcester. I just found the house phone and asked for Theresa Donovan's room.

After six rings, she picked up.

"You really shouldn't leave lasagna on your kitchen floor."

"Who is this?"

"Spenser," I said.

"The guy with Mattie?"

"As I'm known in some circles."

"How'd you find me?"

"I followed a trail of bread crumbs from Dorchester Avenue."

"Are you here?"

"In the lobby."

"Please go away," she said. "They'll find me."

"Red and Moon are dead."

There was a long pause. I could hear her breathing. "I saw the news."

"Can I come up?" I asked.

"Give me a minute," she said. "I'll come down. Wait in the bar."

The bar wasn't much of a bar, either. But they had beer. And the Holiday Inn Worcester was in luck. I happened to like to drink beer.

I got a Sam Adams Noble Pils on tap and found a small table with an excellent view of the parking lot and the interstate. After my beer was half gone, I worried I'd been conned and Theresa had bolted.

That would teach me to drink on the job.

She appeared a minute later. She wore a long coat over jeans and a pajama top. Her hair was pulled tight away from her face in a ponytail. Her face was absent of makeup, and she smelled strongly of cigarettes.

"Drink?"

She shook her head and took off her coat.

"My ma tell you?"

"Nope."

"I called her this morning," she said. "She was sick with worry."

I listened and drank my beer, not telling her about the credit card trace. In case she made like a rabbit again, I didn't want to let her in on my secrets.

She fidgeted with her hands. She looked around the bar and over to the lobby. She pulled out a pack of cigarettes, and then, realizing she couldn't smoke, said, "Fuck."

"We can go outside," I said.

She looked out the window and shook her head. "What do you want?"

"Mickey told me you were with Julie the night she was killed."

"Bullshit."

"If it's bullshit, how come you're running?"

"Because these people are fucking crazy."

"And in saying 'these people,' you mean Jack Flynn."

Theresa stopped fidgeting. She looked me in the eye. I nodded at her.

"Can I still get a drink?" she asked.

"What do you want?"

"Double Black Jack," she said. "Water back."

"Wow."

I complied and joined her with refreshments. I guess it would be too much for the Holiday Inn to offer one of those nut trays like at the Taj. I looked around the room and decided it was.

"Tell me about Julie and Jack Flynn."

"Why should I?"

"Because I'm the only thing between you and Flynn. And because you owe Mattie something. Mickey Green, too."

"You can take on Jack Flynn?"

"You bet."

Theresa just stared at me. But then she nodded, convinced I spoke the truth. I often instilled confidence in young women.

"She met him at Four Green Fields," she said. "He had just got out of jail, just got a job, and had a lot of cash. After that, he called her a lot. Late. She'd get a message and I'd have to drive her to his condo or some motel."

"Was she his girlfriend?"

"I don't know what to call it," Theresa said. "I think he gave her money. I think he liked her. She was a lot younger."

"I heard Flynn nearly took off Touchie Kiley's head one night."

Theresa nodded.

"Yeah, I heard about that," she said. "I think Julie kind of appreciated it. People had stopped respecting her. You know, because of the drugs and all. She wasn't the world's greatest mom, either. But I guess you figured that out from Mattie."

"So they were sort of dating."

"I think Flynn was married," Theresa said. "Or had been married. I didn't like him. He creeped me out. I thought Julie had hit rock bottom. And then she latches on to Jack Fuckin' Flynn, not a month after he gets out of Walpole."

"You knew who he was?"

"He has a rep."

I nodded.

"You know how some people got that?"

"Many would say I have a rep," I said.

I sipped some beer. I studied the view of the interstate and parking lot. A woman passed by the window, pulling her luggage on wheels. When the piece wouldn't jump the curb, she picked it up with a lot of effort. She did not look like she was having a good day.

"Can I have another drink?"

I nodded. I got her another double Jack. I continued sipping my second Noble Pils. Moderation in all things.

I sat down and let her drink. We remained quiet as cars zipped past on the interstate. Rain pattered the windshields of parked cars. People stood outside, smoking under the porte cochere.

"What happened the night she died?"

"Flynn was mad," she said.

"I figured that."

"He snatched me up off a barstool in the pub. He'd parked outside on a curb and tossed me into his car. We drove around for like three hours. He made me call Julie about a dozen times. He was sure she'd gone to the police."

"About what?" I asked.

"I don't know," he said. "He was fucking pissed. I finally found out she was drunk and had gone home."

I nodded. "That's when he sent Red and Moon to pick her up."

"Flynn told them to meet us out at this construction site near The Point," she said. "The university has a couple buildings there now. Why should I tell you all this? Flynn will fucking kill me."

"Is that why you ran?"

"He called me."

I nodded.

"I was scared shitless," she said. "He calls me up a few nights back and asks what I've

330

been saying about him and Jules. He says he wanted to remind me that he let me live. Just like that, let me live. Like he was a great guy or some shit."

"How did he know we talked?"

"Southie ain't very big."

I nodded.

"Can we go outside?" she asked. "I'm dying for a fucking cigarette."

I stood, reached for a few bucks in my pocket, and left a tip. She downed the last gulp of her Jack and grabbed her coat.

We walked to the back of the hotel and the covered swimming pool. The deck tables and chairs were buried in snow and growing thick with ice. The rain pattered on the brim of my ball cap. Theresa smoked, craning her head to study the sky. The cold rain was more an annoyance than a displeasure.

"Flynn told me to stay in the car," she said. "He got out when they drove up. He told Red and Moon to take me home. They'd parked her down a ways. I remember they kept their headlights on. I noticed a lot of bulldozers and stuff. I could see Julie get out of the car while Red and Moon was walking toward me. Flynn dragged her into the car."

"For how long?"

"Five minutes. Long enough," she said. "I

think Red and Moon stayed around for Flynn to tell them what to do. But Flynn was in the car. You know. When he finished, Flynn got out of the car and yanked her with him. Her clothes were all torn and shit. I saw him smack her."

I nodded. I let her talk.

"Red and Moon knew what was about to happen and told me to get in the backseat," she said. She finished the cigarette and started a new one. The wind and rain were very cold. I could feel my face tighten. "I got in back, and I remember asking those pieces of shit to please not kill me."

"What did they say?"

"Red told me to get down low and shut the fuck up. He started the car and started to drive off."

I turned up my collar. A man who worked for the hotel opened a side door and asked if we'd been locked out. I told him we were fine. Theresa was shaking. She smoked and stared at the pool cover. Rain flecked her face.

"They was turnin' around when I saw it," she said. "I didn't want to. But I screamed. You ever screamed like it's involuntary? I mean, I had to cover my mouth, but I couldn't stop it. You couldn't stop it."

"What did you see?"

"I saw her yelling at him, and Flynn's hand come from his pocket with something silver," she said. "He just kept jabbing her with it. I seen her fall to her knees. I seen the blood. *Oh, Jesus.* What the fuck do you want me to say?"

She shook even more, teeth chattering. She tossed the cigarette onto the pool cover, where it went out with a hiss. I took off a glove and put a hand to her cheek. Her nose ran, and she looked as if she might get sick.

I told her I was very sorry. I never felt more awful about saying sorry. Sorry seemed inadequate.

"Last thing I saw was Julie trying to stand," Theresa said. "She was fucking screaming at Flynn, giving him hell. I give her that. She never lost that spirit. I know even cut up like she was, she was telling him he was nothing but a rotten piece of shit."

I took back my hand. I put an arm around her. She was sobbing hard, her body almost in revolt under my shoulder. Her hair was very wet.

"He got in Red's car and fucking ran her down," she said.

"But it was Mickey Green's car," I said.

"I had turned to see the thing out the back window. You could see it all in those headlights. Red told me to look away and to keep my fucking mouth shut. But Flynn knew. He's wanted me dead a long time. But he didn't think I had it in me."

"Did the police talk to you during the investigation?"

Theresa laughed. "Right. They really went all CSI trying to find out who killed the junkie whore from Southie," she said. "No one cared about Julie. I never even saw a single detective. Next thing I know, they've arrested Mickey."

"And you didn't speak up."

" 'Speak up'? Are you not fucking listening? Flynn said he would kill me and my whole family. Hell, no, I didn't speak up. I was relieved that it was over."

"But it's not over. Mattie needs to know. And Flynn probably sees you as a loose end he should've tied up. I can make sure that doesn't happen."

"I don't want to die."

"You won't."

"You promise?"

I nodded. "Let's get you packed."

"Why?"

"You need to change motels," I said. "If I can find you, so can Flynn."

50

Long shadows fell across the Charles River esplanade. Ice hung in the trees, but the paths had been salted and cleared. I wore long underwear under my gray sweatshirt and sweatpants, along with a watch cap and gloves. The grains of salt brought a comforting crunch under my New Balance shoes, rounding the corners, heading back toward the Shell.

I kept a decent pace down to Boston University and the old Braves field. The talk I'd had with Mattie after picking her up at school hadn't been pleasant. She'd been so sure for so long that Red and Moon had killed her mother. She'd felt relief for all of a few hours, and then I had to tell her that another man was still out there. But rules had to be set. I introduced her to a couple Boston police prowl car boys who'd be keeping tabs. I would be there every morning and afternoon until this was done.

The name Jumpin' Jack Flynn meant nothing to her.

Somewhere on my run, I'd picked up a tail. I first noticed the black sedan slowing at the Harvard Bridge. A clean-cut young man in a cold-weather jogging suit and ski hat passed me. He wore Oakley sunglasses and kept a gun under his right arm.

I noted a Bluetooth device over one ear.

I turned as he passed. Another young man in similar dress lagged behind me. Not that I am not stout of heart, but he was loafing it for an athletic guy in his twenties.

I slowed to a walk as I reached the Shell and placed my hands on top of my head. I had worked up a nice sweat under my grays. My breathing was labored but steady. I liked the way I felt after some road work.

My body seemed in balance.

I saw another sedan, or perhaps the same one, parked beyond the Shell toward the Longfellow Bridge. I don't think the Feds were even trying to be covert. Connor wanted to send a message.

I followed the frozen river up to the Longfellow. The streetlamps along the bridge clicked on in the early night. The sedan drove off, and I turned back. I missed the rowers and kids playing Frisbee by the Shell. They were a lot more fun.

I took the footbridge over Storrow Drive toward the Public Garden. I watched for cloven footprints in the snow and ice. Over the thoroughfare, the bridge twisted up and under itself.

When I looped around the next curve, I saw a large man in a heavy overcoat leaning over a railing. He stood staring through Beacon Hill at the gold dome of the State House.

I reached under my sweatshirt for my pistol.

He turned. It was Connor.

He flicked the cigarette over the railing. "You keep in shape for an old fighter," he said.

"Shucks," I said.

We stood maybe six feet apart under the covered walkway. A cold wind blew off the river. The white and red lights of commuter traffic blurred into the gray afternoon.

"A couple of your guys seemed winded," I said. "Don't G-men have to pass a physical anymore?"

"It's all computers," Connor said with a shrug. He tucked another cigarette in his mouth and cupped his hand around a lighter. "It's not the same as when we got into this."

"What are we into?" I asked.

"The game," Connor said. "You like the game same as me."

"Games are more fun to play when you don't cheat."

Connor shrugged. He smoked.

"Have you brought my car back?" I asked.

"You'll get it back," Connor said, smiling. "We just have to put it back together first. Lot of shit gets lost when that happens."

"I'll inform my attorney."

"She's some piece of tail," Connor said. Smoke leaked from the corner of his mouth. "Give me a redhead every time. The problem is getting them to shut up when you're doing it."

"You know, Epstein said you were a great asset to the Bureau, but I guess he could've been off a couple letters."

"You're a funny guy, Spenser," Connor said. "Amazing you've lived this long."

"I'm a people person," I said. "Meeting guys like you makes it all worth it."

Connor shrugged and smoked. "Just seems like you piss off the wrong people. I've checked into your past. Killed a lot of people, too. Some of the shootings seemed suspicious to me."

"If you want to keep leaning on me, Connor, you mind if we set up an appointment?" I asked. "*Jeopardy!* comes on at seven."

"You're fucking up a beautiful investigation," Connor said. "You shot down two key players in a big fucking syndicate. You've destroyed nearly three years of investigative work."

"My condolences."

"You're a real prick," Connor said. "You know that?"

I shrugged. I walked toward him.

Connor puffed up. I shouldered past him, artfully knocking him back a step.

He gripped my arm. I looked down at his fingers on my biceps.

Connor gritted his teeth. More cold wind scattered the snow and ice off the bridge's ledge.

"I don't like to lose," Connor said.

"Federal agent or not, I will toss your ass off this bridge and down into rush hour if you don't let go of my arm."

Connor's eyes shifted across my face. He let go. He snorted and smiled.

"You killed two government witnesses," Connor said. "You've hoodwinked a couple drinking-buddy cops, but you're fucked with us, pal."

" *'To weep is to make less the depth of grief,'* " I said. I kept walking.

"You're fucked," Connor said, yelling down the curving bridge. "You're fucked."

More cold wind blew off the river as I crossed the street to the Garden and then turned right onto Marlborough Street.

51

"Agent Connor does not sound like a very nice man," Susan said.

"No," I said. "He's not. He needs to first love himself in order to love others."

"Do you think he'll try to bring charges against you?"

"Yes."

"But Rita will get them dropped?"

"She will."

I nodded and drank some Ellie's Brown Ale I'd stocked at her place. Susan and I were on the opposite ends of a large clawfoot bathtub. My legs were sore from the run. My ass was sore from all the sitting in cars. The warm water felt great.

"What will you do about the girl who saw the killing?" Susan asked.

"She's safe."

"But for how long?"

"Hawk is watching her."

Susan nodded. "Who's watching Mattie?"

"Boston PD," I said. "Quirk made sure it happened."

"Have you told Quirk what you know?"

I shook my head. I drank more beer. I had to lean up as I did. Some water sloshed out of the tub and onto Pearl, who lay on a bath mat.

Pearl wobbled onto her legs and shook her coat.

"I think she feels left out," Susan said.

"Have to draw the line somewhere."

"This is nice."

"Thank you for not lighting any scented candles," I said.

"A warm bath is good for the soul," she said.

"Even better with a cold beer."

"When will you tell Quirk about the witness?"

"I'm waiting to hear back from Rita," I said. "I'll bring her in tonight if everything lines up with the DA."

"And then what?" Susan asked.

"Depends on Quirk." I finished the beer. "Depends on Rita and the DA."

It had grown very dark outside on Linnaean Street.

"Are you mad about your car?"

"I never liked it," I said. "I'm thinking about getting another Jeep."

"I liked your Jeep."

"You never know when you'll need four-wheel drive," I said.

"Necking adventures?" Susan asked.

"The kids don't call it 'necking' anymore," I said. "It makes me sad."

"What do they call it?" Susan asked.

"You would know better than me," I said. "What do your young patients call it?"

"Lots of things. 'Hooking up.' 'Doing it.' "

I nodded.

"I would like another cold beer, and then I propose that we 'do it.' "

Susan nodded. She stood. I am not ashamed to admit that the bath had been filled with many bubbles. I am equally not ashamed to say they did not hide Susan's nakedness.

Her body was very taut. Her dark hair had been wrapped up in a bun.

"Yowzah," I said.

She stepped out from the bath and wrapped the towel around herself. "What if Rita calls you?"

"I may have to delay our plans. But only because I'm steadfast in my loyalties."

"She hasn't called yet."

"Nope."

"And you could be steadfast in other ways."

"Yep."
"Oh, goody."

52

Early the next morning, Belson and I met at a boutique hotel across the street from Copley Place. Some local uniform guys joined us and waited outside in their prowl cars. We didn't expect trouble. I had taken great care in hiding Theresa Donovan.

Hawk had been watching her. One does not question Hawk's abilities.

Hawk sat cross-legged in the lobby. He was reading the arts section of the *New York Times* and drinking coffee from a tiny cup. He put down the coffee, folded the newspaper, and stood. His chair was purplish velvet with a bright red leather pillow.

The walls were draped in gray curtains. The light was very dim and low.

Belson nodded at Hawk. Hawk nodded at Belson.

"We usually stash witnesses at the Quality Inn in Brookline," Belson said, an unlit cigar clamped in his teeth.

"This is close to my office," I said.

"Bullshit," Belson said. "You're a sucker for a sob story."

Hawk nodded in agreement. "Drinks at the bar cost twenty bucks."

"How's she doing?" I asked.

"Took a shower," he said. "Watchin' a movie on cable. Ordered up some breakfast."

"You check the room-service guy?" Belson asked. He took a cigar out of the corner of his mouth and tucked it into his jacket pocket.

"Nah, man," Hawk said. "I too busy kickin' it with all this ambiance. You notice those candles smell like lavender?"

"Well, get her dressed," Belson said. "I'd prefer to do this at headquarters. Places like this make me uneasy. They charge you every time you fart."

"I did not intend to expense the department," I said.

Belson looked at me with a sideways glance.

"Besides, with all these scented candles, who could tell?" I said.

All three of us rode up in a very old, very cramped elevator. The air did smell of lavender.

We knocked on the door. It took a moment, but Theresa answered.

She was dressed in the same clothes as the night before. I introduced her to Belson. She nodded.

She looked very nervous as she gathered a couple T-shirts, pants, her toothbrush, and a bunch of little shampoos into a paper bag. A plate of half-eaten scrambled eggs, two links of sausage, and toast sat cold on a wheeled cart in the corner.

My stomach grumbled. I had not eaten breakfast. Susan did not stock breakfast food. On the other hand, I was very clean.

We took the elevator back down to the lobby. Belson and Hawk waited for her outside by Belson's cruiser and two marked units.

"You're safe," I said. "Just tell Belson what you told me."

She looked at the elegant carpet. Her face had been scrubbed clean of any makeup. Her hair was again in a ponytail. Theresa Donovan looked about twelve.

"You're stand-up," I said.

"Sure."

"Flynn can't walk on this."

She nodded. I touched her arm.

But she still wouldn't look at me. I caught the eye of the bellhop. He smiled. I'm pretty sure he thought we were in a lover's quar-

347

rel. Or that maybe I was her dad. I preferred the former.

"The guys in Homicide will make sure you're safe," I said. "Belson is a good man."

"Then what?" she asked.

"Hawk and I can help."

"Yeah, right," she said. "I can't live in a hotel my whole freakin' life. I got to go back to my family."

"Flynn will be in jail."

She looked up at me. Her eyes were so clear and blue. She shook her head with a lot of sadness. "Ain't you the dreamer."

53

"You gonna tell Mattie it's over?" Hawk asked.

"Is it over?" I asked.

"You tell me."

"Quirk said they have a pickup order for Flynn," I said. "Looks like he bolted."

"They need to put that motherfucker in the zoo," Hawk said. "His kind should be extinct."

"With a sign reading 'Old School Hood.' "

Hawk drove me in his Jag. We waited like a nice couple of very large dads in the long pickup line outside Mattie's middle school. The principal had even given us a rearview-mirror tag. It was green with a pink flower.

"Got to at least tell her about Theresa being a witness," Hawk said. "Girl like Mattie will hear it anyway."

"With some details left out."

"I'd tell her word for word."

"Hate for her to grow up hard," I said.

"Yeah," Hawk said, driving up into the next slot. "Hate to break down that dream world she livin' in, all full of sunshine and light."

"I'll tell her."

"She a fighter," Hawk said. "Got my respect."

"But she fights everything," I said. "Makes her life harder than it is."

"Can't go back to bein' a kid."

"Nope."

"Don't know if I ever was a kid," Hawk said.

I nodded. "She can't be Hawk."

"She too short and white."

"Maybe she could be like me?"

"She ain't that ugly."

"Life is not always tough."

"That what you want to teach her?" Hawk asked.

"Maybe get Susan to help her with some things," I said. "Mainly that her mother's death does not have to define her."

"And that she can set her own rules, older she get."

I nodded.

We wound our way into the slot by the steps leading down from the front of the school. Mattie wore her blue parka over a school uniform. No Sox cap today. Her reddish hair blew in the cold wind as she stepped up and crawled in back. She again kept the backpack in her lap.

"Where to, missy?" Hawk said.

"Disney World," Mattie said.

"Say the word," Hawk said.

"You want to eat?" I asked.

"No."

"We can grab a burger," I said.

"No."

"Pizza?"

"Spenser ain't bein' nice," Hawk said. "He just like to eat."

"I've got homework," Mattie said. "The girls will be home, too. I need to make dinner. I got laundry."

"You need more groceries?"

"We're fine," Mattie said. "My grandma went to the store. You believe that?"

I nodded. We drove south.

Hawk kept his eyes on the road. I felt his silence as he drummed his fingers on the wheel.

"I have some news," I said.

I told her a PG-13 version of what I learned. Mattie stayed silent as she listened to what Theresa Donovan had witnessed. She stayed silent for a few minutes beyond that, too.

"She's known all this time?" Mattie asked.

"Yep."

"What a freakin' bitch," Mattie said. "Goddamn her."

"She was pretty scared," I said. "But she's doing the right thing now. Doesn't that count for something?"

"She coulda done the right thing four years ago and not left Mickey's ass in the wind."

"Girl got a point," Hawk said.

Hawk took D Street over to Dorchester Avenue, and Dorchester Avenue south. Kemp over to Monsignor O'Callaghan Way. We parked. Hawk shut off the engine. No one moved. The light outside was a pale gray. Everything around us seemed washed of color.

Mattie stayed put.

She was crying. Hawk and I were frozen.

I stared straight ahead out of the windshield. The two- and three-story red-brick buildings surrounded us. There was a lot of chain link and wrought iron. Lots of twisting paths that hadn't been cleared of snow and ice. I watched an old woman in a housecoat and tall rubber boots taking out her trash.

The Jag was very quiet except for Mattie. Hawk's hands remained on the wheel. He had on his sunglasses. I did not turn around.

I placed my leather gloves on top of each other on my right leg.

Mattie's crying came up from somewhere deep. It was so private that I felt a deep shame for hearing it. I just breathed.

The old woman in boots walked back inside. Two teenage boys strolled by, craning their heads to look in the car. I gave them a look to let them know that this wasn't their business. They complied.

After a few minutes, the deep choking wails stopped. There was snuffling and wiping. Mattie opened the car door and without a word got out onto the sidewalk. She closed the door with a light click.

"You want to walk her in?" Hawk said.

"Not much I can do."

"You Irish are softhearted," Hawk said. "You think of somethin'."

"I did what she hired me to do."

"All for a donut," Hawk said.

"A dozen," I said.

"Softhearted." Hawk nodded.

Hawk started the Jag and wheeled around. I told him to wait and reached for the handle to go after Mattie. "Give me a minute."

A white van whipped around the corner and blocked our way. I heard a car behind us. I turned and saw a black SUV zip up within an inch of Hawk's bumper. Hawk jumped out of the car, pulling his .44 Magnum. I followed, drawing the .40-caliber. Everything came in the slow whir of a kaleidoscope. Three men from the van had weapons aimed at me. Two of the men were the guys who chased me into the T station. A heavyset Hispanic in an Army coat and a skinny Anglo with thinning hair and stubbled beard.

The third man was Jack Flynn.

I could take out Flynn. But also Flynn could take me out. *Therein lies the rub.*

Even if he only winged me, his duo of flunkies were probably decent enough shots at ten feet.

Hawk stood tall in my peripheral vision. He faced worse odds with four boys from the SUV. The ambush was a good one, and the only way out was bloody and ugly. Two men carried Mattie down a slushy path. She was kicking, punching, clawing at their faces. One man's cheek was bleeding. She was screaming. Wind rustled Flynn's camel-hair coat as he gripped a .45 automatic. His ruddy Irish face glowed with the cold, his eyes full of heat. "I don't want to hear a fucking word from that Donovan girl," he said.

I kept the .40-caliber aimed right for his

well-sized Irish head.

He smiled at me as if he felt sorry for me. "Give me one reason I don't kill you both right now."

"Because we have such a swell history together," I said.

"Put down your gun, asshole."

"I'd rather not," I said. "No offense. If I'm unarmed, you'll probably shoot me."

"You don't lay down your gun, and we'll shoot the girl."

I didn't like him. But he offered some solid logic.

I did not take my eyes off Flynn as I squatted to the ground and laid my beautiful new Smith & Wesson .40-caliber in the crisp but dirty snow. I stood slowly, hands raised.

We all heard Mattie scream. One of the hoods from the SUV struck her, and you could hear the slap across her face like a rifle shot.

Hawk made a guttural sound. He could not stand it.

Hawk fired his .44. Two men fired their shotguns.

Hawk was knocked two feet back as if sucker-punched by an enormous fist.

I went for my gun.

The men who'd shot Hawk dragged one of their own inside the black SUV and disappeared. Flynn and his boys jumped inside the van as I squeezed off six shots, knocking out its back windows.

I heard sirens.

54

"How is he?" Susan asked.

"Stable," I said.

"You said you saw him shot in the chest," she said. "You said he was blown off his feet."

"I rode with him in the ambulance," I said. "His wounds were not as bad as they first appeared."

Susan let out a very long breath. We stood in a hallway on the third floor of City Hospital. Everything smelled of harsh cleaners and bad food. There was a buzz of activity at the nurses' station. I bet the nurses were buzzing about Hawk.

"He was wearing a vest," I said. "Told me he didn't trust folks in Southie."

Susan let out a little more breath. The tension in her neck and shoulders slackened. "Good to be a little racist."

"I called it being an elitist."

"What did Hawk say?"

"He said he was just being one smart motherfucker."

She squeezed my hand for a moment before we walked to the waiting room. We found a place to sit among a lot of crinkled magazines with health and diet tips. Last weekend's edition of the *Globe,* sans *Arlo & Janis.* It didn't matter. I didn't much feel like heavy reading.

Susan held my hand as we spoke. I felt very hollow.

"Thank God," Susan said.

"If the Ukrainians can't take Hawk out," I said, "nobody can take him out."

She put her arm around me and pulled me in close.

"And Mattie?"

I was quiet. I shook my head.

"Quirk and Belson know everything," I said. "All of the Boston PD and the staties are looking for her and Flynn."

"Why didn't Flynn shoot you?" Susan asked.

It was a good question.

"He had the drop," I said. "He could have. But he needs Theresa Donovan. And to get to Theresa Donovan, he needs me."

"The witness."

"She kinda holds the cards for Jack Flynn."

"Is she safe?"

"Quirk has her in protective custody," I said. "Which is slightly less accessible than Fort Knox."

"Let me get this straight," Susan said. "Flynn kidnaps the daughter of the woman he murdered to stay out of jail? Seems like he's just adding more to his sentence."

"Without Theresa, they can't reopen the case," I said. "And snatching Mattie is also a way to get back at me."

"A warped issue of respect?"

I nodded.

"And rage."

"And whatever business plans he has with Gerry Broz," I said. "Me asking questions and working with the cops is screwing up the rebuilding of the Broz dynasty. That pisses him off a great deal."

"Territory," she said. "How are men different than dogs?"

"I like dogs more."

"How many men came for Mattie?"

"Counting Flynn?" I looked up at the ceiling. "Seven. Altogether, not really great odds."

Susan tilted her head and leaned into my shoulder. After several minutes, she sat up and wiped her eyes. "You both could have been killed."

"Part of the package."

"Doesn't mean I have to like the package."

"I'm not always thrilled by my work conditions."

"But if you die, you die," she said. "I am the one who's left."

"You would manage," I said. "Pearl would mourn."

"It's not funny, goddamn it," she said. "Belson came for me. My heart stopped. I opened the front door, saw Frank, and my heart stopped."

"Frank is thoughtful."

"Damn you."

"I've been doing this my whole adult life, Suze."

"Why couldn't I have met a nice Jewish doctor?"

"Because I'm the thug of your dreams," I said. "Besides, could a nice Jewish doctor try that thing we tried the other night?"

She laughed just a bit. Susan studied me and then shook her head.

"Can we see him?" she asked.

"Maybe we smuggle a couple of bottles of Iron Horse into the emergency ward to revive him."

"You two will go for Flynn?'

I shrugged. "Yes."

"What in the hell do you both have to prove?"

"Mattie is fourteen," I said. "She hired me. She trusts me. This is my fault."

"It's not your fault."

I looked down at the floor. She put a hand to my back, rubbing in strong circles.

"I won't stay," she said. "This is between you and Hawk. But when you get through this, you will take a break for a while. Even if I have to shoot you myself."

I smiled.

Susan did not smile back.

"Are all Harvard-educated Jewesses so tough?"

"You bet your ass."

55

Hawk and I met Vinnie at the ball fields off Commercial Street in the North End. Since Vinnie was Vinnie, the North End was a pretty convenient spot for him. The infields were covered in dunes of shifting snow. You couldn't really tell there were baseball fields right now except for the night lights sticking up by a half-hidden chain-link fence. Hawk and I followed the path around the seawall and found Vinnie alone, drinking from a foam coffee cup.

"Christ," he said. "Couldn't we've met somewheres indoors? I'm freezing my nuts off."

"Hawk's been shot."

"You look okay to me," Vinnie said.

"Got some buckshot in my arm," Hawk said. "I was wearing a vest."

"Hawk's not happy right now," I said. "Flynn and his boys snatched a fourteen-year-old girl. We like her a great deal. We intend to get her back."

Vinnie shook his head. He drank some of the coffee.

"Okay," he said. "Let's go."

I held up my hand. "We need to get to Gerry Broz," I said. "And we need you to tell us how to flip him."

Vinnie shook his head. With his free hand, he turned up the collar on his camel-hair overcoat.

"I like you guys," Vinnie said. "I like you guys a lot. But I can't rat on Joe's boy. I told you that from the start. If I knew how to get to Flynn, I would. But I can't have Gerry killed for this."

"I won't kill Gerry," Hawk said. He took a deep breath. "Unless he get in the way."

"It's talk like that that makes me shut my fucking mouth."

"This ain't a request, Vinnie," Hawk said.

"I can't," Vinnie said. "I'm sorry. You know how this goes."

Hawk stepped up close to Vinnie and stared out at the dark ocean. The wind was very brisk and very cold off the water. He lowered his voice and leaned into Vinnie's ear. "Don't play that honky bullshit code with me. You kill a woman, you kidnap a little girl, there's nothin' left. Ain't no code."

"Gerry knows," I said. "How do we get to

Gerry?"

Hawk stepped back.

"Gerry is afraid of Flynn," Vinnie said. "You'd have to kill him, and then you still won't know. I'm sorry. I can't let that happen."

"Flynn will kill that little girl," I said. "I'm asking for a favor here. You don't owe the Broz family anymore. The old man is long gone."

Vinnie nodded in agreement, finished the coffee, and walked toward a trash can. He threw it away and placed his gloved hands in his pockets. Hawk remained quiet, staring at Vinnie.

"You got to promise not to dust Gerry," Vinnie said.

"Okay," I said.

I looked to Hawk. Hawk shrugged.

"Okay? I seen that look in your eye, Hawk, plenty of times. And it never leads to good things."

"How do we get to Gerry?" Hawk said.

Vinnie reached into his coat and pulled out a notepad and a pen. He carefully wrote out an address in Somerville and drew out a cross street. Like everything else about him, Vinnie Morris had very fine, exact handwriting.

"This is how you get to the kid," Vinnie

364

said. He shook his head with disappointment.

"Again with 'the kid'?" I asked.

"He'll always be a kid," Vinnie said. "I
don't want him hurt. But you go here and
you'll understand."

"I don't get it," I said.

I passed the paper to Hawk. Hawk studied
it and shrugged.

"I ain't into riddles," Hawk said. "Ain't in
the fucking mood."

"It's all I got," Vinnie said. He shrugged.
"What you do from here is your own business. But I got to sit this one out, fellas."

We both watched Vinnie walk away. We
headed back to Commercial Street, where
I'd parked my rental. The rental was still
warm when we got inside. Hawk had
stashed two loaded shotguns in the trunk.

"You think Gerry will give it up?" I asked.

"Vinnie better be playin' straight," Hawk
said. "We called in a favor. He Italian and
knows just what that shit means."

"Against his father?" I cranked the car.

"That *Godfather* bullshit don't apply
tonight," Hawk said. "No sleep till Mattie
safe."

56

The address Vinnie gave us led to a three-story red-brick building off Summer Avenue. The slanted roof was thick with snow. A walkway with a wrought-iron fence zigzagged to a front entrance where an empty flagpole stood between two bare young trees. A small wooden sign by the parking lot read THE SUMMER HOUSE. A man pushed a snow shovel by the sign. He stopped to rest and smoke a cigarette.

"Hospital?" Hawk asked.

"Hospice," I said.

"People on borrowed time."

"Yep."

"Think Gerry doin' charity work?" Hawk said.

"Somehow I doubt it."

At ten minutes after nine a.m., a silver Hummer wheeled into the Summer House parking lot. Gerry Broz stepped out in an ankle-length tan suede coat, black cowboy boots, and narrow wraparound sunglasses. He studied his reflection in the driver's window, tousled the hair over his brow, and shuffled up the zigzagging steps.

He pressed a button. Gerry opened the door and walked inside.

"You ever notice Gerry Broz is a weird dude?" I asked.

" 'Cause how he dress?"

"By what he wears, the way he walks, what comes out of his mouth. Just about everything about him is weird."

"He ain't right."

"An understatement," I said.

"Shall we?" Hawk asked, reaching for the door handle.

"We shall," I said.

We followed the same path. We punched the same intercom button. The door buzzed, and we both walked into a large, empty lobby. The gray linoleum floors had been buffed to a high shine. A grease board proudly listed today's specials as chicken pot pie, cooked carrots, and caramel pudding cup.

"Maybe we should stick around for lunch," Hawk said.

A large dining room with yellowed lace curtains opened up to the left. Pink carnations adorned every table. Pink tablecloths covered every table. Motel art of Cape Cod sunsets and fruit bowls lined the walls. The air smelled of bacon, weak coffee, and heavy doses of Pine-Sol.

There was music while we walked. Several families sat in a large open TV room catching an episode of *The Lawrence Welk Show.* Small children sat on laps of frail, colorless people. Some were old. Some weren't. The ones dying weren't hard to spot. I didn't see peace on their faces, only a grudging bit of understanding. Lawrence conducted on the new modern television. Children giggled and laughed, zipping through legs. They jumped from lap to lap.

From behind a desk, a woman in an orange dress looked us over. She appeared to be in her late fifties or early sixties and wore a lot of blue shadow as once had been the style. Her hair was dyed red and had been recently done. She wore many bright gold chains and rings.

She asked, "Yes?"

"We came with Mr. Broz," I said. "We're his fashion coordinators, Mr. Salt and Mr. Pepper."

Hawk looked at me and raised a single eyebrow. The woman stared at us for a moment.

"Room three-oh-eight," she said.

I nodded. She went back to her computer screen.

We took the elevator to the third floor and quickly found the room. The door was open. More lacy curtains covered a single window. A plush red leather chair and a small chest of drawers sat in a corner. The chest was covered with an old-fashioned lace doily, as if it could make the room feel less like a hospital. The walls were cinder block. Stainless-steel railings had been strategically placed along the way for support. A wooden cross with a golden Christ hung over the washbasin.

The floor was very quiet. There was the smell of sickness and decay that no cleaner could ever remove. A weak winter light bled through the window as we walked inside.

Gerry Broz sat on a small chair with his hands tented in prayer. A shriveled man with tubes up his nose slept on the bed before him.

I knew the old man.

When I'd first met Joe Broz, he'd been full of balls and bluster. I recalled him wearing a white suit, a white vest, a dark blue shirt, and a white tie. He'd sported a gold chain across the vest and a large diamond ring on his little finger. He'd called me a wiseass punk.

Broz was once the most feared man in Boston and the state of Massachusetts. He was petty, greedy, and violent. At the top of his game, he had state senators and police officials in his pocket. He owned the city.

We had an unusual relationship until he disappeared. He kept his word. Often, he tried to have me killed. At least once, he'd expected Vinnie to do it.

What was left of Joe's black hair was white, a few strands falling crookedly off his head. His teeth were still very large and too big for his mouth. The mouth was wide open and rasped with each breath. There were plenty of dials and machines perched over his bed.

Gerry kept his eyes closed for a couple more moments.

I could hear the creaking of Hawk's leather coat as he stood next to me. I dropped my head and waited.

Gerry opened his eyes. He looked both of us over with disgust.

"Goddamn both of you."

"Hello, Gerry."

"What the fuck do you two want?"

Hawk spoke first. "Everything."

57

"How long has your old man been here?" I asked.

"Two years."

"*America's Most Wanted* across the river Styx."

"Why don't you talk like a normal person," Gerry said. "Nobody knows what the fuck you're saying."

" 'Cept me," Hawk said.

Gerry shrugged. He remained seated at the chair beside his old man. He was rubbing his hands together. His face had tightened.

"Where was he before?" I asked.

"Gulf Shores, Alabama."

"No kidding?"

"They got a nice beach," Gerry said. "He liked to fish, feed the seagulls and shit."

"And no one here knows?" I asked.

"Registered him under the name of a dead uncle," Gerry said. "Nobody would recognize him anymore. You mighta noticed he ain't himself."

The tube in Joe Broz's throat made gurgling noises.

"Really?"

"My father thought you were a real piece of shit, Spenser."

"Aw, shucks."

"Should have had you killed a long time ago."

"He had his chance a few times," I said. "I think he took comfort in keeping me around."

"You gotta feel like a big man, droppin' the dime on a dying old man."

I looked at Hawk. He nodded at me.

"Is he?" I asked.

"What the fuck do you think?" Gerry asked. "Does he look like he's taking a fuckin' nap? They got him in diapers. He's fed through a tube."

"You know," Hawk said, giving an appraising look, "Joe has looked better."

"I don't want him dragged into some crazy state place," Gerry said. "They keep 'em in cages like filthy animals, where they piss and shit themselves. Here they keep him clean and safe. These old broads come around twice a day and sing old songs to him. It's got some dignity to it."

"How nice, Gerry," Hawk said.

"Where's Flynn?" I asked.

"Fuck you."

Hawk took a step forward. Gerry stood, sliding a hand under his tan suede coat.

"Whatever you want, kid," Hawk said.

"You feel big? Pickin' on a sick old man? You two feel big?"

"I always feel big," I said. "Hawk?"

"Gargantuan."

"We want Flynn," I said. "That's all. He took a kid and will probably kill her."

Gerry shook his head. He wiped his nose with the back of his hand and then wiped his hand on the suede. It was then that I realized Gerry Broz had started to cry. His head fell forward in his hands. His back shook.

It looked theatrical and silly. But it was real.

"You give us Flynn and we walk," I said. "We leave you and Joe out of this."

Gerry sobbed, head still in his hands. "I knew he'd fuck it up. Flynn fucked me in the ass. Fuckin' stupid. It's all a mess."

"What?"

"Business," Gerry said. "It's all a fucking mess."

Gerry rested his hands on the plastic bed slats running alongside what was left of Joe

373

Broz. He looked down at his old man, his big rolling tears pattering on the laundered sheet running up to his father's sagging neck. The gurgling noises continued.

Hawk and I exchanged glances. I don't know why, but I felt a little ashamed and voyeuristic.

"Why'd you partner with him?" I asked.

"Flynn made me promises," Gerry said. "He said we could get back what had been my dad's after Knocko Moynihan got aced. Now he's gone fucking nuts over what he done to that girl."

"Julie Sullivan."

Gerry kept his head bowed, crying. He nodded. "Pussy makes you crazy."

"Why'd he kill her, Ger?"

Gerry shook his head. He ran the back of his hand under his nose again. I sincerely hoped he wouldn't wipe snot on his jacket again. There were limits. Instead, he shook his head some more.

"Give us Flynn," I said. "He's a sociopath. You have our word we leave your old man alone."

Gerry was silent for a long while. He tilted his head up at me, staring and nodding. He sniffed a little. He looked at Hawk. Hawk looked to me.

Hawk nodded and left the room. The door

behind him closed with a slight click.

I pulled over the red leather chair. Gerry studied my face with a mix of disgust and sadness. Somehow, I didn't really blame him. He'd hated me for a long time. He hated that I'd beat him. More than anything, he hated that his old man respected me and never respected him.

"Sit," I said.

"It's my fuckin' room," he said. "I sit when I want to."

"Sit down, Gerry."

Gerry sat. We stared at each other over the body of Joe Broz. Broz looked like the centerpiece on a dinner table. Lilies would have looked appropriate propped up in his hands.

"That Fed Connor wants your old man bad," I said. "You think Flynn won't give you guys up? You give him up and you have time to move the old man any place you like."

"You always wanted him dead," Gerry said. "You'll sell us both out for a nickel."

"Nope," I said. "Your old man was a lot of things, but his word was good."

"He used to talk to me about ethics and shit," Gerry said. "Since when do crooks have ethics?"

"We only want the kid safe," I said.

Gerry brushed his longish dyed hair from his eyes. On a middle-aged man, long hair looked plain ridiculous. Long strands dropped back over his bloated face. His fingers were stubby and fat.

He patted the old man's wrinkled hand, holding it. He seemed to be willing Joe to sit up and make a decision.

"Hawk and I walk," I said. "You can have your old man FedExed to Boca Raton."

Gerry was silent. I was pretty sure he was thinking. But with Gerry, it was hard to tell. I waited. I crossed my legs. I studied Joe Broz's face, all that cocky swagger and jittery mean gone. He was a shell.

I looked to Gerry. I didn't see the old man in the kid. I never had. Joe was a crook, but he had a code.

"Connor knows," Gerry said. "Of course he fucking knows. Are you mental? Of course he fucking knows."

I nodded. I acted as if I'd known all along. I gave him a slight nod to make it appear I'd been testing him.

"How do you think he and Flynn put the screws to me?" Gerry said. "Jesus H. Are you fucking stupid? Flynn has been ratting to the Feds since they let him out four years ago. That was his deal with Connor. They both have me by the nuts."

"What's Connor get out of it?"

"Dirt on everyone in the city and a single guy he can control," Gerry said. "Or thought he could control. Flynn is batshit crazy. And now he goes off and snatches that broad's daughter. You don't do shit like that."

"Why'd he kill Julie Sullivan?"

" 'Cause she was fucked up," Gerry said. Gerry patted his old man's hands. He slowly let go of Joe Broz's fingers. "She wanted Flynn to leave his fucking wife. When he told her to screw, she came back and says she's dropping the dime on him and Connor bein' buddies. They used to go and have dinners together on Connor's boat. Goddamn, she killed her own fucking self."

I nodded.

"Where's Flynn, Gerry?"

Broz looked at me with his large eyes. His neck had grown even more fat and spilled out over his collar. Buttons looked as if they'd pop down the length of his purple dress shirt. In all the years I'd known him, he'd never worn clothes that fit. He always looked out of breath, red-faced, uncomfortable.

"You and Hawk walk away?" Gerry said.

"My word."

"Your word means shit to my family."

"Meant something to your old man," I said.

Gerry studied my face. He nodded some more in secret Gerry Broz thoughts. Something rattled around in there, and a gumball finally popped out. "Why should I feel bad for rattin' on a rat?"

"There you go."

"Bastard never respected me."

"The shame of it."

"You tryin' to make fun of me?"

"Never."

"I don't know."

"Come on," I said. "What was in it for you? You're too smart for this."

Having to say that last part pained me.

"We were gonna take down the Albanians and Gino Fish," Gerry said, all in a big rush of air. "And then he goes psycho and fucks me in the ass."

"How lovely," I said. "Where's Flynn?"

Gerry stood up. He looked down at his old man. Joe Broz's chest, as thin and delicate as a bird's wrapped in hospital paper, rose and fell.

"Still in Southie," Gerry said. "He's keepin' the girl at this old office building on West Broadway. That's where he keeps his guns. He's got a fuckin' arsenal."

"Good to know."

"You better buckle the fuck up."

"Will he know we're coming for him?" I asked.

Gerry shook his head. "Didn't I say we had a goddamn deal?"

I nodded. I stood.

I reached my hand over what was left of Joe Broz and shook hands with his kid.

His grip was wet and limp.

58

"You know, we could turn all this shit over to Quirk and have a late breakfast at the Russell House Tavern," Hawk said.

"We could."

"Brioche French toast with a big Mescal Mary on the side."

I nodded.

"But we won't."

"That what you want to do?"

"Hell, no."

"Let's check out what Gerry said," I said. "We find Flynn, we hit him hard."

"Plant your feet, bite down on your mouthpiece, and say let's go."

Hawk steered us toward the Mystic River and 93 South. We caught the interstate for a few miles, crossing the channel, and snaked down to the exit in South Boston. The winter light was weak and hazy; snow flurries dissolved against the windshield.

Hawk slowed in front of a long row of

three- and four-story brick storefronts that lined West Broadway. He parked across the street from a defunct bar with a FOR SALE sign hung from a second-floor window. The bar was abandoned. Shades and file cabinets covered most of the windows in the building.

Snow was coming down harder now. It had started to stick.

"How come Flynn does business in plain sight and no one says shit to him?"

"Must have something to do with charisma."

A patrol car pulled right onto the curb by the defunct bar. Officer Bobby Barrett got out and adjusted his cap on his head. He craned his neck up to the second floor and dialed a phone in his hand. A door at street level opened, and he waddled inside.

"Nice to have the law on your side," Hawk said.

"That's the officer who caught Mickey Green washing down the car," I said. "His testimony put Green away."

"Ain't that a coincidence," Hawk said.

Ten minutes later, the side door opened. Barrett walked out alone, got into his patrol car, and drove off.

"He one of the officers watching Mattie's family?"

"One of 'em."

"Nice choice," Hawk said.

"Maybe we should call Quirk."

"Maybe," Hawk said. "Or maybe Flynn see that SWAT team on his ass and starts to clean house. Bein' the psycho we think he is."

I nodded. "Keep it clean and simple."

"If Mattie inside," Hawk said, "time is tight. And we the best she got."

"And if we're the best she's got, that's not too shabby."

"No, it ain't."

"How's the arm?"

"Cool."

"How's the chest?"

"Sore."

"How many men do you think Flynn has?"

"Does it fucking matter?" Hawk said.

"Nope," I said. "Just thinking out loud."

59

The door to the stairwell was metal and well worn and locked. Someone had scrawled some graffiti in big diagonal letters that said BLACK NEVER. SOUTHIE FOREVER. Hawk craned his neck to read it. He turned back to me and shook his head. Snow drifted down along the cracked sidewalks of Broadway. Across the street, thickly bundled people hustled into the T station.

Hawk looked both ways, stepped back, and kicked in the door.

The door slammed open, and light shone into a narrow stairwell covered in dirty red carpet. The light was very dim, burning from a couple of bare bulbs. We moved quickly to the second floor and curved up to the third. Dust motes twirled in the soft gray light.

The third-floor hall seemed to stretch out forever in the dim light. The old building shifted in the darkness; its loose windows battered and thumped against the sills.

I nodded to Hawk. I took the lead.

If Mattie was with Flynn, a pistol was much more precise.

We moved through the hall, checking the first two small offices fronting Broadway. Hawk watched my back, eyeing the length of the hallway, looking for opening doors and waiting for footsteps behind us.

Down the hall, we heard the creak of an office chair.

"Spenser?" a voice called out.

I turned to Hawk. Hawk looked to me. He fitted the stock of the Mossberg into his shoulder. Agent Tom Connor stepped out into the long hallway and lifted his hands. He was dressed in a blue wool suit and red power tie. He held his hands up, smiling in a patronizing way.

"Come on in," Connor said. "We need to have a powwow."

"And you wonder why Native Americans don't like the Feds."

"Let's talk."

"Where's your buddy, Jumpin' Jack?" I asked.

I kept the gun aimed at Connor. Hawk did not lower the shotgun as we walked down the hall. The office was empty except for two rolling office chairs and a file cabinet turned on its side, spilling paper onto the floor. Connor stood, lit a cigarette, and stared out at the snow falling on a pleasant winter afternoon.

People always smoked when trying to look pensive. Connor was very pensive.

"This is a mess, Spenser," Connor said. "What can you say? You've burned a major source of mine. You've scared poor Gerry Broz senseless. He doesn't know which way is up."

"Gerry has often had that problem."

"I don't think you get what's going on here."

"It's become pretty clear."

"No, it's not," Connor said. He blew smoke out of his nostrils. He shook his head like a befuddled parent. "I look out for this entire city, and in doing so, you got to make compromises. I'm not going to lecture a thick-headed guy like you. Or your spook sidekick."

Hawk had not lowered his weapon. It was unwise to call Hawk a spook. Especially when Hawk was armed. Of course, it was an unwise move to call Hawk a spook anytime.

"Where's Flynn?" I said. "Where's the girl?"

"You want to talk about this city's greater

good," Connor said. He shifted his weight, placed his right hand into his pants pocket. I felt for the trigger. But he only jingled the coins or keys inside. "You know what this case means to us?"

Hawk leaned forward with his shotgun.

"Easy there, Hawk," Connor said. "Down, boy."

"I takin' an instant dislike to this mother-fucker," Hawk said.

"Yeah," I said. "He's got a kind of reverse charisma."

"You can never imagine the filth and violent shitbags I have to deal with every day."

"My apologies," I said.

"Sad," Hawk said.

"I have to compromise."

"You said that."

"Jack Flynn goes to jail, this whole thing goes bust."

"Kind of fucked-up logic, Tom."

"I protect my informant."

I nodded. Snow fell softly out onto West Broadway. Smoke billowed up from the diner down the street. A crowd emerged from the T station, and a handful of people replaced them.

Connor blew more smoke from his nose. He ground the cigarette under his tasseled loafer. He looked up at me dramatically. He sneered at Hawk.

"I'm the best chance you got for getting that kid back," Connor said. "I don't want her hurt."

"Then bring in Flynn," I said.

"I can do more damage with Flynn on the outside," he said. "Play the game, the girl goes free. Let me do what I do best."

"C'mon, Spenser," Hawk said. "Trust the nice man."

"Why don't you shut the fuck up," Connor said.

"This Mossberg been modified for military use," Hawk said. "Twelve-gauge, with a kick like a mule. Leaves a nasty hole through a man."

"I don't give a shit who you know with the staties," Connor said. "You shoot a federal officer, and you're toast."

"If you're going to play with us, Connor, please work on your dialogue," I said.

" 'Toast'?" Hawk said. "Shit, this might be worth it."

I lifted up my free hand. "We get the kid. Then talk."

"Flynn won't do it," Connor said. "I swear to Christ I tried. What you don't really get is that Jack Flynn is a sociopath."

"I had a sneaking suspicion."

"He's a suspect in more than fifty killings. I can get him personally on about twelve. But I want it all. I want to use him up till he's dry and then send him to jail for the rest of his life."

"For some reason I don't see how your plan fits with the Bureau's code of conduct."

"Fuck that," Connor said. "I didn't make a name by playing by the rules. How about you?"

I shrugged.

"Just tell me where to find Theresa Donovan," Connor said. "I'll make sure she's safe and can be brought in when it's time. Flynn will calm down and let the kid go."

Officer Barrett didn't know about Theresa being brought in as a witness. Quirk and Belson had kept a lid on it, as I knew they would.

"If we arrange a meet," I said, "I'd prefer it wasn't in Southie. No offense."

Connor looked at me. He tried to give a confused look. Connor wasn't much of an actor.

"Looks like you got at least one patrol guy on the team," I said. "Probably a lot more."

"Ah, shit," Connor said. "You're not from down here. You don't know how the system works."

"Try me," I said.

388

I heard and felt Hawk's breathing behind my right shoulder.

"Give me an address, and I'll make sure the kid goes free."

"You tell Flynn I want to see Mattie in a very public place," I said. "When she's safe, I'll give you an address."

Connor laughed. He placed both hands in his suit pockets. He nodded and grinned. "I get Theresa Donovan, and I'll give the go-ahead to Flynn. Deal?"

"Public place," I said. "And not in Southie."

Connor nodded. He headed past us for the door. "Nobody gets out of this world alive, Spense."

"Again, not so original, Tommy."

"If you want to monkey-fuck us with Boston police, this will all go to hell. Jack Flynn will make her disappear. He's quite talented, you know."

"Me, too." Hawk stepped forward. "Hard to prosecute if they can't find your body."

"What the fuck does that mean?" Connor asked.

"Little girl better not have a hair out of place," Hawk said. "If she do, there gonna be an empty casket at your wake."

Connor just laughed and walked away.

60

"Kind of a theatrical choice, ain't it?" Hawk asked.

"I aim to please," I said.

We stood on the granite steps leading up to the Bunker Hill monument in Charlestown. The battle and monument were actually on Breed's Hill, but after a couple hundred years, I guess the name had stuck. It was still snowing, dusting the steps, and floating past the glowing lamps by the granite obelisk. Over the winter, snow had accumulated on the top of the piked iron fence.

It was almost eight o'clock, and it had grown very cold and very dark. The waiting was always the toughest part. But when the bad guys set the time, you don't have much choice. Flynn wanted us tired. He wanted us nervous. Hawk and I were neither.

The lights were on in the brick town houses surrounding the square. Everything seemed very hushed in the snowfall.

A sign for the Freedom Trail announced the REVOLUTION BEGINS HERE.

"And you tell me how Charlestown is better than Southie."

"It's more integrated," I said.

"Maybe in the projects," Hawk said.

"And they have Old Ironsides."

"We good on your witness?"

"Quirk's got it," I said. "Connor knows how to find her. But she'll be surrounded by about twenty of Boston's finest."

"Wired?" Hawk said.

"They got more bugs in that place than a bait shop."

"Bait shop do have lots of bugs."

"We pull this off, maybe you and I go fishing."

" 'We'll take the car and drive all night,' " Hawk said. " 'We'll get drunk.' "

"Play it, Sam."

"Yes-suh, Mr. Rick."

Hawk began to whistle "As Time Goes By."

"You fish?" I asked. I leaned against the handrail. My hands in my coat pockets. A .38 in my right hand. A .40-caliber strapped under my arm.

"Nope."

"I fished a lot as a kid," I said. "Lots of

391

good places to fish in Wyoming."

"Don't really care to fish," Hawk said.

I nodded.

"Prefer to hunt."

I nodded.

Up the long steps, the statue of William Prescott brandished his sword. Hawk caught me staring. "Don't shoot till you see the whites."

"I think you have that a bit mixed up," I said.

"Do I?" Hawk asked.

He kept the shotgun on a modified rig under his black leather trench coat. He wore the .44 Magnum on his belt. The leather coat covered both very nicely.

I wore my peacoat and Red Sox knitted cap. I had on a well-worn pair of Red Wing boots with steel toes in case the fight got down and dirty. I did not expect the transition to go smoothly. I fingered the S&W .40-caliber in my right pocket.

"Always been guys like Connor."

I nodded.

"Don't make it right."

"Nope," I said.

"You hear him call me a spook?"

"I did."

"Who uses the word 'spook' anymore?"

"Anachronisms."

"And assholes."

"Connor exemplifies both."

My cell phone rang. I took the call. Hawk watched everything without showing a thing on his face.

"We got a visitor," Belson said. "But it ain't Connor. It's fucking Gerry Broz."

"Crapola."

"He's in the lobby with Theresa," Belson said. "Lots of people. We saw him make a call."

At the base of the steps up to the monument, a black Ford SUV pulled to the curb. Jack Flynn stepped out from the passenger side. He looked up at us through the falling snow and climbed the steps. His big face was ruddy and wind-chapped under a thick mop of curly hair.

"Boom," Hawk said, eyeing him.

The SUV took off. I walked down a couple steps and met Flynn halfway.

"Excuse me if we don't shake hands," I said.

"Once we know we're not being followed, you can have the kid."

"Gee," I said. "Such a swell guy."

Jack Flynn studied me without emotion. There were crow's-feet around his pale green eyes, which appraised us quickly, in a way that reminded me of a wild dog. His camel-hair coat fluttered around him while snow caught in his hair and translucent eyelashes. He'd been around a long time, longer than me. He had a lot of confidence.

"Don't make this hard."

"You made the play."

You could smell him. Jack Flynn smelled of sweat and testosterone and a dash of Aqua Velva.

"I don't kill kids," Flynn said.

"Got to draw the line somewhere."

Flynn smiled at me. He buttoned his coat up to his neck. He placed both hands in his pockets. We all had our hands in our pockets. I stole a glance at Hawk. Hawk's eyes were almost sleepy.

"The girl knows I killed her mother," Flynn said.

I nodded.

"Couldn't be helped," Flynn said. "She was a stupid gash."

I watched his face. I didn't see much.

"Doesn't mean jack shit without a witness," Flynn said.

"Nice to have a buddy like Tom Connor."

"I've known him since he was a kid at Old Colony," Flynn said. "Don't take offense at this stuff. Take the girl, tell her to shut the fuck up, and we're good."

Flynn pulled off a leather glove and offered his hand.

I looked at his hand. I looked to Hawk.

"You want to tell me what makes you two shitbirds any better than me?"

"How much time you got?" Hawk asked.

Flynn laughed.

"You want to count bodies with me, Hawk?"

Hawk just stared at Jack Flynn with his sleepy eyes.

"How about you, Spenser?" Flynn said. "How many have you killed?"

Flynn's cell rang, and he took it. He placed it back into his pocket and nodded. Snow continued to fall. His feet crunched on the steps as he shifted his weight.

"Okay," he said. "That was Gerry. He's got Theresa Donovan with him."

"I thought it was going to be Connor."

"You think a federal agent is going to put himself in the middle of this shit pile?" Flynn asked. "Only thugs like us get down and dirty. Guys like Connor watch from the grandstands."

"Connor doesn't know what team he's on."

Flynn watched me. He nodded. "You know," Flynn said, "don't be so sure."

I looked to Hawk. Hawk stared at Jack Flynn. I was getting the impression he didn't care much for him.

"Where's Mattie?" I asked.

"Safe."

"That wasn't the deal."

"She's close."

"Then let's see her."

"You want her, you meet me at the Sully Square Station in thirty minutes," Flynn said. "No cops. No Hawk. You go to the inbound ramp. Mattie will be on the train. You get on. I get off. But if something goes wrong between now and then with the Donovan girl, all bets are off."

"I'm starting to feel like Will Kane," I said.

Flynn didn't hear me. He'd already started back down the steps and to the street. The black SUV pulled up, and Jack Flynn crawled inside. The SUV drove off. A dark green BMW followed a few beats later.

"Don't like it," Hawk said.

"How do you think I feel?"

"You think Quirk and Boston PD have Gerry?"

"Yep."

"You think Flynn will find out in the next thirty minutes?"

"We'll know soon enough."

"Even if he don't, you know Flynn ain't gonna play fair."

"I do."

"And if I go down into the T station with you, they'll spot me."

"You are a big personality."

"That leaves you up shit creek."

"Not my favorite creek."

"Now, ain't this more fun than fishin'?"

61

Sullivan Station was a glorious monument to the Boston transit authority, a slapped-together heap of concrete, wires, and steel below Interstate 93. The T ran aboveground on the north side of the river, and I stood on the inbound platform, waiting for the next train. Snow fell heavier now, and there was talk of canceled flights tomorrow at Logan. There was a lot of wind. I thought about getting a shot of whiskey to warm me. Sully Station wasn't South Station. No bars or boutique cafés.

More snow fell. I waited. Nearly nine o'clock now.

Somewhere in the busted-up concrete-and-steel overpass pilings and general urban mayhem, Hawk was out there. We'd improvised a plan, which was often the way we worked, and now we waited. Hawk had a rifle aimed on that platform. Hawk was watching. I could feel his presence, and that gave me comfort.

Forty minutes had passed since Bunker Hill. The T had come and gone countless times. I kept a good ten feet between me and the train.

At forty-five minutes, another T rambled in from Wellington Station. In the third car, I spotted Mattie. She wore the same blue puffy coat and school uniform as she had the day before.

Two men were with her.

They were Flynn's boys. A Hispanic male and a scruffy old man.

Mattie's eyes were very big when the doors opened with a hiss. The Hispanic man ushered me forward with a rapid hand motion. I walked slowly. I looked in each direction. I studied the other T cars. I peered up to the thick concrete stairwells.

With my hand on the .40-caliber, I stepped inside.

I winked at Mattie.

"Here you go, fuckface," the old man said.

"You kiss your mother with that mouth?" I asked.

"Fuck you," the old man said. His teeth were very crooked, his breath an epidemic.

"Wow," I said. "I guess lackeys don't get the dental plan."

The Hispanic man tried to glower at me.

I winked at him. The glower turned to confusion.

He and the scruffy old man stepped off the train. The train doors closed.

The men remained on the platform as we headed back to the city.

The T bustled and jumped along the track, light flickering past us. A chain-link fence topped with concertina wire separated the tracks. Security lamps spotted portions of a far concrete wall lettered with crude but clever graffiti.

"You okay?" I asked, gripping the overhead rail.

"Sure."

"They hurt you?"

"Nah," Mattie said, still sitting very still, her fists clenched on her lap. "Couple of dickless retards."

"You give them too much credit," I said. "You see Jack Flynn?"

She nodded. I watched the train car as we talked. An old woman in a mustard yellow coat read the *Globe.* A couple of black teens took turns rapping freestyle. A gray-headed vagrant took swigs from a bottle.

We slowed as we reached Community College Station.

The two black teens got off. A slouchy kid in a Levi's jacket with a sherpa collar got

400

on, a backpack slung over a shoulder. He was listening to an iPod and wore an inward smile, enjoying the music.

The vagrant continued to take a swig from the bottle. I almost asked him for a nip.

Doors closed and we moved underground, under the frozen river, whirring and jerking. We rambled through darkness and strobes of white light. I sat down beside Mattie and put my arm around her. She smiled, exhausted. Her body relaxed against me, and tears flowed silently down her face. I don't think she knew she was crying. I decided not to tell her.

"What did Flynn say to you?" I asked.

"Nothin'."

"You say anything to him?"

"Plenty."

"Feel good?" I asked.

Mattie smiled. "You bet."

"Theresa Donovan will testify against Flynn," I said.

"We'll see," she said. "I don't believe she'd say shit if her mouth was full of it."

We soon came out from under the river and into the North Station. We'd head on to South Station. Hawk would meet us at the platform in case anyone followed.

The slouchy kid got off. The old woman got off.

The vagrant left, and sadly took his bottle with him. Two men in their twenties wearing skully caps and thick, dark coats got on board. My hand dropped from Mattie and felt for the S&W as they turned. Both sat at the rear of the train, not once looking at us. The effort of not looking gained my attention.

"Where we headed?" Mattie said.

"A safe place until Flynn's picked up."

One of the skully boys caught my eye. He had a stylized beard cut to make it appear he was too cool to shave.

I nodded. He looked away.

"You won't find him," she said. "He'll walk. Even if he makes it to court, he'll walk. No one gives a shit about my mom."

"That's not true anymore."

I watched the boys. They rested their elbows on their knees and studied the ground between their feet like a couple ballplayers at the ready.

Mattie shook her head as the T rambled on. My heart kept a steady beat. I could almost hear Tex Ritter singing as we approached Haymarket Station.

"They said they'd hurt my sisters," she said. "They said they got policemen on the pad."

The skully-cap boys stood. One absently

felt inside his heavy coat.

"We'll take care of it," I said, my eyes staying with them.

"You and Hawk?"

"And some good policemen I know."

The brakes on the T screeched, and we slowed on the tracks. A dozen or so people waited on the platform. Haymarket Station was dingy and also well graffitied. Small billboards whizzed by for spring water, furniture showrooms, mortgage companies, and shopping malls. The light came in strobes, white and artificial.

The two boys walked toward us. Their full attention was on us. The boy with the stylish beard nodded at me. I wondered how long it took to be artfully scruffy. The other was not so artful, sporting a ragged goatee.

The one with the goatee opened his coat slightly. He displayed his gun.

"Yikes." I grabbed Mattie's arm and said, "Here we go."

62

Mattie stepped with me, weaving through the crowd. People hustled past, brushing us, bumping into one another. I scanned faces, movements. The two boys remained on the train as the doors hissed closed.

I spotted the exit stairs as we crossed the platform. The T rumbled off to the south with great noise and light, picking up speed into the tunnel and darkness. I watched every corner and both stairwells.

It didn't take long before Jack Flynn and two gunmen in black leather jackets walked out from behind a pair of concrete pillars. They pointed their guns at us.

In the spirit of the moment, I pointed the Smith & Wesson at them.

"Broz got picked up," Flynn said. "You fucked me."

"Would it help if I promised to call later?"

"Leave the girl, smart-ass," Flynn said. "She's nothin' but a piece of trash like her

404

ma. Don't get stupid and dead."

"Go ahead and try," I said. "But shut your mouth."

"I heard your mother pulled a train every Saint Pat's Day, Flynn," Mattie said. "Guessin' your father was multiple choice."

Flynn smiled.

"She writes her own material," I said. "Trying to show me up."

There were maybe ten people on the platform, more coming and going up the exit stairs. I pushed Mattie behind me. She kept lurching forward. I pushed her back several more times.

"Your mother was a whore," Flynn said. "She ran her mouth just like you."

Mattie made a deep sound as if all the air had rushed from inside her. She lunged for Flynn. I grabbed her by the arm and pulled her back. She fought me.

Flynn had pointed his gun at her and thumbed back the hammer. His gun was a chrome .357 Magnum with a six-inch barrel. His two boys aimed their weapons at me. I didn't bother to study their makes and models.

"Bad move, Jack," I said. "It's been a pleasure."

"You're fuckin' nuts," Flynn said. "You believe this guy? Shoot the prick."

I saw movement out of the corner of my eye. I knew he was there by his posture and walk. I wrapped my arm around Mattie and pulled her down to the concrete platform.

Three very precise, muffled shots thudded. All of Vinnie Morris's work was neat.

The two gunmen hit the ground, red flowers blooming at their temples. Flynn's side opened up in a red sash as he leapt behind a column and fired his .357 wildly in our general direction.

Footsteps and confusion. Men and women dove to the T platform or ran for the exits. I heard more screams and scattering footsteps. Shooting in a public place inspires a great deal of pandemonium.

I looked up from where I'd covered Mattie. Vinnie Morris wore a Pats jacket, sunglasses, and a dark ball cap pulled down far over his eyes. I did not see a gun. If Flynn had not fired, most people in the station would not have known anything had happened at all. Vinnie was deadly silent. Within seconds, he headed back up the stairs just as an alarm sounded.

Vinnie had tailed Flynn from Bunker Hill as promised and promptly disappeared.

I helped Mattie to her feet. Her face was the color of parchment.

"You've been shot," she said.

I felt my shoulder. "So I have." I yanked her behind a thick tile column with my good arm, peering around it.

A dozen bystanders remained on the ground, hands on heads or curled into fetal positions. A young woman lay next to her spilled purse. She was crying, reaching for her wallet and keys, closing her eyes very tight. Another young man in a rumpled navy overcoat was trying to text-message with one hand.

People stirred from where they lay. The young woman gathered her purse, leaving what had spilled, and ran for the exit. Her footsteps echoed up the stairs. Most people chose to stay where they were.

The gunmen lay in a heap on the ground. Jack Flynn stayed hidden behind another column.

"Ready to renegotiate?" I asked.

Gun drawn, Flynn jumped down onto the second set of tracks and jackrabbited for the gaping mouth of the inbound line.

I walked out from the column and shouted for him to stop. Clever.

He turned and again fired wildly.

I squeezed the trigger on my .40-caliber just as he turned to run and caught Flynn in the back. The old thug stumbled and fell forward like a quarterback from a classic

NFL film. A second shot got him in the leg.

He wavered, but then he was gone.

The station was quiet, all the violence and cracking energy flushed out by a sudden cold rush of air. I pulled out my cell phone and called 911. The bystanders started to get to their feet and do the same. An alarm sounded from the toll booth. I turned to grab Mattie and offer her some reassurance that Flynn would be found. But she'd disappeared.

I spotted the last bit of her darting down the T tracks after Jack Flynn. She didn't give me much of a choice.

I followed her down onto the sunken tracks. My shoulder hurt a great deal. I passed the danger signs, trying my best not to be electrocuted, running between the tracks. Inside the subway, the walls were concrete and tile, and covered in black graffiti and defaced billboards. The tracks ducked into a gentle curve.

I yelled for Mattie.

A single gunshot rang out in the tunnel. It was very loud and harsh and electric. I yelled for her.

My gun stretched out in my left hand. I was breathing very hard. My right arm hung at my side.

The long row of white lights shuddered

off and on.

I turned the corner and spotted Flynn. He'd fallen to his hands and knees in the center of the track. Mattie had Flynn's gun pointed down at his head.

I walked even more slowly. I called to her.

She didn't hear me. She was back to being ten, watching a couple hoods tossing her mom into the back of an old Pontiac.

Flynn was spitting up blood. His coat was filthy. Blood and dirt covered him. He wavered on all fours in the flickering light. Mattie circled him and kicked at him with her little sneaker.

The chrome .357 looked ridiculous in her hands. Almost like an oversized toy.

Her arm was bleeding very badly. She'd been shot taking the gun away from him.

"Would it matter if I said he wasn't worth it?" I said.

Nothing.

"If you kill him, he'll own you," I said. "You'll give his life meaning."

"He called her a whore."

"He's dying, Mattie," I said. "He's been shot three times. Twice by me. Let him go."

"She was not a whore," Mattie said. "She was not a whore."

Flynn choked out more blood. He turned his head to me, staring at me with those pale Irish eyes. I thought I detected something that looked like gratitude. His face had been washed of all color as his body fell into deep shock.

She did not lower the very large gun. She thumbed back the hammer and pressed it to the back of his skull.

"God I'm so sorry," Mattie said. "I'm so goddamn sorry, Ma."

Flynn rolled over to his side, head thumping against a burnished rail. I knew he was either dead or damn near close to it. She dropped the gun. I smiled at her. But Mattie's eyes rolled up into her head and she fell like a limp rag doll.

I pocketed the gun and knelt down, scooping her up in my arms. I had to grit my teeth a fair amount while I walked toward the light. Transit cops scattered down around the edges of the train, coming for us. Guns out, talking on radios.

Little white lights scattered off and on, feathers from her coat flitting in the cavernous draft.

63

Some months later, Boston thawed, and I found myself sitting with Mattie Sullivan right behind home plate at Fenway, as promised. I treated myself to a hot dog and a cold Budweiser. Salted peanuts waited on deck. Miracles never cease.

"Sweet seats," Mattie said. "Too bad the Sox are sucking this year."

"A true fan weathers every game."

"With all the money these guys make, I got a right to complain."

"Glad I don't make much money."

"You did good," Mattie said.

"I bummed the tickets from a fancy law firm."

"You know what I mean."

I toasted her with the half beer that was left.

It was May, and the ballpark was packed despite the gray skies and rain. Lots of people wore ponchos and held umbrellas.

411

The rain fell in soft, gentle waves. What the Irish called a soft day.

I wore my Boston Braves cap. Mattie wore an official fitted Sox cap I insisted on buying her at the team store. It wasn't pink. She balanced the box score sheet on her knee.

"You think you'd see some hustle," Mattie said. "It looks like they got lead in their ass. And against the fucking Halos. Jesus."

"Sometimes a ball game can be enjoyed just for the rhythm of it all," I said. I took a sip of my third beer. "You watch the little details, and it gives the same feeling as listening to good jazz."

"Whatever," Mattie said.

I ate my hot dog. I drank some beer. I opened the sack of peanuts. I wondered if that would be too gluttonous. Since I was on the mend, I figured I needed the nutrition.

We watched Wakefield strike out two Angels.

"How's the shoulder?" Mattie asked.

"Better," I said. "I'm gonna try some heavy-bag work today with Hawk. Slow going."

Mattie's arm was still in a sling. The doctors had inserted pins into the shattered bone, and it would take some time to heal.

There had been a lot of ugly damage and two surgeries, but she kept the arm. Like me, she was on the mend.

"Why don't you come along," I said. "I can teach you how to box."

She laughed and shook her head. Wake struck out the third batter. The crowd cheered. She penciled in the out.

"I'm gonna take a bus out to Walpole and see Mickey."

"I'll drive you," I said. "I promise not to sing anything that's not in the Great American Songbook."

"Rather go myself," she said. "Besides, Mickey doesn't care too much for you."

"I got him a sexy and tough attorney," I said. "She got him a new trial based on DNA evidence and a witness I found."

"Mickey thinks it's bullshit that he hasn't been sprung," Mattie said. She blew a large pink bubble. "Shit, they got Flynn's DNA under my mom's nails."

I nodded. "The wheels of justice turn slowly."

"It's a bunch of crap," she said. "What if Theresa bolts again?"

"I'll track her down."

"What if someone finds her first?"

"Flynn is quite dead."

"Ain't that a shame." She chewed her

gum. She studied the box score.

"You worry about it?"

"Not shooting the bastard myself?"

"Yeah."

"Sometimes," she said. "I guess sometimes I wish I'd had the stuff."

"You got the stuff," I said. "You made a choice that he wasn't worth it. Think on that."

"Figured that's why you wanted me to go shoppin' with Susan," Mattie said. "You wanted her to talk to me about my feelings and shit."

"Talking about feelings and shit can often be therapeutic."

"I don't go for frilly dresses and tea," Mattie said. "Not with Mickey still screwed. There's still a lot to do."

"Mickey will get out," I said. "But it takes time."

"And that crooked Fed?" she asked.

I watched Pedroia loosen up on deck. I felt my face burn. "He's under investigation," I said. "I have a friend who's got him in his sights. He believes me. But he's the only Fed who believes me."

"So this douchebag skates."

"As does Gerry Broz." I sipped the beer. "In my line of work, douchebags often skate."

The rain came down a little harder.

"Bullshit," Mattie said, again. "Just bullshit."

" 'Tis."

Ellsbury struck out. Pedroia sauntered up to the plate. He studied the big Green Monster in left field. I just hoped he connected.

I contemplated another beer. The rain started to fall harder, and the ground crew stood at the ready near the tarp. Pedroia stepped back from the plate and watched the umpire. The game continued.

On the second pitch, Pedroia nicked a line drive past third, making it to first. Adrian Gonzalez was up. Mattie leaned forward. We both liked Gonzalez, curious about what he'd do for us this season. The rain came in a steady, solid patter.

The first pitch was wide. The second a strike. But Gonzalez hammered the next one far into left field. Pedroia made it to third and rounded toward home. Gonzalez rounded second but doubled back, as did Pedroia.

The bottom fell out of the sky.

The umpire held up his hand. The crews hustled out with the tarp.

Mattie and I ran for cover. Inside Fenway, the ballpark smelled of musty old wood, hot dogs, and stale beer. Heaven.

We walked to the gate and waited for the rain to stop.

"Thanks for all you've done," she said. "We'll get square on those donuts."

"Six cinnamon, six chocolate frosted."

"And a tall coffee. I know. I know."

"Cream. Two sugars."

"Quit bustin' my ass. Okay?"

I bought her an umbrella. We walked to my car, and I drove her back to the Mary Ellen McCormack. We sat for a while, waiting for the rain to let up.

"How was that?"

"Nice," Mattie said. "Thanks."

"You do much thinking?"

"I watched the game."

"And now?"

"I'll see Mickey."

"But maybe you give yourself another break soon."

"Like a vacation."

"Yep," I said. "You keep giving yourself breaks, and the time between them will grow shorter. You get into a new normal. Not the same, but not bad, either."

"Guess it's nice knockin' boots with a shrink."

"It is."

"You need breaks sometime, too?"

I nodded.

"Is that how you deal with all the bastards?"

"No harm in being good to yourself," I said. "I know what it's like to show everyone you're tough. It's a form of self-protection. Keeps people from messing with you."

"Is that you or Susan talking?"

"A little of both."

Mattie reached for the door handle.

"I'm always here," I said. "We can always mooch off the firm. Long season this year."

"Maybe the Sox can right things," she said.

"They got time."

I watched her walk away, a lot older and a lot younger than fourteen. I started the car and headed toward the waterfront, knowing lasting change takes time.

At Harbor Health Club, I changed into shorts and running shoes. I pulled on a navy sweatshirt cut off at the elbows and met Hawk in the boxing room, where he had started without me. He'd already worked himself into a shimmering sweat with a leather jump rope.

Hawk could jump rope the way Fred Astaire could dance. He crossed and switched feet as delicately and quickly as he had when he was a teenager.

Hawk hung up the rope. I wrapped my hands and fitted on a pair of sixteen-ounce gloves.

He hung the heavy bag on loose chains. Hawk told me to take it slow.

"Promised Susan," he said.

"She call you?"

"Five times."

"What does that mean?" I asked.

"Means take it easy," he said. "Until that shoulder heals."

"And you?"

"I heal by magic."

"Must be nice," I said.

"I often marvel at myself," Hawk said, getting a good grip of the heavy bag. I started with some short jabs with my left and then worked in a few light crosses with the right. The bullet had torn through muscle and cartilage, and the best I could get was a solid tap. I tapped a few crosses and jabbed hard again with the left.

"Hmm," Hawk said.

"It will come."

Hawk nodded.

I did some speed-bag work. The work from the right was pathetic at best.

Hawk thought it was funny.

The rain was gone, and the sun had started to set with all that bold color that comes after a long rain. The gym was filled with a brilliant gold light coming through the window and reflecting across the mirrors. I turned away from it and faced the waterfront. Sailboats zipped through the Atlantic. Tourist boats crisscrossed their wakes.

"You don't deserve it," Hawk said. "But after you done, I'll buy you a drink."

"Gee, thanks."

"Might be good to keep you around," Hawk said. "That right hook good enough to knock some old lady flat."

"I greatly appreciate your support."

Henry Cimoli stepped out of his office in a red satin sweatsuit. Gray-haired, skinny, and five-five on his tiptoes, Henry had a distinct banty rooster quality. He held out a cordless phone in his hand and called to me.

"Who is it?" I asked.

"How the hell should I know?" Henry asked. "That right is pathetic, by the way."

"I heard."

"Whatta I tell 'im?"

"Ask who it is."

Henry asked. He put his hand over the mouthpiece. "Some lawyer," Henry said. "Wants to hire you. You gonna take it or what?"

ABOUT THE AUTHORS

Robert B. Parker was the author of seventy books, including the legendary Spenser detective series, the novels featuring Jesse Stone, and the acclaimed Virgil Cole–Everett Hitch westerns, as well as the Sunny Randall novels. Winner of the Mystery Writers of America Grand Master Award and long considered the undisputed dean of American crime fiction, he died in January 2010.

Ace Atkins is the author of eleven novels, including the true crime-based *White Shadow, Wicked City, Devil's Garden,* and *Infamous.* He is also the author of the Quinn Colson series, which includes *The Ranger* and the forthcoming *The Lost Ones.* Bestselling author Michael Connelly has called Atkins "one of the best crime writers working today." He lives on a farm outside Oxford, Mississippi.